RANDOM HOUSE

LARGE PRINT

THE
MOTHERS

THE MOTHERS

|||||| A NOVEL ||||||

BRIT BENNETT

RANDOM HOUSE
LARGE PRINT

Copyright © 2016 by Brittany Bennett

Published in the United States of America by Random House Large Print in association with Riverhead Books, an imprint of Penguin Random House LLC.

Cover design Rachel Willey

The Library of Congress has established a Cataloging-in-Publication record for this title.

ISBN: 978-1-5247-0986-0

www.randomhouse.com/largeprint

FIRST LARGE PRINT EDITION

Printed in the United States of America

10 9 8 7 6 5 4 3 2 1

This Large Print edition published in accord with the standards of the N.A.V.H.

For Mom, Dad, Brianna, and Jynna

THE
MOTHERS

ONE

We didn't believe when we first heard because you know how church folk can gossip.

Like the time we all thought First John, our head usher, was messing around on his wife because Betty, the pastor's secretary, caught him cozying up at brunch with another woman. A young, fashionable woman at that, one who switched her hips when she walked even though she had no business switching anything in front of a man married forty years. You could forgive a man for stepping out on his wife once, but to romance that young woman over buttered croissants at a sidewalk café? Now, that was a whole other thing.

But before we could correct First John, he showed up at Upper Room Chapel that Sunday with his wife and the young, hip-switching woman—a great-niece visiting from Fort Worth—and that was that.

When we first heard, we thought it might be that type of secret, although, we have to admit, it had felt different. Tasted different too. All good secrets have a taste before you tell them, and if we'd taken a moment to swish this one around our mouths, we might have noticed the sourness of an unripe secret, plucked too soon, stolen and passed around before its season. But we didn't. We shared this sour secret, a secret that began the spring Nadia Turner got knocked up by the pastor's son and went to the abortion clinic downtown to take care of it.

She was seventeen then. She lived with her father, a Marine, and without her mother, who had killed herself six months earlier. Since then, the girl had earned a wild reputation—she was young and scared and trying to hide her scared in her prettiness. And she was pretty, beautiful even, with amber skin, silky long hair, and eyes swirled brown and gray and gold. Like most girls, she'd already learned that pretty exposes you and pretty hides you and like most girls, she hadn't yet learned how to navigate the difference. So we heard all about her sojourns across the border to dance clubs in Tijuana, the water bottle she carried around Oceanside High filled with vodka, the Saturdays she spent on base playing pool with Marines, nights that ended with her heels pressed against some man's foggy window. Just tales, maybe, except for one we now know is true: she spent her senior year of high school rolling around in bed with Luke Sheppard and come springtime, his baby was growing inside her.

LUKE SHEPPARD WAITED TABLES at Fat Charlie's Seafood Shack, a restaurant off the pier known for its fresh food, live music, and family-friendly atmosphere. At least that's what the ad in the **San Diego Union-Tribune** said, if you were fool enough to believe it. If you'd been around Oceanside long enough, you'd know that the promised fresh food was day-old fish and chips stewing under heat lamps, and the live music, when delivered, usually consisted of ragtag teenagers in ripped jeans with safety pins poking through their lips. Nadia Turner also knew things about Fat Charlie's that didn't fit on a newspaper ad, like the fact that a platter of Charlie's Cheesy Nachos was the perfect drunk snack or that the head cook sold the best weed north of the border. She knew that inside, yellow life preservers hung above the bar, so after long shifts, the three black waiters called it a slave ship. She knew secret things about Fat Charlie's because Luke had told her.

"What about the fish sticks?" she would ask.

"Soggy as shit."

"The seafood pasta?"

"Don't fuck with that."

"What could be so bad about pasta?"

"You know how they make that shit? Take some fish that's been sitting around and stuff it in ravioli."

"Fine, the bread, then."

"If you don't finish your bread, we just give it to another table. You about to touch the same bread as some dude that's been digging in his nuts all day."

The winter her mother killed herself, Luke saved Nadia from ordering the crab bites. (Imitation crab deep-fried in lard.) She'd begun disappearing after school, riding buses and hopping off wherever they took her. Sometimes she rode east to Camp Pendleton, where she watched a movie or bowled at Stars and Strikes or played pool with Marines. The young ones were the loneliest, so she always found a pack of privates, awkward with their shorn heads and big boots, and by the end of the night, she usually ended up kissing one of them until kissing made her feel like crying. Other days she rode north, past Upper Room Chapel, where the coast became frontier. South, and she hit more beach, better beaches, beaches with sand as white as the people who lay on it, beaches with boardwalks and roller coasters, beaches behind gates. She couldn't ride west. West was the ocean.

She rode buses away from her old life, where after school, she'd lingered with her friends in the parking lot before driver's ed or climbed the bleachers to watch the football team practice or caravanned to In-N-Out. She'd goofed around at Jojo's Juicery with her coworkers and danced at bonfires and climbed the jetty when dared because she always pretended to be unafraid. She was startled by how rarely she had been alone back then. Her days felt like being handed from person to person like a baton, her calculus teacher passing her to her Spanish teacher to her chemistry teacher to her friends and back home to her parents. Then one day, her mother's hand was gone and she'd fallen, clattering to the floor.

She couldn't stand to be around anyone now—

her teachers, who excused her late work with patient smiles; her friends, who stopped joking when she sat down at lunch, as if their happiness were offensive to her. In AP Government, when Mr. Thomas assigned partner work, her friends quickly paired off with each other, and she was left to work with the other quiet, friendless girl in the class: Aubrey Evans, who skirted off to Christian Club meetings at lunch, not to pad her college resume (she hadn't raised her hand when Mr. Thomas asked who had turned in applications) but because she thought God cared if she spent her free period inside a classroom planning canned food drives. Aubrey Evans, who wore a plain gold purity ring that she twisted around her finger when she talked, who always attended service at Upper Room by herself, probably the poor holy child of devout atheists who was working hard to lead them into the light. After their first time working together, Aubrey had leaned closer to her, dropping her voice.

"I just wanted to say I'm sorry," she said. "We've all been praying for you."

She seemed sincere, but what did that matter? Nadia hadn't been to church since her mother's funeral. Instead, she rode buses. One afternoon, she climbed off downtown in front of the

Hanky Panky. She was certain someone would stop her—she even looked like a kid with her backpack—but the bouncer perched on a stool near the door barely glanced up from his phone when she ducked inside. At three on a Tuesday, the strip club was dead, empty silver tables dulled under the stage lights. Black shades pulled in front of the windows blocked the plastic sunlight; in the man-made darkness, fat white men with baseball caps pulled low slouched in chairs facing the stage. Under the spotlight, a flabby white girl danced, her breasts swinging like pendulums.

In the darkness of the club, you could be alone with your grief. Her father had flung himself into Upper Room. He went to both services on Sunday mornings, to Wednesday night Bible study, to Thursday night choir practice although he did not sing, although practices were closed but nobody had the heart to turn him away. Her father propped his sadness on a pew, but she put her sad in places no one could see. The bartender shrugged at her fake ID and mixed her a drink and she sat in dark corners, sipping rum-and-Cokes and watching women with beat bodies spin onstage. Never the skinny, young girls—the club saved them for weekends or nights—just older women thinking about grocery lists and child care, their bodies stretched and pitted from age. Her mother would've been horrified at the thought—her in a strip club, in the light of day—but Nadia stayed, sipping the watery drinks slowly. Her third time in the club, an old black man pulled up a chair beside her. He wore a red plaid shirt under suspenders, gray tufts peeking out from under his Pacific Coast Bait & Tackle cap.

"What you drinkin'?" he asked.

"What're **you** drinking?" she said.

He laughed. "Naw. This a grown man drink. Not for a little thing like you. I'll get you somethin' sweet. You like that, honey? You look like you got a sweet tooth."

He smiled and slid a hand onto her thigh. His fingernails curled dark and long against her jeans. Before she could move, a black woman in her forties wearing a glittery magenta bra and thong appeared at the table. Light brown streaked across her stomach like tiger stripes.

"You leave her be, Lester," the woman said. Then to Nadia: "Come on, I'll freshen you up."

"Aw, Cici, I was just talkin' to her," the old man said.

"Please," Cici said. "That child ain't even as old as your watch."

She led Nadia back to the bar and tossed what

was left of her drink down the drain. Then she slipped into a white coat and beckoned for Nadia to follow her outside. Against the slate gray sky, the flat outline of the Hanky Panky seemed even more depressing. Further along the building, two white girls were smoking and they each threw up a hand when Cici and Nadia stepped outside. Cici returned the lazy greeting and lit a cigarette.

"You got a nice face," Cici said. "Those your real eyes? You mixed?"

"No," she said. "I mean, they're my eyes but I'm not mixed."

"Look mixed to me." Cici blew a sideways stream of smoke. "You a runaway? Oh, don't look at me like that. I won't report you. I see you girls come through here all the time, looking to make a little money. Ain't legal but Bernie don't mind. Bernie'll give you a little stage time, see what you can do. Don't expect no warm welcome, though. Hard enough fighting those blonde bitches for tips—wait till the girls see your light-bright ass."

"I don't want to dance," Nadia said.

"Well, I don't know what you're looking for but you ain't gonna find it here." Cici leaned in closer. "You know you got see-through eyes? Feels like I can see right through them. Nothin' but sad on the other side." She dug into her pocket and pulled out a handful of crumpled ones. "This ain't no place for you. Go on down to Fat Charlie's and get you something to eat. Go on."

Nadia hesitated, but Cici dropped the bills into Nadia's palm and curled her fingers into a fist. Maybe she could do this, pretend she was a runaway, or maybe in a way, she was. Her father never asked where she'd been. She returned home at night and found him in his recliner, watching television in a darkened living room. He always looked surprised when she unlocked the front door, like he hadn't even noticed that she'd been gone.

In Fat Charlie's, Nadia had been sitting in a booth toward the back, flipping through a menu, when Luke Sheppard stepped out of the kitchen, white apron slung across his hips, black Fat Charlie's T-shirt stretched across his muscular chest. He looked as handsome as she'd remembered from Sunday School, except he was a man now, bronzed and broad-shouldered, his hard jaw covered in stubble. And he was limping now, slightly favoring his left leg, but the gimpiness of his walk, its uneven pace and tenderness, only made her want him more. Her mother had died a month ago and she was drawn to anyone who wore their pain outwardly, the way she couldn't. She hadn't even cried at the funeral. At the repast, a parade of guests had told her how well she'd done and her father placed an arm around her shoulder. He'd hunched over the pew during the service, his shoulders quietly shaking, manly crying but crying still, and for the first time, she'd wondered if she might be stronger than him.

An inside hurt was supposed to stay inside. How strange it must be to hurt in an outside way you couldn't hide. She played with the menu flap as Luke limped his way over to her booth. She, and everyone at Upper Room, had watched his promising sophomore season end last year. A routine kick return, a bad tackle, and his leg broke, the bone cutting clear through the skin. The commentators had said he'd be lucky if he walked normal again, let alone played another down, so no one had been surprised when San Diego State pulled his scholarship. But she hadn't seen Luke since he'd gotten out of the hospital. In her mind, he was still in a cot, surrounded by doting nurses, his bandaged leg propped toward the ceiling.

"What're you doing here?" she asked.

"I work here," he said, then laughed, but his laugh sounded hard, like a chair suddenly scraped against the floor. "How you been?"

He didn't look at her, shuffling through his notepad, so she knew he'd heard about her mother.

"I'm hungry," she said.

"That's how you been? Hungry?"

"Can I get the crab bites?"

"You better not." He guided her finger down the laminated menu to the nachos. "There. Try that."

His hand curved soft over hers like he was teaching her to read, moving her finger under unfamiliar words. He always made her feel impossibly young, like two days later, when she returned to his section and tried to order a margarita. He laughed, tilting her fake ID toward him.

"Come on," he said. "Aren't you, like, twelve?"

She narrowed her eyes. "Oh fuck you," she said, "I'm seventeen."

But she'd said it a little too proudly and Luke laughed again. Even eighteen—which she wouldn't turn until late August—would seem young to him. She was still in high school. He was twenty-one and had already gone to college, a real university, not the community college where everyone loafed around a few months after graduation before finding jobs. She had applied to five universities and while she waited to hear back, she asked Luke questions about college life, like were dorm showers as gross as she imagined and did people actually stick socks on door handles when they wanted privacy? He told her about undie runs and foam parties, how to maximize your meal plan, how to get extra time on tests by pretending you had a learning problem. He knew things and he knew girls, college girls, girls who wore high heels to class, not sneakers, and carried satchels instead of backpacks, and spent their summers interning at Qualcomm or California Bank & Trust, not making juice at the pier. She imagined herself in college, one of those sophisticated girls, Luke driving to see her, or if she went out of state, flying to visit her over spring break. He would laugh if he knew how she imagined him in her life. He teased her often, like when she began doing her homework in Fat Charlie's.

"Shit," he said, flipping through her calculus book. "You a nerd."

She wasn't, really, but learning came easily to her. (Her mother used to tease her about that—must be nice, she'd say, when Nadia brought home an aced test she only studied for the night before.) She thought her advanced classes might scare Luke off, but he liked that she was smart. See this girl right here, he'd tell a passing waiter, first black lady president, just watch. Every black girl who was even slightly gifted was told this. But she liked listening to Luke brag and she liked it even more when he teased her for studying. He didn't treat her like everyone at school, who either sidestepped her or spoke to her like she was some fragile thing one harsh word away from breaking.

One February night, Luke drove her home and she invited him inside. Her father was gone for the weekend at the Men's Advance, so the house was dark and silent when they arrived. She wanted to offer Luke a drink—that's what women did in the movies, handed a man a boxy glass, filled with something dark and masculine—but moonlight glinted off glass cabinets emptied of liquor and Luke pressed her against the wall and kissed her. She hadn't told him it was her first time but he knew. In her bed, he asked three times if she wanted to stop. Each time she told him no. Sex would hurt and she wanted it to. She wanted Luke to be her outside hurt.

By spring, she knew what time Luke got off work, when to meet him in the deserted corner of the parking lot, where two people could be alone. She knew which nights he had off, nights she listened for his car crawling up her street and tiptoed past her father's shut bedroom. She knew the days he went to work late, days she slipped him inside the house before her father came home from work. How Luke wore his Fat Charlie's T-shirt a size too small because it helped him earn more tips. How when he dropped to the edge of her bed without saying much, he was dreading a long shift, so she didn't say much either, tugging his too-tight shirt over his head and running her hands over the expanse of his shoulders. She knew that being on his feet all day hurt his leg more than he ever admitted and sometimes, while he slept, she stared at the thin scar climbing toward his knee. Bones, like anything else, strong until they weren't.

She also knew that Fat Charlie's was dead between lunch and happy hour, so after her pregnancy test returned positive, she rode the bus over to tell Luke.

"FUCK" was the first thing he said.

Then, "Are you sure?"

Then, "But are you **sure** sure?"

Then, "Fuck."

In the empty Fat Charlie's, Nadia drowned her

fries in a pool of ketchup until they were limp and soggy. Of course she was sure. She wouldn't have worried him if she weren't already sure. For days, she'd willed herself to bleed, begging for a drop, a trickle even, but instead, she only saw the perfect whiteness of her panties. So that morning, she rode the bus to the free pregnancy center outside of town, a squat gray building in the middle of a strip mall. In the lobby, a row of fake plants nearly blocked the receptionist, who pointed Nadia to the waiting area. She joined a handful of black girls who barely glanced up at her as she sat between a chubby girl popping purple gum and a girl in overall shorts who played Tetris on her phone. A fat white counselor named Dolores led Nadia to the back, where they squeezed inside a cubicle so cramped, their knees touched.

"Now, do you have a reason to think you might be pregnant?" Dolores asked.

She wore a lumpy gray sweater covered in cotton sheep and spoke like a kindergarten teacher, smiling, her sentences ending in a gentle lilt. She must've thought Nadia was an idiot—another black girl too dumb to insist on a condom. But they had used condoms, at least most times, and Nadia felt stupid for how comfortable she had felt with their mostly safe sex. She was supposed to be the smart one. She was supposed to understand that it only took one mistake and her future could be ripped away from her. She had known pregnant girls. She had seen them waddling around school in tight tank tops and sweatshirts that hugged their bellies. She never saw the boys who had gotten them that way—their names were enshrouded in mystery, as wispy as rumor itself—but she could never unsee the girls, big and blooming in front of her. Of all people, she should have known better. She was her mother's mistake.

Across the booth, Luke hunched over the table, flexing his fingers like he used to when he was on the sidelines at a game. Her freshman year, she'd spent more time watching Luke than watching the team on the field. What would those hands feel like touching her?

"I thought you were hungry," he said.

She tossed another fry onto the pile. She hadn't eaten anything all day—her mouth felt salty, the way it did before she puked. She slipped out of her flip-flops, resting her bare feet against his thigh.

"I feel like shit," she said.

"Want something different?"

"I don't know."

He pushed away from the table. "Let me get you something else—"

17

"I can't keep it," she said.

Luke stopped, halfway out his seat.

"What?" he said.

"I can't keep a baby," she said. "I can't be someone's fucking mother, I'm going to college and
my dad is gonna—"

She couldn't bring herself to say out loud what
she wanted—the word **abortion** felt ugly and
mechanical—but Luke understood, didn't he?
He'd been the first person she told when she
received her acceptance e-mail from the University of Michigan—he'd swept her into a hug
before she even finished her sentence, nearly
crushing her in his arms. He had to understand
that she couldn't pass this up, her one chance to
leave home, to leave her silent father whose smile
hadn't even reached his eyes when she showed
him the e-mail, but who she knew would be happier with her gone, without her there to remind
him of what he'd lost. She couldn't let this baby
nail her life in place when she'd just been given a
chance to escape.

If Luke understood, he didn't say so. He didn't
say anything at first, sinking back into the
booth, his body suddenly slow and heavy. In that
moment, he looked even older to her, his stubbled

face tired and haggard. He reached for her bare feet and cradled them in his lap.

"Okay," he said, then softer, "okay. Tell me what to do."

He didn't try to change her mind. She appreciated that, although part of her had hoped he might do something old-fashioned and romantic, like offer to marry her. She never would've agreed but it would've been nice if he'd tried. Instead, he asked how much money she needed. She felt stupid—she hadn't even thought of something as practical as paying for the surgery—but he promised he'd come up with the cash. When he handed her the envelope the next day, she asked him not to wait with her at the clinic. He rubbed the back of her neck.

"Are you sure?" he said.

"Yes," she said. "Just pick me up after."

She'd feel worse if she had an audience. Vulnerable. Luke had seen her naked—he had slipped inside her own body—but somehow, his seeing her afraid was an intimacy she could not bear.

THE MORNING OF HER APPOINTMENT, Nadia rode the bus to the abortion clinic downtown.

She had driven past it dozens of times—an unremarkable tan building, slunk in the shadows of a Bank of America—but she had never imagined what it might look like inside. As the bus wound its way toward the beach, she stared out the window, envisioning sterile white walls, sharp tools on trays, fat receptionists in baggy sweaters herding crying girls into waiting rooms. Instead, the lobby was open and bright, the walls painted a creamy color that had some fancy name like **taupe** or **ochre,** and on the oak tables, beside stacks of magazines, there were blue vases filled with seashells. In a chair farthest from the door, Nadia pretended to read a **National Geographic.** Next to her, a redhead mumbled as she struggled with a crossword puzzle; her boyfriend slumped beside her, staring at his cell phone. He was the only man in the room, so maybe the redhead felt superior—more loved—since her boyfriend had joined her, even though he didn't seem like a good boyfriend, even though he wasn't even talking to her or holding her hand, like Luke would have done. Across the room, a black girl in a clingy yellow dress sniffled into her jean jacket sleeve. Her mother, a heavy woman with a purple rose tattooed on her arm, sat beside her, arms folded across her chest. She looked angry or maybe just worried. The girl looked fourteen, and the louder she sniffled, the harder everyone tried not to look at her.

Nadia thought about texting Luke. **I'm here. I'm okay.** But he'd just started his shift and he was probably worried enough as it was. She flipped through the magazine slowly, her eyes gliding off the pages to the blonde receptionist smiling into her headset, the traffic outside, the blue vase of seashells beside her. Her mother had hated the actual beach—messy sand and cigarette butts everywhere—but she loved shells, so whenever they went, she always spent the afternoon padding along the shore, bending to peel shells out of the damp sand.

"They calm me," she'd said once. She'd clutched Nadia on her lap and turned a shell carefully, flashing its shiny insides. In her hand, the shell had glimmered lavender and green.

"Turner?"

In the doorway, a black nurse with graying dreadlocks read her name off a metal clipboard. As Nadia gathered her purse, she felt the nurse give her a once-over, eyes drifting past her red blouse, skinny jeans, black pumps.

"Should've worn something more comfortable," the nurse said.

"I am comfortable," Nadia said. She felt thirteen again, standing in the vice-principal's office as he lectured her on the dress code.

"Sweatpants," the nurse said. "Someone should've told you that when you called."

"They did."

The nurse shook her head, starting back down the hall. She seemed weary, unlike the chipper white nurses squeaking down the hallways in pink scrubs and rubber shoes. Like she'd seen so much that nothing surprised her anymore, not even a girl with a sassy mouth wearing a silly outfit, a girl so alone, she couldn't find one person to sit with her in the waiting room. No, there was nothing special about a girl like this—not her good grades, not her prettiness. She was just another black girl who'd found herself in trouble and was finding her way out of it.

In the sonogram room, a technician asked Nadia if she wanted to see the screen. Optional, he said, but it gave some women closure. She told him no. She'd heard once about a sixteen-year-old girl from her high school who'd given birth and left her baby on the beach. The girl was arrested when she doubled back to tell a cop she'd seen a baby and he discovered that she was the mother. How could he tell, Nadia had always wondered.

Maybe, in the floodlights of his patrol car, he'd spotted blood streaking the insides of her thighs or smelled fresh milk spotting her nipples. Or maybe it was something else entirely. The ginger way she'd handed the baby over, the carefulness in her eyes when he brushed sand off its downy hair. Maybe he saw, even as he backed away, the maternal love that stretched like a golden thread from her to the abandoned baby. Something had given the girl away, but Nadia wouldn't make the same mistake. Double back. She wouldn't hesitate and allow herself to love the baby or even know him.

"Just do it already," she said.

"What about multiples?" the technician asked, rolling toward her on his stool. "You know, twins, triplets . . ."

"Why would I want to know that?"

He shrugged. "Some women do."

She already knew too much about the baby, like the fact that it was a boy. It was too early to actually tell, but she felt his foreignness in her body, something that was her and wasn't her. A male presence. A boy child who would have Luke's thick curls and squinty-eyed smile. No, she couldn't think about that either. She couldn't allow herself to love the baby because of Luke. So when the technician swirled the sensor in the blue goo on her stomach, she turned her head away.

After a few moments, the technician stopped, pausing the sensor over her belly button.

"Huh," he said.

"What?" she said. "What happened?"

Maybe she wasn't actually pregnant. That could happen, couldn't it? Maybe the test had been wrong or maybe the baby had sensed he wasn't wanted. Maybe he had given up on his own. She couldn't help it—she turned toward the monitor. The screen filled with a wedge of grainy white light, and in the center, a black oval punctuated by a single white splotch.

"Your womb's a perfect sphere," the technician said.

"So? What does that mean?"

"I don't know," he said. "That you're a super-hero, maybe."

He chuckled, swirling the sensor around the gel. She didn't know what she expected to see in the sonogram—the sloping of a forehead, maybe, the outline of a belly. Not this, white and bean-shaped and small enough to cover with her thumb. How could this tiny light be a life? How could something this small bring hers to an end?

When she returned to the waiting room, the

girl in the jean jacket was sobbing. No one looked at her, not even the heavy woman, who was now sitting one seat over. Nadia had been wrong—this woman couldn't be the girl's mother. A mother would move toward a crying child, not away. Her mother would've held her and absorbed her tears into her own body. She would've rocked her and not let go until the nurse called her name again. But this woman reached over and pinched the crying girl's thigh.

"Cut all that out," she said. "You wanted to be grown? Well, now you grown."

THE PROCEDURE only takes ten minutes, the dreadlocked nurse told her. Less than an episode of television.

In the chilly operating room, Nadia stared at the monitor that hung in front of her flashing pictures from beaches around the world. Overhead, speakers played a meditation CD—classical guitar over crashing waves—and she knew she was supposed to pretend she was lying on a tropical island, pressed against grains of white sand. But when the nurse fit the anesthesia mask on her face and told her to count to a hundred, she could only think about the girl abandoning her baby in

25

the sand. Maybe the beach was a more natural place to leave a baby you couldn't care for. Nestle him in the sand and hope someone found him— an old couple on a midnight stroll, a patrol cop sweeping his flashlight over beer cases. But if they didn't, if no one stumbled upon him, he'd return to his first home, an ocean like the one inside of her. Water would break onto the shore, sweep him up in its arms, and rock him back to sleep.

WHEN IT WAS OVER, Luke never came for her.

An hour after she'd called him, she was the only girl still waiting in the recovery room, curled in an overstuffed pink recliner, clutching a heat pad against her cramping stomach. For an hour, she'd stared into the dimness of the room, unable to make out the faces of the others but imagining they looked as blank as hers. Maybe the girl in the yellow dress had cried into the arms of her recliner. Or maybe the redhead had just continued her crossword puzzle. Maybe she'd been through this before or she already had children and couldn't take another. Was it easier if you already had a child, like politely declining seconds because you were already full?

Now the others were gone and she had pulled

out her phone to call Luke a third time when the dreadlocked nurse dragged over a metal chair. She was carrying a paper plate of crackers and an apple juice box.

"Cramps'll be bad for a while," she said. "Just put some heat on 'em, they'll go away. You got a heat pad at home?"

"No."

"Just heat you up a towel. Works just as fine."

Nadia had hoped she might get a different nurse. She'd watched the others swish through the room to dote on their girls, offering smiles, squeezing hands. But the dreadlocked nurse just shook the plate at her.

"I'm not hungry," Nadia said.

"You need to eat. Can't let you go until you do."

Nadia sighed, taking a cracker. Where was Luke? She was tired of this nurse, with her wrinkled skin and steady eyes. She wanted to be in her own bed, wrapped in her comforter, her head on Luke's chest. He would make her soup and play movies on his laptop until she fell asleep. He would kiss her and tell her that she had been brave. The nurse uncrossed, then recrossed her legs.

"Heard from your friend yet?" she asked.

"Not yet, but he's coming," Nadia said.

"You got someone else to call?"

"I don't need someone else, he's coming."

"He's not coming, baby," the nurse said. "Do you have someone else to call?"

Nadia glanced up, startled by the nurse's confidence that Luke would not show, but even more jolted by her use of the word **baby.** A cotton-soft **baby** that seemed to surprise the nurse herself, like it had tripped off her tongue. Just like how after the surgery, in her delirium, Nadia had looked into the nurse's blurred face and said "Mommy?" with such sweetness, the nurse had almost answered yes.

TWO

If Nadia Turner had asked, we would've warned her to stay away from him.

You know what they say about pastors' kids. In Sunday School, they're running around the sanctuary, hollering, smearing crayons on the pews; in middle school, a pastor's son chases girls, flipping up their dresses, while his sister smears on bright lipstick that makes her look like a harlot; by high school, the son is smoking reefer in the church parking lot and the daughter is being felt up in a bathroom stall by the deacon's son, who is quietly unrolling the panty hose her mother insisted she wear because ladies don't show their bare legs in church.

Luke Sheppard, bold and brash with wispy curls, football-built shoulders, and that squinty-eyed smile. Oh, any of us could've told her to stay away from him. She wouldn't have listened, of course. What did the church mothers know anyway? Not how Luke held her hand while they slept or played with her hair when they cuddled or how after she'd told him about the pregnancy test, he cradled her bare feet in his lap. A man who laced his fingers through yours all night and held your feet when you were sad had to love you, at least a little bit. Besides, what did a bunch of old ladies know?

We would've told her that all together, we got centuries on her. If we laid all our lives toes to heel, we were born before the Depression, the Civil War, even America itself. In all that living, we have known men. Oh girl, we have known littlebit love. That littlebit of honey left in an empty jar that traps the sweetness in your mouth long enough to mask your hunger. We have run tongues over teeth to savor that last littlebit as long as we could, and in all our living, nothing has starved us more.

———

TEN YEARS BEFORE Nadia Turner's appointment, we'd already made our first visit to the abortion clinic downtown. Oh, not the way you're thinking. By the time that clinic was built, we would've laughed like Sarah at the thought of having babies, unwanted or otherwise. Besides, we were already mothers then, some by heart and some by womb. We rocked grandbabies left in our care and taught the neighborhood kids piano and baked pies for the sick and shut-in. We all mothered somebody, and more than that, we all mothered Upper Room Chapel, so when the church started a protest out front, we joined too. Not like Upper Room was the type of church to fuss at every little thing it didn't like. Shake fists at rated-R movies or buy armloads of rap CDs just to crush them or write letters to Sacramento to ensure the state's list of banned books stayed long and current. In fact, the church had only protested once before, back in the seventies, when Oceanside's first strip club was built. A strip club, minutes from the beach where children swam and played. What next, a brothel on the pier? Why not turn the harbor into a red-light district? Well, the Hanky Panky opened and even though it was a blight to the community, everyone agreed that the new abortion clinic was much worse. A sign of the times, really. An abortion clinic going up downtown just as easy as a donut shop.

So the morning of the protest, the congregation gathered in front of the unbuilt clinic. Second John, who had driven the carless in the church van, and Sister Willis, who had instructed her Sunday School students to help color in the protest signs, and even Magdalena Price, who could hardly be bothered to do anything around Upper Room that required her to step out from behind her piano bench, had come down to the protest to, as she put it, see what all the fuss was about. All of us had circled around the pastor and the first lady and their son—a boy then, kicking dirt clods onto the sidewalk—while the pastor prayed for the souls of innocents.

Our protest only lasted three days. (Not because of our wavering convictions but because of the militants who joined us, the type of crazed white people who would end up on the news someday for bombing clinics or stabbing doctors. The last place any of us wanted to be was near the scene when one went off the deep end.) All three days, Robert Turner drove downtown at six a.m. to deliver a new batch of picket signs from the church. He and his wife were not the protesting type, he told the pastor, but he'd figured that transporting the signs was the least he could do, truck and all.

This was ten years before he would be known around Upper Room as the man with the truck, a black Chevy pickup that had become Upper Room's truck because of how often Robert was seen driving from church, an arm hanging out the window, the truck bed filled with food baskets or donated clothes or metal chairs. He wasn't the only member with a truck, of course, but he was the only one willing to lend his at any moment. He kept a calendar by the phone and whenever anyone from Upper Room called, he carefully scheduled them in with a tiny golf pencil. Sometimes he joked that he should add the truck to his answering machine greeting because the truck would earn more messages than he did anyway. A joke, although he wondered if it was true, if the truck was the only reason he was invited to picnics and potlucks, if the true guest was the truck, needed to haul speakers and tables and folding chairs, but no one minded if he tagged along too. Why else would he receive such warm greetings when he stepped into Upper Room each Sunday? The ushers clapping his back and the ladies at the welcome table smiling at him and the pastor mentioning, once, in passing, that he wouldn't be shocked if Robert's good stewardship landed him on the elders board one day.

The truck, Robert believed, had turned things around for him. But there was also his daughter. People are always tenderhearted toward single fathers, especially single fathers raising girls, and folks would have cared for Robert Turner still, even if that terrible thing hadn't happened with his wife, even if she had just packed a suitcase and left, which to some, it seemed like she did anyway.

THAT EVENING, when her father pulled his truck into the garage, Nadia was curled in bed, clutching her twisting stomach. "The cramps might be bad," the dreadlocked nurse had told her. "Expect them a few hours or so. Call the emergency number if they're severe." The nurse didn't explain the difference between bad cramps and severe ones, but she'd handed Nadia a white bag curled at the top like a sack lunch. "For the pain. Two every four hours." A clinic volunteer offered to drive Nadia home, and when she climbed into the white girl's dusty Sentra, she glanced out the window at the nurse, who watched them drive off. The volunteer—blonde, twentyish, earnest—chatted nervously the whole drive, fiddling with the radio dials. She was a junior at Cal State San Marcos, she said, volunteering at the clinic as part of her feminist studies major. She looked like the type of girl who could go to college, major in something like feminist studies, and still expect to be taken seriously. She asked if Nadia planned to go to college and seemed surprised by her response. "Oh, Michigan's a good school," she said, as if Nadia didn't already know this.

That was two hours ago. Nadia clenched her eyes, passing through the cold center of the pain into its warmer edges. She wanted to take another pill even though she knew she should wait, but when she heard the garage door rumble, she shoved the orange vial into the white bag, everything inside her nightstand drawer. Anything unusual might tip her father off, even that nondescript bag. Since she discovered that she was pregnant, she'd been sure that her father would notice something was wrong with her. Her mother had been able to tell when she'd had a bad day at school moments after she climbed into the car. What happened? her mother used to ask, even before Nadia had said hello. Her father had never been that perceptive, but a pregnancy wasn't a bad day at school—he would notice that she was panicking, he would have to. She was grateful so far that he hadn't, but it scared her, how you could return home in a different body, how something big could be happening inside you and no one even knew it.

Her father knocked three times and nudged her bedroom door open. He wore his service khakis today, which seemed like a second skin, how naturally he fit within sharp pleats, a row of badges across his chest. Her friends used to be surprised that her father was a Marine. He didn't seem like the boys they'd grown up seeing around town, cocky and buff and horsing around in front of the Regal, flirting with passing girls. Maybe her father had been like that when he was younger but she couldn't imagine it. He was quiet and intense, a tall, wiry man who never seemed to relax, like a guard dog on his haunches, his ears always perked up. He leaned in her doorway, bending to unlace his shiny black boots.

"You don't look so good," he said. "You sick?"

"Just cramps," she said.

"Oh. Your . . ." He gestured to his stomach. "Need anything?"

"No," she said. "Wait. Can I use your truck later?"

"For what?"

"To drive."

"Where are you going, I mean."

"You can't do that."

"Do what?"

"Ask where I'm going. I'm almost eighteen."

"I can't ask where you're taking my truck?"

"Where do you think I'm taking it?" she said. "The border?"

Her father never cared about where she went, except when she asked to borrow his precious truck. He spent evenings circling the truck in the driveway, dipping a red velvet square into a tub of wax until the paint shone like glass. Then as soon as someone from Upper Room called for a favor, he jogged out the door, always running to his truck, as if it were the only child, needy and demanding of his love. Her father sighed, running a hand over the graying hair she cut every two weeks, the way her mother used to, her father sitting in the backyard with a towel draped around his neck, her hands guiding the clippers. Cutting his hair was the only time she felt close to him.

"Downtown, okay?" she said. "Can I borrow your truck, please?"

Another wave of cramps gripped her, and she

37

flinched, pulling her blanket tighter around herself. Her father lingered in the doorway a moment before dropping his keys on her dresser.

"I can make you some tea," he said. "It's supposed to—your aunts, they'd drink it, you know, when—"

"You can just leave the keys," she said.

THE DAY AFTER she was accepted into Michigan, Luke brought Nadia to the Wave Waterpark, where they rode inner tubes down the Slide Tower and the Flow Rider until they were soaked and tired. At first, she'd worried that he'd suggested a water park because he thought she was childish. But he had as much fun as she did, yelping as they splashed into pools, or dragging her to the next ride, water beads clinging to his chest, his wet sideburns glinting in the sun. After, they ate corn dogs and churros at the tables outside Rippity's Rainforest, where kids too small for the slides padded in floaties. She licked cinnamon sugar off her fingers, sun-heavy and happy, the type of happiness that before might have felt ordinary, but now seemed fragile, like if she stood too quickly, it might slide off her shoulders and break.

She hadn't expected a gift from Luke, not when her father had barely congratulated her. Look at that, he'd said when she showed him the e-mail, offering her a side hug. Then he'd passed her in the kitchen later that night, eyes glazing over her as if she were a once-interesting piece of furniture he'd since tired of. She tried not to take it personally—he wasn't happy about anything these days—but she still teared up in the bathroom while brushing her teeth. The next morning, she awoke to a congratulations card on her nightstand with twenty dollars folded inside. **I'm sorry**, her father had written, **I'm trying**. Trying what? Trying to love her?

She stretched her legs across Luke's lap and he kneaded the smooth skin near her ankles while he finished his corn dog. He'd never seen her like this before—hair wet and kinky, her face clean of makeup—but she felt pretty as he smiled at her across the table, touching her ankle, and she wondered if his gentle touch meant more, if he might even be in love with her a little bit. Before they left, she tried to take a picture of the two of them but Luke cupped his hand around her phone. He wanted to keep their relationship a secret.

"Not a secret," he said. "Just private."

"'That's the same thing," she said.

"It's not. I just think we should be low-key about this. That's all."

"Why?"

"I mean, the age thing."

"I'm almost eighteen."

"'Almost' ain't eighteen."

"I wouldn't get you in trouble. Don't you know that?"

"It's not just that," he said. "You don't know how it is. You're not a pastor's kid. The whole church in my business all the time. They'll be up in your business too. Let's just be smart, that's all I'm saying."

Maybe there was a difference. You hid a secret relationship out of shame, but you might keep a relationship private for any number of reasons. All relationships, in some way, were private— why did anyone else need to know as long as you were happy? So she learned how to be private. She didn't reach for his hand in public or post photos of them online. She even stopped going to Fat Charlie's after school every day, in case one of his coworkers began to wonder about them. But after Luke had left her at the abortion clinic, she forgot about being private and drove her father's truck to Fat Charlie's. She knew he closed on Thursday nights, but when she arrived, she didn't see him on the floor. At the bar, she waved down Pepe, a burly Mexican bartender with a graying ponytail. He glanced up from drying a glass with a brown rag.

"Go ahead and put that cheap-ass fake away," he said. "You know I ain't serving you."

"Where's Luke?" she asked.

"Hell if I know."

"Doesn't he get off soon?"

"I ain't in charge of his schedule."

"Well, have you seen him?"

"You okay?"

"Did you see him earlier?"

"Why don't you just call him?"

"He's not answering," she said. "I'm worried."

It wasn't like Luke to disappear like this, to not answer his phone, to promise he'd be somewhere, then not show. Especially on a day like today when she needed him, when he knew she needed him. She was worried that something bad had happened to him, or even worse, that nothing had. What if he had abandoned her at that clinic because he'd simply chosen to? No, he would never do that—but she thought about him at the water park, clamping his hand over her phone, that brief moment when she had felt safe and loved right before Luke had pulled away.

Pepe sighed, setting the glass on the bar. He had four daughters, Luke had told her once, and she wondered if this was why Pepe always refused her fake ID, always shooed away men who hit on her, always asked her how she was getting home.

"Look, hon," he said. "You know Sheppard. Probably just wanted to go out with his buddies. I'm sure he'll call you tomorrow. Just go home, won't you?"

IN THE END, she found Luke at a party.

Not just any party but a high school party, although Cody Richardson would've been offended to hear his parties referred to as such. He had graduated ten years ago, after all, but his parties would always be high school parties because Nadia, and everyone else at Oceanside High, had spent countless weekends partying at his house. He was a sandy-haired skater, the type of white boy she had nothing in common with. But even though she normally hated white boy parties—the repetitive techno music, the smothering Abercrombie and Fitch cologne, the terrible dancing—she had gone to Cody Richardson's parties because everyone did. She had piled inside his beach bungalow every weekend, where you never worried about anyone's parents coming back to town early or the cops shutting the party down, and now his floor plan read like a map of her teenage firsts: the balcony where she'd first smoked weed, hacking into the beach air; the corner of the kitchen where she'd broken up with her first boyfriend; the hallway in front of the bathroom where she had drunk-cried the weekend after they buried her mother.

She hadn't been back to Cody's since. The yellow house already felt like something she'd outgrown and once she'd graduated, she promised herself that she would never return. She had always been bothered by how many people did, how everyone seemed stuck in time, the years since high school collapsing as soon as they stepped through the door. Still, Cody's house was the only place she could think to find Luke after she'd driven past his parents' house and seen his truck missing from the driveway. Somehow, she knew he would be at Cody's. She felt him as she walked, lovesick and angry, across the damp beach sand. She followed the footprint trail leading to the beach house, wondering if she might find the footprints that belonged to Luke, her feet stepping inside his the entire time.

Techno pulsed through the open door in green waves as she padded up the lopsided driftwood steps. Bass rumbled through wooden floors sticky with beer, and she paused in the doorway, her eyes adjusting to the dimness. She wouldn't have noticed Luke at first if it weren't for his walk. Past the crowd of white kids thrashing together, past kitchen counters covered in half-empty bottles of liquor and two triangles of cups from an abandoned game of beer pong, she caught Luke's silhouette crossing the darkened room. That slight limp, subtle enough for most to ignore it but as familiar to her as his voice. He looked drunk, a near-empty pint of Jim Beam dangling from his hand. When she neared, he swayed a little, as if the sight of her was enough to knock him off balance.

"Nadia," he said. "What're you doing here?"

"What the fuck are you doing here?" she said. "I called you a hundred fucking times."

"You shouldn't be here. You should be in bed or something—"

"Where were you?" she said. "I waited for hours."

"Some shit came up, okay? I knew you were gonna find a way home."

But he stared at the ground when he said it and she knew he was lying.

"You left me," she said.

He finally looked up at her, and it startled her, how he looked the same as he always had. Shouldn't someone look different once you've caught them in a lie, once you've seen them truthfully for the first time?

"Look, this shit was supposed to be fun," he said, "not all this fucking drama. I got you the money. What else do you want from me?"

Then he brushed past her, pushing through the crowd and lurching unevenly toward the door. She should've known. She should've known when he'd brought her an envelope with six hundred dollars that the money was his part, the rest hers. He'd slipped her the money, and now she was a problem that he'd already dealt with. In a way, she had known this—or at least suspected it—but she'd wanted to believe in Luke, in love, in people who did not leave. She squeezed into the kitchen, past a group of giddy high schoolers playing flip cup, and reached for a bottle of Jose Cuervo on the counter. The dreadlocked nurse

had told her no alcohol for forty-eight hours—
thins the blood, increases the bleeding—but she
poured a shot of tequila anyway. She felt a hand
on her waist and when she turned, Devon Jackson lingered behind her, a joint pressed between
his fingertips. She hadn't spoken to him since
they fooled around once her freshman year; he
looked the same, almost delicate, tall and lean
with long eyelashes except his skin was now covered in tattoos. Even his neck was darkened with
ink, a fleur-de-lis stretching up his throat.

"Jesus," she said. "You're stained now."

He laughed. "Where the fuck you been?"

Nowhere. Everywhere. He passed her the joint
and she felt fifteen again, smoking with a boy
who had fingered her once at the top of a Ferris
wheel, gently, the car swaying like it was rocking
them to sleep. The last she'd heard, Devon was
modeling now, mostly on gay websites. Two years
ago, a friend had sent her a link to a photo spread
where Devon stretched out along white sheets in
nothing but his briefs, a blond man's face inches
from his crotch.

"I heard you're famous now," she said, passing
the joint.

She didn't mean to get drunk. She poured herself another drink because Devon asked why her

cup was empty, what, did she become a nun or something? She poured a shot of tequila into a cup of lemonade, then another shot, then another, then she let Devon pull her onto the dance floor. Not because she wanted to dance but because dancing was an excuse to be close, to touch, to be comforted by the press and pull of Devon's body against hers without having to talk. And the drinks made her feel nice, although the room was warm and she felt disgusted by Devon's swampy T-shirt as she draped an arm around his waist. Her blood was probably thinning as she danced, but how nice it was to feel drunk and relaxed and warm and touched and touching.

Devon kissed her neck, squeezing her ass with both hands.

"You're so fuckin' fine," he said, breath hot against her ear.

He grinded against her, biting his lip in that serious way of anyone trying hard to be sexy. She giggled. He laughed too, squeezing her again.

"What?" he said.

"I thought you like boys now," she said.

"Who the fuck told you that?"

"People."

"Does this feel like I like boys?"

He pressed her hand against his bulge and she

wrested her wrist out of his grasp, pushing him away. She felt trapped, suddenly, like she was suffocating. Blurry-eyed, she felt along the wall, past bodies bumping into her, the frenetic rhythms pumping out the speakers, through the sticky humidity to the back door. On the other end of the balcony, Cody Richardson leaned against the wooden railing. He was taller, thinner now, his dirty-blond hair shaggier, his plaid shirt hanging off his angular shoulders. He smiled, flashing his silver lip ring, and she eased toward him, gripping the rail.

"Don't you think it's weird?" he said.

"What?"

He pointed over her shoulder. Beyond the lavender roofs of other beach houses, she could see the top of the San Onofre nuclear power plant, two white domes that kids on the school bus used to call "the boobs" when they drove past on field trips.

"Any minute—boom." Cody's eyes widened, his hands exploding away from each other. "Just like that. I mean, all it takes is a storm and we all blow up."

Nadia rested her head on the railing, closing her eyes.

"That's how I wanna go someday," she said.

"Really?"

"Boom."

THIS IS HOW she imagined it:

Her mother driving around town, her husband's service pistol in her lap. A curve, then another curve, the morning light as pink as a baby girl's nightgown. She was groggy or maybe clearheaded, as clear as she'd ever been. She thought first about driving to the beach because it'd be a good place to die. Warm enough. A dying place ought to be warm—enough coldness waiting in the afterlife. But it was too late. Surfers were already padding across the sand and dying should be private, like humming a little song only you can hear.

So she drove on, half a mile up the hill from Upper Room where her car was shielded by branches. She shut off her engine and picked up the gun. She had never shot anything before but she'd seen animals die, pigs squealing as they bled out, chickens flapping as her mother wrung their necks. You could coax out life or you could end it at once. A slow death might seem gentler but a sudden death was kinder. Merciful, even.

She would be merciful to herself, this once.

———

WHEN HER FATHER ASKED, Nadia told him she hadn't seen the tree. In the darkness, the tree in front of their house was nearly impossible to see, so she'd made too sharp a turn. It was nearly four a.m., and they were both standing in the driveway, her father in his green plaid robe and slippers, her leaning against the truck door, her shoes in her hands. She had planned to sneak back inside the house, but her father had run outside as soon as he heard the crash. Now he crouched in front of his dented bumper, feeling the jagged metal.

"Why the heck weren't your headlights on?" he said.

"They were!" she said. "I just—I looked down to shut them off and then I looked up and then the tree."

She swayed a little. Her father frowned, straightening.

"Are you drunk?" he said.

"No," she said.

"I can smell it on you from here."

"No—"

"And you drove home?"

He stepped toward her and the sudden movement made her drop everything in her hands, her purse and shoes and keys clattering to the driveway. She jutted her arms out before he could come closer. He stopped, his jaw clenched, and she couldn't tell whether he wanted to slap her or hug her. Both hurt, his anger and his love, as they stood together in the dark driveway, his heart beating against her hands.

THREE

We pray.
   Not without ceasing, as Paul instructs, but often enough. On Sundays and Wednesdays, we gather in the prayer room and slip off jackets, leave shoes at the door and walk around in stocking feet, sliding a little, like girls playing on waxed floors. We sit in a ring of white chairs in the center of the room and one of us reaches into the wooden box by the door stuffed with prayer request cards. Then we pray: for Earl Vernon, who wants his crackhead daughter to come home; Cindy Harris's husband, who is leaving her because he'd caught her sending nasty photographs to her boss; Tracy Robinson, who has

taken to drinking again, hard liquor at that; Saul
Young, who is struggling to help his wife through
the final days of her dementia. We read the request
cards and we pray, for new jobs, new houses, new
husbands, better health, better-behaved children,
more faith, more patience, less temptation.

We don't think of ourselves as "prayer war-
riors." A man must've come up with that term—
men think anything difficult is war. But prayer is
more delicate than battle, especially intercessory
prayer. More than just a notion, taking up the
burdens of someone else, often someone you don't
even know. You close your eyes and listen to a
request. Then you have to slip inside their body.
You are Tracy Robinson, burning for whiskey.
You are Cindy Harris's husband, searching your
wife's phone. You are Earl Vernon, washing dirty
knots out of your strung-out daughter's hair.

If you don't become them, even for a second, a
prayer is nothing but words.

That's why it didn't take us long to figure out
what had happened to Robert Turner's truck.
Ordinarily waxed and gleaming, the truck hobbled into the Upper Room parking lot on Sunday
with a dented front bumper and cracked head-
light. In the lobby, we heard young folks joking
about how drunk Nadia Turner had been at some

beach party. Then we became young again, or that is to say, we became her. Dancing all night with a bottle of vodka in hand, staggering out the door. A careless drive home weaving between lanes. The crunch of metal. How, when Robert smelled the liquor, he must have hit her or maybe hugged her. How she was probably deserving of both.

The truck was the first sign that something wasn't right that summer, but none of us saw it that way. The banged-up truck only meant one thing to us then.

"Look what she done."

"Who done?"

"That Turner girl."

"Which one is that?"

"You know the one."

"Redbone, clear-eyes like."

"Oh, that girl?"

"What other Turner girl is there?"

"Don't she look—"

"Sure do."

"Like she spit her out."

"Y'all see his—"

"Mhm."

"How much you think that costs to fix?"

"Why she do that?"

"She wild."

"Poor Robert."

"She wild wild."

We only felt sorry for Robert Turner. He'd already been through too much. Half a year earlier, his wife had stolen his gun and blown her head clean off her body. A little past sunrise, she'd parked her blue Tercel along some back road and sent her car rocking from the gun blast. A jogger had found her an hour later. Robert had driven the Tercel home from the police station, the headrest still darkened with his wife's blood. No one knew what had happened to that car. Rumor was that after combing it for the rest of his wife's things—her pocketbook, overdue library paperbacks, a ruby red hair clip he'd bought her, years ago, from Mexico—he'd put a brick on the gas pedal and sent it right into the San Luis Rey River. But a man as sensible as Robert had probably sold it for parts, and sometimes we wondered if a passing car had Elise Turner's muffler, if her turn signal blinked at us from the next lane.

All of that, and now a reckless daughter too. No wonder Robert looked so troubled.

That evening, we found a prayer card with his name on it in the wooden box outside the door. In the center, in all lowercase, the words **pray for**

her. We didn't know which **her** he meant—his dead wife or his reckless daughter—so we prayed for both. It's more than just a notion, you know. Praying for someone dead. When there's no body to slip into, you can only try to find their spirit, and who wants to chase down Elise Turner's, wherever it's hiding?

Later that night, when we left the prayer room, we felt something in Upper Room shift. Couldn't explain it, something just felt different. Off. We knew the walls of Upper Room like the walls of our own homes. We'd soft-stepped down hallways as the choir practiced, noticing that corner in front of the instrument closet where the paint had chipped, or the tile in the ladies' room that had been laid crooked. We'd spent decades studying the splotch that looked like an elephant's ear on the ceiling above the water fountain. And we knew the exact spot on the sanctuary carpet where Elise Turner had knelt the night before she killed herself. (The more spiritual of us even swore they could still see the indented curve from her knees.) Sometimes we joked that when we died, we'd all become part of these walls, pressed down flat like wallpaper. Near the stained-glass windows in the sanctuary or in a corner of the Sunday School room or even attached to the ceiling in the prayer room, where we met every Sunday and Wednesday to intercede.

We didn't know then that the banged-up truck had knotted Nadia Turner's future to our own, that we would watch her come and go over the years, each time tugging that knot a little tighter.

ON SUNDAY NIGHT, the Turners received a visitor.

Nadia had spent most of the weekend in bed, not because her stomach still hurt but because she had nowhere else to go. She wasn't pregnant anymore but she had wrecked her father's truck. What if it took weeks to fix? How would he stand it, no truck to turn to, no errands to run, only work and home? He loved one thing, her father, and she had ruined it. Worse, her father hadn't even yelled at her. She wished he would rage when he was angry—it'd be easier that way, quicker—but instead, he coiled up tight inside himself, moving silently around her in the kitchen or avoiding her altogether. She felt herself disappearing into the silence until she heard two high-pitched notes stepping through the air, so light she thought she dreamed them. Then she heard three knocks and a brief stab ran through her. Luke. She jumped up, finger combing her hair into a ponytail, tucking her bra strap under her tank top, adjusting her shorts. She padded barefoot across the cold tile and opened the door.

"Oh," she said. "Hi."

Pastor Sheppard smiled from the doorstep. She had never seen him look this casual before, not in his church robes or a three-piece suit but a polo shirt and jeans and black sneakers with special soles he wore, Luke said, because his knees were bad. She'd always imagined pastors as mousy old men in sweaters and glasses but Pastor Sheppard looked more like the bouncers she sweet-talked outside of clubs, tall and wide, his shiny mahogany head nearly touching the doorframe. He seemed even larger on Sunday mornings, stalking across the altar in his long black robe, his voice booming to the rafters. But in his polo shirt, standing on her front steps, he looked relaxed. Kind, even. He smiled at her and she saw Luke for a second, a fragment of him, like a vein of light through smashed glass.

"Hi honey," the pastor said. "Is your dad around?"

"In the yard."

She backed up, letting him inside. He filled the entrance, gazing around the living room, and she

wondered what he made of her house. He probably visited so many homes, he could read them
as soon as he stepped inside. Some houses filled
with sickness, some with sin, others with sorrow.
But hers? It probably just seemed empty. The
silent, uncluttered rooms, the whole house open
like a wound that would never scab over. She led
the pastor to the backyard, where her father was
bench-pressing on the concrete slab. He racked
his weights with a loud clink.

"Pastor." He wiped his face with his gray USMC
T-shirt. "Didn't know you were stopping by."

She slid the screen door shut and started back
down the hallway. As she turned, she felt the pastor watching her and she wondered, for a second,
if he knew. Maybe his calling had imbued him
with divine knowledge and he could see it hanging off her shoulders, the heaviness of her secrets.
Or even if he had no holy power, maybe he just
sensed it. Maybe he could feel the once-connection
between the two of them, and as soon as she'd
turned, he'd reached up to touch its frayed edges.

She tiptoed down the hall to the bathroom and
perched on the toilet lid, listening through the
cracked window.

"I was in the area," the pastor was saying. "Saw
your truck earlier. Everything okay?"

"It'll be fine," her father said. "Just needs a little bodywork. Sorry about the picnic—I know I said I'd haul those chairs—"

"We'll manage." The pastor paused. "Folks are saying your girl crashed it."

She gripped her knees tighter on the toilet lid.

"Were we that crazy when we were young?" her father said.

"Crazier, maybe. She okay?"

"She's a smart girl," her father said. "A lot smarter than me, that's for sure. Going off to college soon. She should know better. That's what worries me."

"You know how these kids are—they just want to push the limits. Think they're invincible."

"She wasn't like this before," her father said. "Or maybe she was. Maybe I just didn't know her before. Elise was always there to . . . they were so close, I couldn't get between them and didn't hardly want to. Mothers are selfish. You know she wouldn't even let me hold Nadia at first? Not until the doctor made her rest. You can't get between no mother and child. I don't know, Pastor. I'm trying to raise her right. Maybe I just don't know how."

She eased back down the hallway. She didn't want to hear more. She hated hearing her father blame himself for her mistakes, even though she knew she blamed him too. After all, she had been the one who held it together. She'd answered the door when the Mothers visited with food, while her father disappeared into the darkness of his bedroom. She had eaten the food the Mothers brought until she sickened of it, until she felt she could taste exactly who'd made what. Mother Hattie had brought the macaroni and cheese, so rich that butter pooled in the corner of the pan. Mother Agnes, rail thin, had made the apple pie, its lattices straight and ruler made. For weeks Nadia ate donated food, each bite soured by grief, until she grew tired of the old ladies, their kindly smiles masks for nosiness. So one day, she left their dishes on the front steps and ignored the doorbell. Then she drove her father's truck to the grocery store and for dinner, she cooked meatloaf. It came out dry and brick-like, suspended in a pan of brown gel, but her father ate it anyway.

After the pastor left, she carried her mother's clippers to the living room, where her father was watching a cowboy movie. Though it was their usual time, she thought he might ignore her, but he stood silently and stepped into the backyard.

They could talk this way, over the buzz of the clippers, not having to look at each other.

"Pastor asked about you," her father said.

The sky was filmy and light, like lavender silk rippling above her. She guided the clippers across his hair, clumps of black and gray wool falling to his shoulders.

"Okay," she said.

"The first lady needs an assistant," he said. "Just for the summer. Nothing fancy, but it's money and you'll learn some good skills."

"I can't work there," she said.

"Why not?"

"I just can't," she said. "I'll find something else."

"It's a good job—"

"I don't care, I'll find something else—"

"You'll pay to fix my truck and everything else will go to your books and schooling," he said. "It's a good job and it'll be good for you. Spending some time at Upper Room. It'll help you. God will—you have to trust Him, see? You trust Him and stay in His presence and He'll carry you through like He's carrying me."

He sounded like he was trying to convince himself this was a good idea. As if by spending enough time in church, she might absorb holiness into her bones. She sighed, brushing hair off his shoulders. What did her father know about what would be good for her? What did he know about her at all?

On her first morning of work, she slumped against the window as her father guided his loaner car up the hill toward Upper Room. The church—tan, with a tall steeple—rose in hills of wild brush, the worst place to be in a county that burned. Out-of-towners never ventured this far north. Anyone visiting a beach town wanted sparkling oceans and cool breezes, so they stayed downtown, strolling across the long wooden pier where fishers lounged in metal chairs, poles propped over the edge, and children skipped with red pails to the Dairy Queen. But north of the beach was miles of coastal sagebrush that became kindling during wildfire season. In springtime, fires were distant from everyone's mind, but as her father drove, she stared out the window at black stumps jutting out of the charred ground. Even though Upper Room sat in a nest of kindling, even though it would only take a gust of wind carrying a single ember to its steps, the church had never burned. A sign, the congregation often said, of divine favor. God so loved Upper Room, He spared them from the flames.

These were the stories people told themselves. She'd heard, time and time again, her mother's own story about how God had led her to Upper Room. She had been a young mother then, a military wife new to California and lonely. She didn't even have a high school diploma, so she cleaned rooms at the Days Inn downtown, a job her supervisor, an older black woman, told her she was lucky to have.

"Used to be a way for us to make a living," she said. "But nowadays? They only want to hire those Mexicans. Can't speak a drop of English but dirt cheap. Pay them right under the table. You speak Spanish?"

"No," her mother had said.

"That's all right. You'll learn."

She did, over time. Basic phrases, like **How are you** or **Can you pass me that** and all the swear words. Sometimes, when her child care fell through, she brought Nadia to work with her and the other ladies cooed over her, singing Spanish lullabies as they rocked her on balconies overlooking the beach. Her mother could barely understand the songs herself but she had heard on **Oprah** that it was good to expose a baby's brain to different languages. That, she would later say, was how Nadia got to be so smart. How she'd read her first book before kindergarten, stumping the other parents so much that one mother had brought in her own book to test her, convinced she had just memorized the story. But Nadia's mother remembered the Mexican women circling around her, cocooning her in Spanish, her brain sopping up words until it hung heavy and full.

Her own patchy Spanish only took her so far. Her husband had been deployed to the Persian Gulf, and even though she had lived in Ocean-side for a year, she had not made a true friend. So in her loneliness, she'd sought out a church home. She hadn't been sure where to begin looking. Besides the Catholic churches, dutifully named after saints, most of the San Diego churches bore nautical names like Coastline Baptist or Seacoast Community Church. With names like that, she imagined congregations filing into pews wearing swim trunks, a minister who climbed the altar with a surfboard under his arm. She tried Calvary Chapel and Emmanuel Faith, but neither felt right. Emmanuel Faith had a woman pastor who had gone to Harvard, which she'd mentioned three times in the sermon. At Calvary

THE MOTHERS

Chapel, a woman behind her had gotten filled
with the spirit and started flailing, nearly knocking everyone in the head. For years, she bounced
from church to church, each one too small or
too big, too modern or too traditional. Then one
afternoon, she was emptying a room's trash can
when a bulletin from Upper Room Chapel fluttered onto her foot.

"It was my Goldilocks church," she used to tell
Nadia. "I knew it as soon as I walked in. Everything about it, just right."

On Sunday mornings, Upper Room Chapel
crowded and bustled, men in suits pulling each
other into rough hugs, ladies planting cheek kisses
before scribbling brunch dates on scrap paper
sticking out of Bibles, toddlers skirting around
flowerpots in makeshift games of tag, and the
Mothers, strutting past in colorful hats crowned
with feathered plumes. Her first time in Upper
Room, Nadia had watched from behind her
mother's knee, mystified, as their feathers bobbed
up and down past her. White gloves were pulled
up to their elbows, their tambourines jingled
as they walked, and she'd wondered if jingling
came with age, if one day, when she was wrinkled
and gray, her own steps would make music. Her
mother had laughed at the question.

67

"Oh, your body'll make some sounds all right," she'd said, wrapping her hand around Nadia's.

That first Sunday, her father had not been with them. Her mother had apologized for his absence to the pastor after service when she shook his hand in the receiving line.

"My husband, he just got back from overseas," she'd said. "And he's not much the churchly type."

Nadia's father had arrived home a week ago. She was four then and she barely remembered him, although she was old enough to understand that was a shameful thing to admit. In the months counting down to his return, her mother had gathered Nadia into her lap and pulled out a photo album, flipping slowly past pictures of her father holding her as a baby. In one, she was curled up like a kitten against his chest and her father, young and strapping in dress blues, smiled into the camera. He had a mole by his nose and short dark hair that looked plushy, like the bristles on her mother's makeup brush. She studied his face, searching for features that were also hers. People had always said she looked exactly like her mother.

She had been wary around him at first, shy even. He'd knelt to hug her outside of the terminal and she had drawn back, startled by this man in camouflage hefting a giant duffel bag, his face darkened by desert sun. The time she'd spent studying his photographs had not prepared her for the reality of him, his size and smell. He frowned.

"She don't remember me?" he said to her mother.

"Well, she was nothin' but a baby when you left." Her mother gave her a little push. "Go on and hug your daddy. Go on."

She took a few steps forward and her father pulled her into a hug. His chest felt hard. She smiled at him, even though the hug hurt. Her father held her in his lap on the drive back home, while her mother complained that she ought to be in a car seat.

"She ought to be getting used to me," he said.

"It just takes a little time, Robert," her mother said.

"I don't care," he'd said. "I don't care how long it takes. She's gonna love me."

Now her father paused at an intersection, before turning onto the road that led to the church. She hadn't been on this ride since the morning of her mother's funeral. That drive had been a blur— she'd felt like she'd been cast in a play she hadn't tried out for and was suddenly expected to know all the lines. Would she have to speak at the service? What did anyone expect her to say? That one day, she'd had a mother, and the next, she didn't? That the only tragic circumstance that had befallen her mother was her own self? In the backseat of the hearse, she'd found a run in her panty hose and quietly picked at it until it became a gaping hole, finding peace in the unraveling.

"I need you to take this seriously," her father said. "Nice thing Mrs. Sheppard is doing for you."

Maybe, but she didn't understand why the first lady had felt inclined to help her at all. Luke's mother hated her, ever since the seventh grade when she'd caught Nadia kissing Deacon Lou's nephew behind the church. He was the type of boy she'd liked then—tall and rangy, draped in a T-shirt three times too big—and she'd traced his zigzag cornrows, pressing him against the side of the church as they panted into each other's mouths. She'd never kissed a boy before, really kissed him. Earlier that year she'd dated a boy for three weeks, but they'd only kissed once after a circle of their friends dared them, so it didn't really count. But this kiss was a real kiss. She felt it burning through her as he slipped his hand up her shirt and rubbed her through her training bra, and she thought he might have felt it too when he suddenly pulled away, as if he'd touched something hot. Then she followed his gaze over her shoulder to where the first lady stood. She'd snatched Nadia by the arm and dragged her back into the church, shaking her wrist as she fussed at her.

"I've never seen such a thing in my life! Carrying on like that behind the church!" Mrs. Sheppard gave her wrist another good shaking, leaning her face close to hers. "Don't you know nice girls don't do that? Don't you know that?"

She still remembered the way the first lady's face had suddenly loomed close to hers. She had one brown eye and one blue eye, and in that moment, both became a disorienting blur. She'd dragged Nadia back to Sister Willis's class. For the rest of Sunday School, Sister Willis made Nadia sit in the back of the room by herself, writing **My body is a temple of God** a hundred times before she could be dismissed. Her mother hadn't said much on the ride home, but when they pulled into the garage, she'd quietly shut off the engine and sat in the car a minute, still holding the steering wheel.

"My mama tried to keep me away from boys," she said. "Obviously it didn't work, so I won't tell you that. You just gotta be smart and you gotta be careful. Boys, they can go around careless their whole lives. But you can either be careful now or careful later. That's your only choice, really. You got big things ahead of you. Don't you give that up for nobody."

"But it's just kissing," Nadia said.

"Don't let it be more than that," her mother said. "Don't end up like I did. That's the only thing you could do that would break your daddy's heart."

Her father was a Marine, stoic and tough with a chest so hardened with muscle that his hugs even hurt. She'd never thought herself capable of breaking anyone's heart, let alone his. But her mother was seventeen when she'd gotten pregnant. She must've known from experience how that had hurt her own parents. And if getting pregnant was the most harmful thing Nadia could do, then how much pain had her unexpected arrival caused? How much had she ruined her mother's life, if her mother told her that a baby was the worst thing that could happen to her?

Nadia had told Luke the kissing story once and he'd laughed into his pillow.

"It's not funny," she said.

"Aw, come on," he said. "That shit was so long ago. And how you think she hates you? You never even talk to her."

"I can tell by the way she looks at me."

"She looks at everyone like that. That's just how she looks."

He'd rolled over in bed, burying his face in her neck, but she twisted out of his arms, feeling under the covers for her panties. She never stayed long when she visited him. It was thrilling at first— fucking in a pastor's house—but after, the thrill faded into panic and she imagined footsteps out-side the door, keys jingling, cars pulling into the driveway. Luke's mother dragging her naked out of the bed, shaking her wrist. Luke thought her paranoia was funny but she didn't want to give his mother another reason to hate her. She had hoped someday that Luke might bring her home, not sneak her in his bedroom when his parents were gone, but invite her to dinner. He would intro-duce her as his girlfriend and his mother would drape an arm across her shoulders and guide her to the table.

Her father turned the silver Chevy Malibu into the parking lot, cruising toward the church entrance. She felt her stomach thrum.

"I could find another job," she said. "If you just give me a little time—"

"Go on," her father said, unlocking the door. "You don't want to be late."

She had never been in Upper Room during the week, and as soon as she pushed open the heavy double doors, she felt like she was trespassing. The church, crowded and bustling on Sunday morning, was now wrapped in quiet, the halls darkened, the main foyer, with its sprawling blue carpet, empty. She felt almost disappointed by how plain the unoccupied building seemed, like how once at Disneyland, Space Mountain had stopped mid-ride and the lights flashed on, revealing that she was only in a gray warehouse, riding along a track with tiny drops that had only seemed exciting in the haze of special effects. She followed a dark corridor toward the back of the building, past the Sunday School room where she had reported, dutifully, from kindergarten to the eighth grade, past the choir room and the pastor's office, down to the first lady's office at the end of the hall. The room spread regally in front of her, mahogany furniture gleaming under the sunlight, tiny potted palm trees sprouting out of every corner. Mrs. Sheppard leaned against the desk, her arms folded. She was tall—at least six feet—and in her red skirt suit and matching high heels, she towered over Nadia.

"Well, come on in," she said. "Don't just stand there."

She had always seemed intimidating, if not because of her height or her title or the way she walked slowly as she talked, like a panther stalking its prey, then because of her odd eyes. One brown and one blue, the coldness of that blue eye forcing Nadia to stare at the ground whenever the first lady passed her in the church lobby.

"How old are you, honey?" Mrs. Sheppard asked.

"Seventeen," Nadia said softly.

"Seventeen." Mrs. Sheppard paused, glancing in the doorway as if she expected a better girl to walk through it. "And you going off to school somewhere in the fall?"

"Michigan," she said, but her response felt bare, so she added, "ma'am."

"Studying what?"

"I don't know yet. But I want to go to law school."

"Well, college girl like you must be smart. You ever work in an office?"

"No ma'am."

"But you worked before. Right?"

"Of course."

"Doing what?"

"I was a cashier once, in the mall. And I also worked at Jojo's Juicery."

"Jojo's Juicery." Mrs. Sheppard pursed her lips. "Well, look. I never had an assistant and I never needed one. But my husband seems to think I could use some help. So let's find you something to do, okay?"

She sent Nadia to bring her a cup of coffee from the pastor's office. As she headed down the hall, Nadia glanced out the window overlooking the parking lot. On the lawn in front of the church, little children played tag in the grass. Summer day camp, she figured, but she still paused, squinting, as she spotted, in the midst of the chaos, Aubrey Evans. Of course Aubrey would spend her summer at church—of course she had nothing better to do. She was wearing a stupid safari hat and baggy cargo shorts, and she loped slowly toward kids who scattered as soon as she drew near. She let most escape her grasp, but in the end, she caught a slow one, sweeping him into her arms as he squealed, kicking his little legs in the air. In another life, maybe, Nadia could have been like her. Playing in the summer morning, scooping up a child who smiled, grateful to be caught by her.

HER FIRST WEEKS working at Upper Room, Nadia and her father fell into a routine: wake early, eat silently, and climb into the loaner car. He would drop her off on his way to work. On the drive over, her father would complain about the different steering or how he hated sitting this low in traffic, but she knew he only missed his truck because while it was in the shop, he couldn't serve Upper Room. After work, he lingered in the kitchen, patting his pockets like he'd stepped inside a stranger's house and didn't know what to do with himself. Should he leave his shoes by the door? Where was the bathroom? He eventually filed outside to lift weights in the backyard, like a prisoner quietly biding his time.

At work, Nadia did the tasks Mrs. Sheppard assigned her: calling caterers for the Ladies Auxiliary luncheon, proofreading the church bulletin, scheduling toy donations at the children's hospital, photocopying registration forms for the summer day camp. She tried to do everything perfectly because when she made a mistake, Mrs. Sheppard gave her a look. Eyes narrowed, lips pursed somewhere between a frown and a smirk, as if to say, look what I have to put up with.

"Honey, you need to do this again," she would say, waving Nadia over. Or, "Come on, now, pay attention. Isn't that what we hired you for?"

To be honest, Nadia wasn't exactly sure why

the pastor and his wife had hired her. They pitied her, she knew, but who didn't? At her mother's funeral, in the front pew, she'd felt pity radiating toward her, along with a quiet anger that everyone was too polite to express, though she'd felt its heat tickling the back of her neck. "Who is in a position to condemn? Only God," the pastor had said, opening his eulogy. But the fact that he'd led with that scripture only meant that the congregation had already condemned her mother, or worse, that he felt her mother had done something deserving of condemnation. At the repast, Sister Willis had pulled her into a hug and said, "I just can't believe she did that to you," as if her mother had shot Nadia, not herself.

On the Sunday mornings that followed, her father never gave up knocking on her door but Nadia always turned away in bed, pretending to be asleep. He wouldn't force her to go to church with him. He didn't force her to do anything. Asking her already required enough energy. Sometimes she thought that she ought to join him; it would make him happy if she did. But then she remembered Sister Willis whispering into her ear and her stomach turned cold. How dare anyone at that church judge her mother? No one knew why she'd wanted to die. The worst part was that

Upper Room's judgment had made Nadia start to judge her mother too. Sometimes when she heard Sister Willis's voice in her head, a part of her thought, I can't believe she did that to me either.

At Upper Room, Nadia tried not to think about the funeral. Instead, she focused on the little jobs assigned to her. And they were all little because Mrs. Sheppard, brusque and businesslike, was the type of person who'd rather do something herself than show you how. (The type who would prefer to give a man a fish not only because she could catch a better one herself, but because she felt important being the only thing standing between that man and starvation.) Nadia hated how much time she spent studying Mrs. Sheppard and anticipating her desires. In the mornings, Nadia stood in front of her closet, searching for an outfit the older woman would like. No jeans, no shorts, no tank tops. Only slacks and blouses and modest dresses. As a California girl who rarely wore anything that didn't show her legs or shoulders, Nadia didn't own many outfits that met Mrs. Sheppard's standards. But she hadn't been paid yet and she couldn't bring herself to ask her father for money, so a few nights a week she hunched over the bathroom sink, dabbing at the deodorant stains on the armpits with a wet towel. If Mrs. Sheppard noticed the repeated outfits, she didn't say anything. Most days, she barely acknowledged Nadia at all, and Nadia couldn't decide which was worse, the criticism or the indifference. She saw the way the first lady looked at Aubrey Evans—softly, as if a hard look might break her. What made that other girl so special?

Nadia had run into Aubrey one morning outside the bathroom, both girls jolting at the sight of each other. "Hi," Aubrey said. "What're you doing here?" She was still wearing that floppy hat and baggy cargo shorts that made her look like a mailman.

"Working," Nadia said. "For Mrs. Sheppard. I do her bitch work, basically."

"Oh." Aubrey had smiled but she seemed skittish, like a delicate bird landing on your knee. Too loud a motion, too wild a gesture, and she'd be sent flapping back into the trees. Her yellow flip-flops had sunflowers in the center, as if they were blooming from between her toes. Watching her flounce around in them, Nadia wanted to rip the flowers off. How dare she enjoy something so stupid? She imagined Aubrey Evans in the shoe store, passing rows of sensible black sandals and plucking that sunflower pair off the shelf instead. As if she believed herself deserving of every flourish.

One afternoon, when the campers had gone home, Mrs. Sheppard hugged Aubrey and guided her into her office for tea. What would it be like to sit in there? Not drop envelopes on the desk or duck her head in the doorway to ask a question but to sit. Did the pink curtains look more purple? Were the photos of Luke on the desk angled so that she might be able to see his smile from the couch? Nadia tried to refocus then on the envelopes she was stuffing, but it was too late. Her mind was flooded. Luke, the boy, squeezing between his parents in the front pew and tugging at his tie, or sitting in front of her in Sunday School, where she studied him instead of the Bible, memorizing the swirl of his curly hair. Luke clomping around in cleats after football practice, or ripping through the church parking lot blasting music that made the old folks clamp hands over their ears. Her stomach leapt, like she'd missed a stair. Grief was not a line, carrying you infinitely further from loss. You never knew when you would be sling-shot backward into its grip.

THAT NIGHT, before falling asleep, Nadia opened her nightstand and felt around for the baby feet. A gift, if you could call it that, from the free pregnancy center after she'd learned her test was positive. The counselor Dolores gave her a plastic bag full of pamphlets with titles like "Caring for Your Preborn Baby," "Secrets of the Abortion Industry," and "Can the Pill Kill You?" Under a handout titled "True Love Waits," the counselor had tucked a purple Precious Milestones card, explaining the stages of a baby's development, week by week. Attached to the card was a lapel pin, a pair of tiny golden feet in the exact shape and size, Dolores told her, as those of her own eight-week-old baby.

Before leaving, Nadia had thrown up quietly inside the clinic bathroom. Then she'd dumped the pamphlets in the trash, shoving all of them through the narrow slot until she reached the card on the bottom, the one attached to the baby feet. She had never seen such a thing before—a pair of disembodied feet—and maybe the sheer oddness compelled her to keep the pin. Or maybe she had known then that she would have an abortion. She had felt her choices strung in a tight balance, and when she hadn't been able to throw the pin away, she knew that there would be no baby, that this pin was all that would remain. She had hidden the lapel pin in the back of her drawer, past old notebooks and hair ties and an empty jewelry box her father had bought her years ago. Every night before bed, she dug through the drawer for the pin and held it in her palm, stroking the bottom of golden feet still glinting in the dark.

IN LATE SPRING, Oceanside was blanketed in so much mist, the locals called it May Gray. When darkened skies lasted into summer, it became June Gloom. No Sky July. Fogust. That spring, the fog was so thick, the beaches were empty until noon, surfers, unable to see ten feet in front of them, abandoning the coast. The type of thick, billowing fog that rolled fat and lazy, so much fog that the ladies at Upper Room covered their hair in hats and scarves to protect press-and-curls on their way into the church. The fog had brought with it news: the first lady had hired a new assistant and her name was Nadia Turner.

Latrice Sheppard had never had an assistant before and everyone doubted she would be able to keep one. She was tall and demanding, not some meek wife who sat in the front pew, silent and smiling. When the elders, and sometimes her husband, suggested she had too much on her plate, she said that she had not been called to sit, but to serve. And she served with the homeless ministry, the children's ministry, the sick and shut-in ministry, the drug recovery ministry, and the women's ministry, where she personally led outreach to the battered women's shelter. She'd grown used to the chaos of her life, running around Upper Room from meeting to meeting, stuffing clothes donations for the homeless into the trunk of her car, hopping on the freeway to bring toys to the children's hospital. To the battered women's shelter, to the youth detention center, to everywhere that needed going until she ended up back home to cook dinner for her husband. But she'd never had an assistant and she didn't want one now.

"I just don't like the look of her," she told her husband one morning.

"You don't like the look of a lot of folks," he said.

"And am I wrong?"

"It isn't a reason to fire someone."

Behind his desk, John sipped his coffee and Latrice sighed, pouring herself another cup. Out the window, she could see the fog rolling into the church parking lot. Enough to make her about sick of it. She was from Macon, Georgia. She knew rain and she knew humidity, but she hated this strange in-between, especially since springtime in Georgia was when azaleas and peach blos-

THE MOTHERS

soms and magnolias bloomed and the weather was perfect for barbecues and porch-sitting and driving with the windows down. But here, she could barely see out to the road. It was enough to make her more frustrated than she already was.

"Honey, we all like Brother Turner," she said, "but I don't need some fast-tailed, know-nothing girl following me around all summer!"

"Latrice, the Word says that the good shepherd leaves the ninety-nine—"

"Oh, I know what the Word says. Don't you preach at me like I'm some little woman in your congregation."

John slipped his glasses off his face, the way he always did when he wanted to make a point. Maybe some things were easier for him to say once she was blurred, out of focus.

"We owe her," he said.

She scoffed, turning in front of the window. She refused to be indebted to anyone, let alone a girl she'd done nothing but help. She had been the only one quick enough to act. That morning, her son had sat slumped over the kitchen table, his head in his hands, while her husband paced across the kitchen floor. Both her son's stillness and her husband's constant movement irritated her. She had barely woken up, hadn't even taken

85

the rollers out of her hair. A pregnant girl before she drank her morning coffee.

"You couldn't have found you a girl who didn't go to Upper Room?" she'd finally asked.

"Mama—"

"Don't Mama me. You know it's yours? Who knows how many of these boys she been with?"

"It's mine," he said. "I know it."

"A high school girl," she said. "Is she even eighteen?"

"Almost," he said softly.

"After everything we taught you," John said, "after we raised you up in the Word, after we told you about living in sin, you go out and do something as dumb as this?"

She had witnessed this scene dozens of times before, her husband yelling at Luke. For joyriding with his friends, theater-hopping, sneaking beer onto the beach in old Coke bottles, smoking reefer in Buddy Todd Park, goading Marines into fights. He wasn't a bad kid but he was reckless. Black boys couldn't afford to be reckless, she had tried to tell him. Reckless white boys became politicians and bankers, reckless black boys became dead. How many times had she told Luke to be careful? But he'd messed around with a girl who was not even legal yet—what would Robert think? He would be angry, of course, but how angry? Angry enough to haul Luke to the police station?

"She wants to get rid of it," Luke said.

He looked defeated, brushing tears from the corner of his eye. She hadn't seen him cry in years. Her boy, like all boys, had long outgrown her mothering. She'd watched Luke's growth spurts, the stretch marks on his shoulders from summers of weight lifting, and the more mannish he became, the less he felt like her son. He was someone else now, a furtive and cagey person who disappeared behind closed doors and stopped talking on the phone when she entered the room. In elementary school, he'd wrestled with his friends on the living room rug, but in high school, she'd seen him shove a friend into a wall so hard, a picture fell off its hook. What bothered her most was the surprise on his face when she'd yelled at him to stop, as if roughness came so naturally, he was startled to find it a problem.

A daughter grows older and draws nearer to her mother, until she gradually overlaps her like a sewing pattern. But a son becomes some irreparably separate thing. So even though she hated to see her son cry, she was grateful for the chance to mother him again. She pulled him to her shoulder, stroking his hair.

"Shh now," she said. "Mama's taking care of it."

At the bank, she withdrew six hundred dollars, and slid the cash in an envelope for Luke to give the girl. John hadn't slept that night, tossing in bed, then pacing across the bedroom floor.

"We shouldn't have done this," he said. "My spirit-man is grieved."

But Latrice refused to feel guilty about it. They hadn't forced the girl to do anything she didn't already want to do. A girl who didn't want a baby would find a way to not have one. The good thing to do—the Christian thing—would be to make it a little easier on her. Now the girl could go off to college and leave their lives. It wasn't a perfect solution, but thank God it wasn't the disaster it could have been.

Still, John felt grieved, and when Robert Turner had arrived at church on Sunday, his wrecked truck already felt like a sign, the beginning of a long judgment. So John had gone to Robert's house and offered the girl a pity job without even consulting Latrice first. Now the girl would be all under her this summer, only because John wanted to atone for undeserved grief.

"I don't owe her a thing," she said. "I'm all paid up."

FOUR

At Elise Turner's funeral, the whole church arrived early, spilling out of the pews.

We have known hard deaths before. Sammy Watkins, who'd been stabbed outside a bar, his body crumpled and wedged between two trash cans. Moses Brewer, who'd been found in Buddy Todd Park, bludgeoned to death. Kayla Dean, a fourteen-year-old shot by Mexican Bloods because she'd been wearing her boyfriend's bright blue jacket. For a week, her high school had erupted in brawls between blacks and Mexicans until police arrived in riot gear and sheriff's helicopters circled overhead. All the while, Upper Room remained a source of calm, Pastor Sheppard urging sense in a situation that made none. To be killed over a jacket. A child, waiting for fish tacos outside Alberto's, who'd borrowed a jacket because she was cold, because her mother had fussed at her for coming home without one and tempting sickness. At Kayla Dean's funeral, Upper Room had encircled the wailing mother and held her up, soundlessly, because hard deaths resist words. A soft death can be swallowed with **Called home to be with the Lord** or **We'll see her again in glory,** but hard deaths get caught in the teeth like gristle.

We have known hard deaths, but the difference was that Elise Turner had chosen one. Not a handful of pills to stretch sleep, not a running motor in a closed garage, but a pistol to the head. How could she choose to destroy herself so violently? We'd all squeezed into pews, not knowing what to expect. What would the pastor say? Not the usual funeral scriptures, those would not do. We wouldn't see her again in glory because what glory awaited a woman who'd sent a bullet into her own head? She had not been called home to be with the Lord—she had simply chosen to leave. Imagine, having the gall to choose when so many had that choice taken away from them.

How dare she opt for a hard death when the rest of us were trying to manage the hard lives we'd been given?

We have never understood it, although maybe we should. We are, after all, the last ones to have seen Elise Turner alive. The morning she killed herself, we'd gone to Upper Room early to get started on our praying. At first, when we'd peeked through the sanctuary doors, we only saw a person wrapped in a down coat, slumped forward in front of the altar in what looked like prayer or sleep. A bum, probably. We stumbled across them sometimes in the mornings, sleeping across the pews.

"All right now," Betty said, "you got to go. We won't tell nobody we seen you but you got to go on now."

No response. Probably a drunk bum. Lord, now those we couldn't deal with. Passed out drunk after mistaking the offering basket for a toilet, leaving broken beer bottles around for the babies to cut their feet.

"Okay," Hattie said, "now why don't you hop on up? We don't wanna have to call the police."

We edged closer, noticing, for the first time, past the fur collar, long, dark hair swept up away from a slender yellow neck. A neck that looked too clean for a bum's, too delicate for a man's. Agnes touched the strange woman's back.

"Elise! What you doin' in here?"

"I . . . I came in here last night and . . ." Elise looked dazed as Flora helped pull her to her feet.

"Girl, it's morning already," Agnes said. "You better get on home to your child."

"My child?"

"Yes, honey. What you doin' sleepin' in here all night?"

"Robert probably worried sick," Hattie said. "Get on home, then. Go on."

At the time, we'd laughed as we watched Elise head through the morning fog to her car. Oh, wait till we told the ladies at bingo about this. Elise Turner, asleep in the church like an ordinary bum. They would have a field day with that one. She had always seemed a little strange to us anyway—dreamy, like her mind was a balloon on a long string and she forgot to reel it in sometimes.

For years, we've fixated on that final conversation. Elise had hesitated before going out to her car, a pause that varies in length throughout our memories; Betty says it was a long moment, Flora, a brief hitch. Should we have known Elise would drive off and shoot herself? Was there any way of

knowing? No, nobody could've predicted it, not
if Robert hadn't even known. Elise Turner was
beautiful. She had a child and a husband with a
good government job. She had gone from clean-
ing white folks' toilets to styling hair at the salon
on base. A pretty black woman living as fine as
any white woman. What did she have to complain about?

THAT SUMMER, Nadia Turner haunted us.

She looked so much like her mother that folks
around Upper Room started to feel like they'd
seen Elise again. As if her restless spirit—and no
one doubted it was restless—was roaming the
place where it had last been seen. The girl, who
haunted the church halls with her beauty and her
sullenness, barely noticed the stares, until one
evening, when Second John offered her a ride
home from work in the church van. He pulled
onto the street, and for a second, their eyes met in
the rearview mirror.

"You look so much like your mama," he said.
"Gives me chills to look at you."

He glanced away, bashful almost, like he'd said
the wrong thing. At dinner that night, she mentioned his comment to her father and he glanced

up, as if he'd needed to remind himself of what her face looked like.

"You do," he finally said, cutting his meat, his jaw set the way it always did whenever she tried to bring up her mother. Maybe that was why he always ran off to Upper Room, why he couldn't stand to be around her. Maybe he hated looking at her because she only reminded him of all that he'd lost.

The night before her mother died, Nadia had caught her staring out the kitchen window, arms deep in soap suds, so gone in her own mind that she hadn't noticed the sink almost overflowing. She'd laughed a little when Nadia shut off the water.

"Look at me," she'd said. "Off daydreaming again."

What had she been thinking about in that moment? Weren't your final hours supposed to be dramatic and meaningful? Shouldn't their last conversation have been emotional, even if it hadn't registered to her at the time? But there was nothing special about that last moment. She had laughed too and brushed past her mother to the refrigerator. The next morning, she'd woken to find her father sitting on the edge of her bed, his face in his hands, so quiet she hadn't even felt him sit on her mattress, weightless in his grief.

She still searched for clues, for strange things her mother had done or said, for signs that she should've noticed. At least then, her mother's death would make sense. But she couldn't think of any hints that her mother had wanted to die. Maybe she'd never really known her mother at all. And if you couldn't know the person whose body was your first home, then who could you ever know?

She was lonely. How could she be anything else? Each morning, her father dropped her off at Upper Room, and each afternoon, she sat on the church steps, waiting for him to pick her up. After work, she passed the hours in bed, watching old episodes of **Law & Order,** waiting for the next morning when she would awake and start her routine all over again. Sometimes she thought she could pass time like this, one day falling into another until autumn. The hot winds would arrive and she would blow out with them, on to a new school in a new state where she would start a new life. Other times, she felt so miserable, she thought about calling her old friends. But what would she say to them? She'd had a mother and now she didn't, and she'd been pregnant but now she wasn't. She'd thought with time the distance between her and her friends would narrow, but that gap had only widened and she couldn't find the energy to pretend otherwise. So she remained alone, working silently in the first lady's office all morning, then shuffling outside at noon to eat lunch on the church steps. One afternoon, she was picking at her peanut butter sandwich when she noticed Aubrey Evans heading toward her. The girl smiled, clutching a sky blue lunch bag that matched her sundress. Nadia should have known she couldn't just bring a brown bag like everyone else.

"Can I sit here?" she asked.

Nadia shrugged. She didn't want to invite the girl to join her but she couldn't very well tell her not to. Aubrey squinted into the sunlight and lowered herself onto the step. Then she unzipped her bag and pulled out tiny plastic containers, carefully arranging them on the step beside her. Nadia stared at tubs filled with macaroni and cheese, slices of steak, potato salad.

"That's seriously your lunch?" she said. Of course it was. Of course Aubrey Evans's parents cooked her elaborate feasts for her lunch, because

God forbid, she should have to eat something as normal as a sandwich.

Aubrey shrugged. "Want some?"

Nadia hesitated before reaching for the brownie and breaking off a corner. She chewed slowly, almost disappointed by how delicious it was.

"Wow," she said. "Your mom made this?"

Aubrey carefully zipped up her lunch bag. "I don't live with my mom," she said.

"So your dad, then."

"No," she said. "I live with my sister, Mo. And Kasey."

"Who's Kasey?"

"Mo's girlfriend. She's a really good cook."

"Your sister's gay?"

"So?" Aubrey said. "It's really not a big deal."

But she'd gotten prickly, so Nadia knew that it was. She still remembered how years ago, the congregation had been convinced that Sister Janice's daughter had been turned into a lesbian because she'd started playing rugby at the junior college. For weeks, the old folks had whispered about how no girl should be playing football—it just wasn't **right**—until she showed up on Easter Sunday holding hands with a shy boy and that was that. At Upper Room, a gay sister was a big deal and she wondered how she'd never heard about Aubrey's. Maybe because Aubrey didn't want anybody to know. Nadia couldn't help it, she was surprised. The life she'd imagined for Aubrey— a stay-at-home mother, a doting father—was melting away into something murkier. Why did Aubrey live with her sister, not her parents? Had something terrible happened to them? She felt a sudden kinship with a girl who didn't live with her mother either. A girl who was also a keeper of secrets. Aubrey tilted the brownie toward her and Nadia silently broke off another piece.

THIS IS WHAT SHE KNEW about Aubrey Evans: She'd appeared one Sunday morning, a strange girl wandering into Upper Room with nothing but a small handbag, not even a Bible. She'd started crying before the pastor asked who needed prayer and she'd cried even harder as she rose and walked to the altar. She was saved at sixteen, and since then, she'd attended church services each week and volunteered for the children's ministry, the homeless ministry, the bereavement committee. Babies, bums, grief. A hint about where she'd come from, maybe, although Nadia only knew what most people did: that Aubrey had arrived at

Upper Room suddenly and within a year, she'd seemed like she'd always belonged.

Now, each afternoon, the girls ate lunch together on the church steps. Each afternoon, Nadia learned more about Aubrey, like how she'd first visited Upper Room because she'd seen it on television. She was new to California then and camped out in front of the TV, watching the wildfire coverage. She had never heard of wildfire season and she had lived all over, so she thought she'd heard of everything. She'd spent two damp years in Portland, where she wrung rain out of her socks, then three years freezing in Milwaukee, another muggy year in Tallahassee. She'd dried out in Phoenix, then re-frosted in Boston. She felt like she'd been everywhere and nowhere at all, like she had flown to thousands of airports but never ventured outside of the terminal.

"Why'd you move so much?" Nadia asked. "Was it, like, a military thing?"

She had lived in Oceanside her whole life, unlike all the military kids from school who had followed a parent from Marine base to Marine base until they'd ended up at Camp Pendleton. She had never lived outside of California, never gone on exciting vacations, never left the country. Her life already seemed so singular and flat and dull, and she could only comfort herself with the fact that the good stuff was ahead.

"No," Aubrey said. "My mom would just meet a man. And he'd move somewhere, so we'd go too."

She had accompanied her mother as she followed boyfriends from state to state. A mechanic she'd loved in Cincinnati, a grocery store manager in Jackson, a truck driver in Dallas. She had never married although she'd wanted to. In Denver, she'd dated a cop named Paul for three years. One Christmas, he gave her a small velvet box and her hands shook while opening it. It was just a bracelet, and even though she cried later in the bathroom, she still wore it around her wrist. Aubrey never mentioned her father. She told one or two stories about her mother, but only stories that had happened years ago and Nadia began to wonder if her mother was even still alive.

"Did she—I mean, your mom isn't—" But Nadia stopped herself before she could finish. She barely knew this girl. She couldn't ask if her mother was dead too. But Aubrey understood and quickly shook her head.

"No, no, nothing like that," she said. "I just—we don't get along, that's all."

Could you do that? Leave your mother because

you two fought sometimes? Who didn't fight with her mother? But Aubrey said nothing more and her reticence only made Nadia even more intrigued. She imagined the lovesick mother chasing men from state to state, how, when each affair ended, the mother would have cursed and cried, flinging clothes into a suitcase; how Aubrey and her sister must have known that when love left, they would have to leave too.

"WHAT WERE YOU LIKE," Nadia asked once, "as a little kid?"

She was sitting in the passenger's seat of Aubrey's Jeep, her bare feet warming on the dashboard. They were stuck in the perpetually long drive-thru line at In-N-Out, behind a brown minivan full of jostling kids. Earlier, Aubrey had suggested they go somewhere for lunch—Del Taco or Carl's Jr. or even Fat Charlie's. Luke Sheppard worked there and maybe he'd recognize them from church and offer a discount. But Nadia had shaken her head and said that she hated seafood.

"What was I like?" Aubrey smiled, her fingers dancing on the steering wheel. She always did that, repeated the question. Like she was stumped in a job interview and needed to buy time.

"Yeah, you know, as a little kid. I was a brat. No one could tell me shit. Surprise, right?"

She laughed, then Aubrey laughed. Another one of her habits, waiting for someone else to laugh before she joined in.

"I was . . . I don't know. I played soccer. I had a lot of friends." Aubrey shrugged. "My best friend had this trampoline. We'd jump on it for hours. My mom told me not to—she said I'd break my neck. So I always lied to her."

"What a badass."

"One time," Aubrey said, "we were super hungry, so we brought out this leftover cornbread to eat. It was really crumbly, though, but we kept jumping and eating and all the crumbs were flying up with us and we couldn't stop laughing."

She smiled, like she was still proud of this tiny childhood rebellion, but the smile didn't reach her eyes. Another thing she did all the time: smile when she didn't mean it.

When the fire season began, Aubrey had been living in California for three months. She had not known that wildfires could be a normal part of the calendar year, an event you expected as regularly as snow or rain, and the idea terrified her. Her sister told her that she shouldn't worry about wildfires, not in Oceanside at least. Along the coast, you were as safe as anyone could be. But she still followed the local news as reporters coughed in fields where flames licked behind them and helicopters swept over scorched ground, and that was how she first saw Upper Room. The church was serving as a temporary evacuation site, and a reporter interviewed the pastor, a large, dark man named John Sheppard.

"We're just glad to help," he said. He had a deep, sonorous voice, like the type of man who might narrate a book-on-tape. "We're grateful God has placed us in a position where we can give back to our community. So if you've been forced out your home, come to Upper Room and let us be a home to you."

Later, she told Nadia, she realized that the pastor's plea had drawn her in. She was between homes then—she had been between homes her whole life—and she still felt like a guest in Mo and Kasey's house. Each time she did her laundry, she folded her clothes and returned them to her suitcase, afraid to fill the drawers. But no one made her leave Oceanside, so she'd visited Upper Room one Sunday and that was that.

That year had been the worst fire season Nadia could remember. The local news ran flashy graphics calling October "The Fire Siege" and even after the peak months had passed, fifteen wild-fires burned throughout Southern California that winter. If you had to evacuate, the sheriff's office left an automatic phone call, but her mother had always said that if you waited for the call, it was already too late. A sheriff's call only gave you a fifteen-minute warning, so last fall, her mother had packed bags in advance and left them by the front door.

"You think this is silly," she told Nadia, "but you always got to be prepared. Even for things you can't see."

She had grown up in Texas, in between tornado and hurricane country, so she knew how to prepare for disaster. Unlike you California girls, she used to tell Nadia, who never thought about earthquakes until the world started shaking right under them.

That winter, her mother's death would be an earthquake jolting her out of her sleep. But earlier, in September, Nadia had watched her mother pack bags of clothes, water jugs, and photo albums. Then they'd left for church, where a cry-ing girl had appeared in a light blue dress that fit her too tightly around the middle, as if she had just put on weight. Her curly hair was tied back in a ponytail and she wore white canvas sneakers scuffed at the toes. She dressed like someone who had never been to church before imagined she ought to dress. The girl was mourning, and months later, in her own grief, whenever Nadia saw Aubrey at school, she envied how easily the girl had shown her sadness, how completely the church embraced her. Was that all it took, kneeling at the altar and asking for help? Or did you have to invite everyone in on your private sorrow to be saved?

Later, in the dying evening light, the girls swung gently in the ratty old hammock hanging in Nadia's backyard. Her father never used his hammock anymore—she couldn't remember the last time she'd seen him relaxed enough to enjoy it—but Aubrey had wanted to lie in it as soon as she followed Nadia outside. "It feels like such a California thing to do," she'd said, so every evening that week, they'd swung in the hammock and talked as the sun lowered in the sky.

Nadia glanced at her father through the screen door. He'd cooked them dinner each night that week and hadn't complained about fixing Aubrey an extra plate. He seemed pleased to do it, almost. He smiled and tried to tell jokes about his day on base that would've been swallowed with mouthfuls of food had he and his daughter been alone.

Maybe he was glad to have company again, or maybe there was something special about Aubrey that made him open up.

Across from her, Aubrey licked a dab of ice cream off her thumb and asked Nadia what her father was like.

"What do you mean?" Nadia said. "You know what he's like. You see him around."

"As a person. He's nice, but he doesn't talk much."

"I guess he's nice. I don't know. Serious. Likes to be by himself. Why? What's your dad like?"

"I don't know. He left when I was little."

"Fine. Your mom, then."

Aubrey chewed on her thumbnail. "We haven't talked in a while."

"How long is a while?"

"Almost a year."

Nadia had since grown used to the ebb and flow of their conversations, the opening up and shutting down, the ease forward, the retreat, so she just nodded and pretended to understand, the way she would pretend all her life when friends complained about their mothers. Rolling her eyes along with them while they ranted about mothers who disapproved of their jobs or their boyfriends, always sympathizing, always smiling, even though she hated them for complaining. She understood Aubrey even less. What did it feel like, she wondered, to be the one who'd left?

IF YOU DROVE east from the beach, if you left behind the surf shacks and bait shops and ice cream parlors, the lean surfers, the rent-a-cops cruising along the harbor, you'd reach the Back Gate. The entry to Camp Pendleton was guarded by armed Marines, but outside its border was a not-bad, not-good neighborhood. Here's how you could tell: the fences were higher but the houses wore no metal gates over their windows; the Pizza Hut hid behind bulletproof glass but they stayed open late at night; and cops still patrolled, more than they did in good neighborhoods, but more than they did in bad neighborhoods already abandoned to their own chaos. In this not-bad, not-good neighborhood, Aubrey lived with her sister and her sister's girlfriend in a little white house. The house itself was simple, but Aubrey's bedroom was surprisingly ornate. The walls were painted a dusty green with silver flowers, and white Christmas lights traced the ceiling. Silver curtains rippled in the windows and swaths of lace draped over the bed like a wedding veil. Her first visit, Nadia had wandered through the room slowly, her arms behind her back, afraid to touch anything, as if she were in a museum.

"I couldn't sleep when I first moved in," Aubrey said, pointing to a dream catcher that hung from the ceiling. "Kasey thought this might help."

Kasey was slender and lean like an alley cat, and she had long, dirty-blonde hair she liked to rumple in the middle of conversations, as if to prove how little she cared about how her hair looked. She was a bartender downtown at the Flying Bridge and she liked telling stories about her regulars. A man who hated touching dry glass. A woman who was deathly afraid of pickles.

"You know, them big ones they give you with your sandwich? Scared shitless. Runs and screams if you bring one near her, even if it's still in a jar. Wild, huh?"

Kasey had traveled west eight years ago with her big brother, who was stationed at Camp Pendleton. She was lovesick over a straight girl and had fled to California to forget about her. On the long drive from Tennessee, she'd plucked the dream catcher off a shelf at a truck stop, wanting it for no other reason than the fact that she could want it. Now the dream catcher drifted inside a bedroom almost painful in its effort. Aubrey said that her sister helped her decorate the room after she'd moved in.

"Mo thought we needed to do something together," she said. "We hadn't seen each other in a few years."

"Why not?" Nadia said.

"She left for college."

"And she just never came back?"

Aubrey shifted slowly, one foot to the other. "Well, she didn't like Paul."

"What was wrong with him?"

"He hit my mom," she said.

"Oh." Nadia paused in front of the bookshelf. "Did he hit you?"

"Sometimes."

Nadia couldn't imagine a grown man hitting her. Even when she'd misbehaved as a child, her father had always carried her to her mother, who did the spanking, as if discipline were something to be dealt with between women.

"Well, what'd your mom say?" she said.

"She's still with him." Aubrey shrugged, then hopped off the bed. "Come on. Let's go outside."

Nadia finally understood, why Aubrey had left and why her mother had let her, why her sister had helped her create a bedroom out of a Disney movie, why Mrs. Sheppard cherished her. In a way, Nadia almost felt lucky. At least her mother had been sick—at least she'd only tried to hurt herself. At least her mother would've never let a man hit her child. Her mother was dead, but what could be worse than knowing that your mother was alive somewhere but she wanted a man who hit her more than she wanted you?

On the Fourth of July, Nadia sat on Aubrey's porch, watching the neighbors set up fireworks in the street. The city was hosting a fireworks show downtown at the pier, but it wasn't the Fourth of July without illegal fireworks, Kasey had said. She was appalled by the strictness of California fireworks law, so she cheered on the people who smuggled them over from Tijuana to set off in the neighborhood. What was the harm? It wasn't as if people were setting off bombs. She sipped her beer, wrapping an arm around Monique, who watched the neighbors in the street and shook her head.

"Someone's gonna blow a hand off," she said. "I just know it."

She was not a mother but she had a mother's gift of rushing to the worst possible outcome. She was a trauma nurse at Scripps Mercy Hospital, so she encountered the worst possible outcome daily. But even if she hadn't been a nurse, she was the type to worry. When she came home from work, she always asked if they had eaten. She reminded Aubrey to take her vitamins and called after her to grab a jacket, it gets chilly downtown, oh don't look at me like that, you know you always get cold. A man in the middle of the street squawked as a car swerving around the display nearly hit him. Monique shook her head again.

"You warm enough, babe?" she said.

Aubrey was sitting under a blanket with Nadia. She rolled her eyes a little.

"I'm not a baby, Mo," she said.

"You're **my** baby," her sister said.

Kasey laughed and Aubrey rolled her eyes again, but she didn't look upset, not really. It was the fake-annoyed look you give to someone who could never actually bother you. Sometimes Nadia envied Aubrey, even though she felt guilty for considering the thought. Aubrey had lost her mother too, but she was loved by her sister and her sister's girlfriend and even the first lady, three women who cared for her only because they wanted to. Both girls had been abandoned in the sand. But only Aubrey had been found. Only Aubrey had been chosen.

Monique and Kasey's love for Aubrey hung in their eyes, and even though it wasn't meant for

Nadia, she inched closer, holding her hands up to the warmth. In the street, the neighbors huddled around, giving directions in Spanglish. Teenage girls herded babies onto the grass, while old men in flannel shirts redirected traffic and boys on skateboards looked out for cops. Reggaeton and rap blasted out windows, rattling through cars parked in driveways. Soon, fireworks would illuminate the pier, but Nadia wanted to be nowhere else but here, in a house where everyone was wanted, with a family where anyone could leave but nobody ever did. A firecracker lit up the sky, and she jumped, delighted and a little surprised, at the first spark.

LATRICE SHEPPARD HAD GHOST EYES.

One brown and one blue, which meant, her granddaddy had told her, that she could see heaven and earth at the same time. Her mother had gasped the first time she'd held her—something must be wrong, the blue eye blinded, maybe, already filmy with disease—but the doctor had said it was too soon to tell. "Takes time for a baby's eyes to adjust to the world," he'd said. "Just pay attention. If the eyes squint or cloud, there may be cause for concern." So she'd spent the first years of her life with her mother's face always inches from hers, studying her eyes. Maybe that was why she'd always felt there was something wrong with them, even though she could see fine. The brown eye seemed ugly next to the blue, the blue next to the brown, and she learned that it was better to just be one thing, to distill yourself into something as simple as you could. She had already begun her unending growth spurt—by the second grade, she was the first to line up in the school picture—and at lunch, she ate alone on the playground while the other girls double-Dutched to a rhyme they'd made up about her:

> **Latrice, the beast**
> **She'll make you her feast**
> **Got two odd eyes and two big feet**

The height she couldn't hide, but the odd eyes, she tried to. She started wearing sunglasses whenever she could, in the grocery store, in her bedroom, even in the classroom, handing her teacher a fake note from her doctor describing her sensitivity to light. Later in life, she would consider her odd eyes a blessing. Not ghost eyes, but she had been gifted with a second sight nonetheless: she could look at a girl and tell if she'd been hit before.

113

Forget bruises and scars—hit women learned to hide or explain those away. No need for stories about running into doorknobs or tripping down stairs—all she needed to do was lock her odd eyes onto theirs and she knew a woman surprised or outraged by pain from a woman who'd learned to expect it. She saw past flawless skin to diamond-shaped iron burns, gashes from golden belt buckles, necks nicked by steak knives, lips split by class rings, faces blooming purple and deep blue. She'd told Aubrey this the third time she'd invited her for tea, and after, Aubrey had stared into the mirror, wondering what else the first lady saw. Was her entire past written on her skin? Could Mrs. Sheppard see everything that Paul had done to her? At least now she knew why Mrs. Sheppard had been so kind to her. Why, after the altar call, Mrs. Sheppard had found her in the church lobby and offered her a hug; why, the following Sunday, Mrs. Sheppard had given her a small Bible with a floral cover; and why, the Sunday after that, Mrs. Sheppard had invited her into her office for tea. Aubrey didn't even drink tea, but for months she'd sat on the other side of the gray striped settee, dropping sugar cubes into her cup. She took her tea sweet—sugar, honey, and cream.

"That's fine in here," Mrs. Sheppard had told

her once, "but out in public, folks might think it's juvenile, a young lady doctoring up her tea with all those sweets." She'd corrected Aubrey gently, but Aubrey had felt so embarrassed that weeks later, she'd only added a single sugar cube to her tea.

One afternoon, she sipped the bitter tea and asked Mrs. Sheppard what had happened to Elise Turner. She lofted the question casually, as if she hadn't been wondering it for weeks—no, months, ever since Pastor Sheppard had somberly announced the news to the congregation. At the time, he hadn't offered a cause of death, which had raised suspicions the way only a sudden, unexplained death could. A woman Elise Turner's age didn't just die naturally; she hadn't seemed ill and if she hadn't suffered some terrible accident, then what could've happened to her?

"I just don't know," Sister Willis had said in the ladies' room after service. "Somethin' just don't sound right to me." And even though the other women around the sink had nodded, no one had expected the news that trickled in, days later, that Elise Turner had shot herself in the head. The congregation had already imagined possible shameful tragedies—an accidental drug overdose, a drunk-driving accident, even a murder caused by circumstances the pastor had thought it best to obscure. Maybe Elise had taken a lover (she could do better than Robert, couldn't she?) and in the seedy motel room where they'd conducted their affair, the lover had killed her.

Despite the lurid speculation, no one had been prepared for the reality of Elise Turner's death, especially not Aubrey. She had never known Mrs. Turner but she'd felt as if she did, at least a little, the way you could know someone you'd only seen from a distance. On Sundays, she'd seen the Turners enter Upper Room—the husband stiff-backed in his suit, the wife smiling at the greeters in the lobby, the daughter a spitting image of the mother. They'd reminded her of a family out of television. The strong, manly father, the beautiful mother, and the daughter, who had somehow been blessed with beauty and smarts. In AP Government, Aubrey sat near the back, watching Nadia breeze into class with her friends, and whenever she slipped through the door after the bell rang, she appeased Mr. Thomas with a smile before he could write her up for detention. How could he punish her? Week after week, when he listed the top ten test-scorers, her name was on the whiteboard, as if it had been written in permanent marker. She was going to a big univer-

sity someday, everyone knew it, while Aubrey
would shuffle off to the community college with
the rest of their class. On Sunday mornings, she
watched this girl—this Nadia Turner—slide into
the church pew beside her mother and her father,
and she wondered what it would be like, to go
to church with your family. Mo didn't believe
in God. Kasey did, only abstractly, the way she
believed in the universe's ability to right itself.
Neither was happy that Aubrey had started going
to church, although they hadn't said so directly.

"Are you sure you want to spend so much time
there?" Mo would say. "I mean . . . don't you
think it's maybe a little too soon?"

Too soon for what, she'd never said, but she
didn't have to. She worried that Aubrey had
turned into some religious nut. That she would
start seeing images of Jesus in burnt toast, or
speaking in tongues mid-conversation, or pick-
eting outside gay weddings. When Aubrey had
seen the Turners on Sundays, she wondered what
it would be like to be their child, to be smart and
beautiful, to have a father and a mother who held
your hands during prayer. She thought about the
mother especially, who seemed nothing like her
own. Elise Turner, young and energetic and beautiful, who laughed in the lobby before service,

always greeted as soon as she stepped inside, who had spoken to Aubrey once before, when they'd passed each other before the Christmas play.

"You dropped something, honey," Elise Turner had said, pointing at Aubrey's program, which had fluttered to the carpet. Her voice was cool and silky, like milk.

How could a woman like that kill herself? Aubrey knew it was a stupid question—anyone could kill herself, if she wanted to badly enough. Mo said that it was physiological. Misfired synapses, unbalanced chemicals in the brain, the whole body a machine with a few tripped wires that had caused it to self-destruct. But people weren't just their bodies, right? The decision to kill yourself had to be more complicated than that. Across the couch, the first lady raised an eyebrow as she leaned forward to refill Aubrey's teacup.

"What do you mean?" Mrs. Sheppard said. "You know what happened to her."

"I just know she shot herself."

"Well, that's all there is to it, honey."

"But why?" Aubrey said.

"The devil attacks all of us," Mrs. Sheppard said. "Some folks just aren't strong enough to fend him off."

She sounded matter-of-fact as she slowly stirred her tea, the spoon clanging against the cup. She was also nothing like Aubrey's mother—too assertive and steady and sure of herself. Her mother was one of the weak women Mrs. Sheppard would pity or scorn, depending on how much she knew. Right now, she didn't know much. Only that Aubrey had moved in with her sister because she and her mom hadn't gotten along. She hadn't told Mrs. Sheppard about Paul, who drank bottles of whiskey on weekends and sometimes hit them but always cried about it after because he didn't mean to, his job was so stressful, they just didn't know what it was like, being out on the streets all the time, not knowing if you'd make it home. He'd moved in a year before she'd left, and for a year, he had made nightly trips to her room, pushing her door open, then her legs, and for a year, she had told almost no one. Almost, because she'd told her mother after the first time it happened and her mother had shook her head tightly and said "No," as if she could will it to be untrue.

Across the couch, Mrs. Sheppard reached for a cookie.

"Now, why do you want to know about all this?" she asked.

"I don't know," Aubrey said. "Nadia never talks about it."

She couldn't exactly ask Nadia herself, although she thought about it often when they were together. Did Nadia know why her mother had killed herself? Was it even better to know?

"I see you two out there eating lunch all the time." Mrs. Sheppard smiled, brushing sugar dust from her fingers onto a napkin. "I didn't know you got on like that."

"She's nice." Aubrey paused, taking a sip. "She's . . . I don't know. Funny. She makes me laugh. And she doesn't let people run over her. She's not afraid of anything."

"I just wouldn't get too attached if I was you," Mrs. Sheppard said.

Aubrey frowned. "Why?"

"Now, don't look at me like that. You know she's runnin' off to school in the fall. Making new friends in the dorms. Folks change, that's all. I just don't want you to get hurt, honey."

Mrs. Sheppard passed her the plate of short-bread cookies and Aubrey silently took one. The first time she'd visited Nadia's house, she'd spotted on her bookshelf a clay Noah's Ark statue small enough to fit in her palm. A white-haired Noah stood on the deck, tiny giraffe and chimp and

120

elephant heads poking out the portholes. She'd reached for it but Nadia had grabbed her hand.

"Don't," she'd said. "My mom gave me that."

Aubrey had drawn her hand back, embarrassed for violating a rule she hadn't known existed. But she saw then that Nadia didn't speak about her mother because she wanted to preserve her, keep her for herself. Aubrey didn't speak about her mother because she wanted to forget that she'd ever had one. And it was easier to forget when she was with Nadia.

She didn't want to think about Nadia leaving for college. She felt at home in Nadia's motherless world. Later that evening, she drove her friend home. They went out in the backyard and rocked in Mr. Turner's hammock until the sky faded into black. Nadia stretched a long leg over the side and pushed her bare toes against the grass, careful not to upset their delicate balance.

FIVE

We were girls once. As hard as that is to believe.

Oh, you can't see it now—our bodies have stretched and sagged, faces and necks drooping. That's what happens when you get old. Every part of you drops, as if the body is moving closer to where it's from and where it'll return. But we were girls once, which is to say, we have all loved an ain't-shit man. No Christian way of putting it. There are two types of men in the world: men who are and men who ain't about shit. As girls, we've lived all over. Sharecropping in the cotton fields of Louisiana until the humid air sucked our shirts to our backs. Shivering in freezing kitchens while packing lunches for daddies heading to Ford plants. Shuffling slowly over icy Harlem sidewalks, stuffing ripped fabric in coat-pocket holes. Then we'd grown up and met men who wanted to bring us to California. Military men, stationed out at Camp Pendleton, who promised us marriage and babies and all that sunshine. But before we woke to pink clouds drifting over the coastline, before we found Upper Room and each other, before we were wives and mothers, we were girls and we loved ain't-shit men.

You used to be able to spot an ain't-shit man a lot easier. At pool halls and juke joints, speak-easies and rent parties and sometimes in church, snoring in the back pew. The type of man our brothers warned us about because he was going nowhere and he would treat us bad on the way to that nowhere. But nowadays? Most of these young men seem ain't-shit to us. Swaggering around downtown, drunk and swearing, fighting outside nightclubs, smoking reefer in their mamas' base-ments. When we were girls, a man who wanted to court us sipped coffee in the living room with our parents first. Nowadays, a young man fools around with any girl who's willing and if she gets in trouble—well, you just ask Luke Sheppard what these young men do next.

A girl nowadays has to get nice and close to tell if her man ain't shit and by then, it might be too late. We were girls once. It's exciting, loving someone who can never love you back. Freeing, in its own way. No shame in loving an ain't-shit man, long as you get it out your system good and early. A tragic woman hooks into an ain't-shit man, or worse, lets him hook into her. He will drag her until he tires. He will climb atop her shoulders and her body will sag from the weight of loving him.

Yes, those are the ones we worry about.

SINCE HE'D SEEN NADIA TURNER LAST, Luke had broken seven plates, two bowls, and six glasses. "A personal record," his boss Charlie had announced during the morning's staff meeting. "No, scratch that—a company best. Give it up for Sheppard, folks. Making history one fuckup at a time." Luke never dropped dishes. He'd spent years grabbing footballs out of the air, snagging them out of the reach of defenders, cupping his hands underneath them before they hit the grass. In fact, he was heralded throughout Fat Charlie's Seafood Shack for his miraculous catches; the highlight reel, if one existed, would have consisted entirely of Luke Sheppard: Luke grabbing sippy cups before they teetered to the floor, Luke palming bowls tipped by wayward elbows, Luke righting trays sliding off their stands as customers applauded and coworkers clapped him on the back. But since Cody Richardson's party, there'd been no heroics, no last-minute saves, no godlike displays of reflex and awareness. The commentators on **SportsCenter**, if **SportsCenter** covered workplace athleticism, would've hung their heads and said, "Too bad, that Sheppard kid sure had shown a lot of promise." Now glasses slipped right through his hand or slid off his tray, and Luke, who worshipped the save, the graceful leap into the end zone, found himself instead kneeling on the sticky floor, watery Sprite soaking his pant leg.

"Oh, for fuck's sake," Charlie said, hovering over him.

"I know, I know."

"You trying to break every dish I own?"

"I said I'm sorry. What you want me to do? I'm cleanin' it."

"I want you to learn how to hold a cup. A monkey can hold a cup, Sheppard. A fucking chimp."

Luke pushed past Charlie on his way to the trash can and that slight shoulder tap—the inch of space he'd forced Charlie to yield—felt like that moment after the doctor injected pain medicine into his leg. A pinch, and then relief.

Focus, that's what Luke needed to do. Concentrate on one thing at a time. The smooth motion of his arm when he reached for the cup, the way the glass felt against his palm as he tightened his grip. And he did focus, from time to time. He survived a shift without dropping anything. Then Nadia returned to him, a sharp, sudden pain like hunger. Kissing her in the beach shower, his hands, still gritty with sand, on her stomach, his lips passed against the back of her suntanned neck. Later kneeling at the edge of his bed, hooking his fingers under the sides of her bikini bottom, her skin smoldering under his hands. She smelled like the ocean. She felt like the ocean when he was inside of her, rocking and rocking and calm. When it was over, he'd kissed the side of her face, the soft skin near her ears, the light baby hair turned curly from their sweat. His mouth had never touched anything that delicate.

He spent his dinner break smoking in the alley behind Fat Charlie's with CJ. They used to play high school football together. CJ, a burly Samoan with long, curly hair, had been a decent nose tackle and earned a few letters from Division III schools, nothing like the recruitment packets and personal visits Luke had received. Still, they'd both ended up here, in an alley that smelled like wet garbage and sea air and cat piss. Luke leaned against the wall, passing the joint.

"You good, **uso**?" CJ said. "You got a weird look on your face."

"Just some shit with this girl," Luke said.

"Who? Shorty with the books?"

Luke hesitated, then needing to tell someone, said, "She told me she was pregnant."

CJ laughed, a strange, wheezing laugh.

"Oh, that's easy," he said. "Real simple. Don't give her shit until you know it's yours. I don't care how fuckin' cute that kid looks, don't even buy his ass some diapers before you swab him—"

"She ain't been with no one but me," Luke said.

He didn't know that, of course, but he knew he'd been her first. She hadn't admitted that she was a virgin but he'd felt it from her tightness, from the little gasp she'd made once he'd entered her, from the way she clenched her eyes when he'd barely moved. Three times he asked if she wanted him to stop. Three times she shook her head. She was the type of girl who never wanted to admit that she was in pain, as if not confessing it made her stronger. Her mother had died two months ago and he knew that was the reason she was fucking him. Why she hadn't mentioned his limp, why she'd pulled his Fat Charlie's shirt over his head, even though it smelled like sweat and grease. She was a seventeen-year-old with a dead mother and she wanted him to fuck the sadness out of her. Every time he felt guilty for hurting her, she wrapped her arms tighter around his back so he sank deeper, moving as slowly as he could until he finished with a tiny shudder. Later, he pretended not to notice the blood on her sheets. He rolled closer to her and slept on top of the uneven spots.

CJ blew a puff of smoke toward the crumbling tile roof and tossed what was left of the joint in a puddle.

"Still," he said. "You better get that kid tested. If you even act like he's yours, the state's taking all your money. Happened to a dude I know. The laws are all fucked up."

"She didn't keep it," Luke said.

"Well, shit." CJ clapped him on the back. "That's even easier. You got lucky, homie."

Luke didn't feel lucky. When Nadia had first told him, he'd felt wired, the way he used to feel right after he'd finished lifting, like little sparks were running under his skin. Just to think, that morning his biggest worry had been getting to work on time so he wouldn't get fired from his shitty job. And now a baby. A whole fucking baby. He felt terrible—she looked miserable, barely eating anything—but a small part of him had felt amazed by what they'd done. He'd helped create a whole new person, a person who'd never existed before in the entire world. Most days, the biggest thing he managed to accomplish was to recite the lunch specials from memory. He imagined rushing to the break room, once she left, to log on to the work computer and Google when pregnancy shows, how to stop pregnancy sickness, how much it costs to raise a child. Then Nadia told him she wanted an abortion. He'd promised he'd get her the money, even though he'd only saved two hundred for his apartment, wads of cash tucked in an orange Nike box under his bed. It had been all too easy to blow his paychecks on beer and sneakers, and he'd felt stupid, pulling his life's savings out of a shoebox. How had he ever thought he could find a way to raise a kid?

He hadn't planned to leave her at the clinic. But the day of the appointment, when he slid his cell phone into his work locker like he did every day, it dawned on him how easy it was to walk away. He had done his part and she had done hers, and he would never have to see her again. He wouldn't have to imagine what she might look like after the surgery—grief-stricken, in pain—or find the right words to comfort her. He wouldn't have to tell her that she had made the right decision or that he felt like he had barely made a decision at all. He could just lock the phone up and walk away. This was his gift, a body tied to no one.

But then he'd seen her at Cody Richardson's party. And she hadn't looked unpregnant. He'd only seen the word once before, years ago, when his father's congregation had joined a protest out in front of the abortion clinic. He was just a boy then, clinging to his mother's side because the other marchers made him nervous. A red-faced man in a camouflage puffy vest stomped around, chanting, "It's a war out here, man, and we're the front line." An old black man held a sign that said ABORTION IS BLACK GENOCIDE. A nun carried a photo of a bloody baby's head squeezed by forceps. THERE'S NO SUCH THING AS AN UNPREGNANT WOMAN, the sign read, JUST A MOTHER OF A DEAD BABY. Years later, Luke hadn't forgotten that sign. The word unpregnant had stuck with him even more than the graphic photograph—its finality, its sheer strangeness, not not pregnant but a different category of woman altogether. An unpregnant woman, he'd always thought, would somehow wear her unpregnancy as openly as pregnant women did. But when Nadia Turner had pushed inside the party, she looked no different than when he'd last seen her. Leggy in her high heels, a red blouse hugging her breasts, paining him with her prettiness. She wasn't even crying. He was the weak one who couldn't bring himself to face her.

Now he couldn't stop breaking things. If you dropped one dish during your shift, Charlie just humiliated you at the next staff meeting. Two and he took you off tables for the rest of the night. Luke counted the tip money in his pockets— fifteen dollars in crumpled ones and a few nickels. Not even gas money. He glanced at CJ, who was still grinning at him, in awe of his good fortune.

"Guess I am lucky," Luke said, blowing smoke into the sour air.

THAT SUMMER, Nadia spent more nights in Aubrey Evans's bed than in her own.

She slept on the right side, farthest from the bathroom, because Aubrey got up more in the middle of the night. In the morning, she brushed her teeth and left her toothbrush in the holder by the sink. She ate breakfast in the chair nearest the window, her feet bunched up on the edge of her seat. She drank her juice out of Kasey's bright orange Vols cup. She left clothes in Aubrey's room, accidentally at first—a sweatshirt forgotten on the back of a chair, a swimsuit left in the dryer—then she forgot things on purpose. Soon, when Monique dumped a laundry basket on the bed, the girls' clothes tangled into an indistinguishable knot.

It wasn't hard to move into someone else's life if you did it a little at a time. Aubrey no longer asked if she wanted to spend the night—after work, when they walked out to the parking lot, Aubrey unlocked the passenger's side and waited for Nadia to climb inside. Aubrey was lonely too. She hadn't made many friends at school. She'd spent more time volunteering at church than going to football games or dances. It was strange, learning the contours of another's loneliness. You could never know it all at once; like stepping inside a dark cave, you felt along the walls, bumped into jagged edges.

"You sure you're not wearing out your welcome over there?" her father asked one night.

"No," she said. "Aubrey invited me."

"But you're over there all the time now."

"So now you care where I go," she said.

He paused in her doorway. "Don't get smart with me," he said.

She went anyway, even though on most nights, she and Aubrey did nothing at all, lounging on the couch, watching bad reality TV and painting each other's nails. They drove downtown and ducked inside little shops at the harbor. Last summer, Nadia had worked there at Jojo's Juicery, smiling plaintively while people squinted at the rainbow-colored menu above her head. She had daydreamed while following smoothie recipes on laminated index cards taped to the counter. She served rich white people, mostly, who strolled with pastel sweaters tied around their shoulders, as if carrying them was too much work. She had never been inside any of the harbor restaurants like Dominic's Italian or Lighthouse Oysters—fancy places she could never afford—but she joked with the waiters sometimes when they came inside Jojo's. A waitress at D'Vino's told her how a Hollywood producer had yelled "**Al dente! Al dente!** That means 'to the tooth'!" at her and sent his linguine back three times until it was firm enough. He was trying to impress his date, a weathered blonde woman who barely reacted, which just seemed sad—what was the point of being a Hollywood producer if you had to yell at waitresses to impress women? At least no one would try to impress a date at Jojo's. During work, she liked to stare out the glass at the boats docked along the harbor, their colorful sails furled, but sometimes it made her sad. She'd never been inside a boat and they were docked twenty feet away. She'd never been anywhere.

Some evenings, she stayed after work to help Aubrey volunteer. They packed food baskets for the homeless and cleaned Sister Willis's classroom, scrubbing the chalkboards and scraping Play-Doh off the tables. On Friday nights, they hosted senior bingo, dragging in stacks of metal chairs, setting up snacks, and calling out numbers the seniors asked them to repeat at least three times. Other nights, the girls sipped smoothies along the harbor and peered into shop windows at trinkets. In the coming darkness, the boats bobbed and swayed, and later, when she crawled into Aubrey's bed, Nadia felt like one of those boats, bobbing in place. She was leaving for college in two weeks. She was drifting between two lives, and as excited as she felt, she wasn't quite ready to lose the life she'd found this summer.

Sometimes Kasey grilled and they all ate dinner in the backyard, then walked down the street for Hawaiian shaved ice. Monique told them stories about work, about a hallucinating man who'd gouged his own eye out, a woman who'd fallen asleep at the wheel and crashed into a fence, nearly impaling herself on the post. One evening, she told them about a girl who had taken illegal abortion pills from Mexico and couldn't bring herself to admit it until she almost bled out on the E.R. floor.

"What happened to that girl?" Nadia asked later, while they all washed the dishes.

"What girl?" Monique handed her a wet plate.

"That girl. The one who took those pills from Mexico."

She still couldn't bring herself to say the word **abortion.** Maybe it would sound different falling out of her mouth.

"Horrible infection. But she pulled through. These girls are so afraid to tell someone they're pregnant, they get these pills cheap online and no one knows what's in them. She would've died if she hadn't had enough sense to get help." Monique handed Aubrey a plate. "Don't you girls ever do something like that. You call me, okay? Or Kasey. We'll take you to a doctor. Don't ever try to do something like that on your own."

Nadia had read online about abortion pills,

forty dollars and delivered to your door in a plain brown box. She would've ordered them herself if Luke hadn't found her the money for the surgery. You didn't know how desperate you could be until you were.

"Do you think it's bad?" she asked Aubrey later. "What that girl did?"

"Of course. Mo said she almost died."

"No, not like that. I mean, do you think it's wrong?"

"Oh." Aubrey flipped off the lights and the other half of the bed lowered beneath her weight. "Why?"

"I don't know. Just asking."

In the darkness of the room, she could barely make out Aubrey's outline, let alone her face. In the darkness, talking felt safe. She lay on her back, staring up at the ceiling.

"Sometimes I wonder—" She paused. "If my mom had gotten rid of me, would she still be alive? Maybe she would've been happier. She could've had a life."

Any of her other friends would have gasped, turning to her with wide eyes. "Why would you even think that?" they would say, chiding her for entertaining such darkness. But Aubrey just squeezed her hand because she too understood

137

loss, how it drove you to imagine every possible scenario that might have prevented it. Nadia had invented versions of her mother's life that did not end with a bullet shattering her brain. Her mother, no longer cradling a tiny, wrinkled body in a hospital bed, an exhausted smile on her face, but seventeen and scared, sitting inside an abortion clinic, waiting for her name to be called. Her mother, no longer her mother, graduating from high school, from college, from graduate school even. Her mother listening to lectures or delivering her own, stationed behind a podium, running a toe up the back of her calf. Her mother traveling the world, posing on the cliffs of Santorini, her arms bent toward the blue sky. Always her mother, although in this version of reality, Nadia did not exist. Where her life ended, her mother's life began.

THAT SUMMER, the girls drove to Los Angeles to explore different beaches. Somehow, sun and sand and salt water seemed better, more glamorous even, in the shadows of Hollywood. They wandered down Venice Beach, past weight-lifting jocks and weed dispensaries, T-shirt shops and churro stands and bucket drummers. They swam at Santa Monica Beach and drove through the winding cliffs to Malibu. Other places they went: downtown San Diego, where they rode trolleys across the city, window-shopping at Horton Plaza and walking around Seaport Village and sneaking into nightclubs in the Gaslamp district. Nadia sweet-talked a bouncer who let them into an underground club where shot glasses glowed red over the bar, industrial fans spun lazily overhead, and she had to scream into Aubrey's ear to talk. They met boys. Boys tossing footballs on the beach, boys hanging out of car windows, boys smoking cigarettes in front of water fountains, boys, barely still boys, offering to buy them drinks in clubs. Boys bunched around them at the bar, and while Nadia flirted, Aubrey seemed to shrink within herself, her arms folded tightly across her chest. She'd never had a boyfriend before but how did she expect to ever find one if she never loosened up? So on one of her last nights in Oceanside, Nadia knew exactly where she wanted to take Aubrey: Cody Richardson's house. Aubrey had never been, and in her waning days at home, Nadia felt nostalgic enough to return. Besides, if she was honest with herself, she also hoped she might see Luke. She'd imagined their good-bye—not dramatic, they weren't dramatic people, but some final conversation where she would see, in his eyes, the realization that he'd hurt her. She wanted to feel his regret, for leaving her, for not loving her like he was supposed to. For once in her life, she wanted an ended thing to end cleanly.

The night of the party, she sat on the edge of Aubrey's bed, helping her friend with her makeup. She tilted Aubrey's face toward her, gently sweeping gold eye shadow across her lids.

"You have to wear the dress," she said.

"I told you, it's too short."

"Trust me," she said. "Every guy's gonna want to hook up with you tonight."

Aubrey scoffed. "So? That doesn't mean I want to hook up with them."

"Don't you at least want to know what it's like?"

"What?"

"Sex." She giggled. "Just don't expect it to be all beautiful and romantic. It's gonna be awkward as hell."

"Why does it have to be awkward?"

"Because—look, has any guy ever seen you naked?"

Now Aubrey opened her eyes. "What?" she said.

"I mean, what's the furthest you've ever gone?"

"I don't know. Kissing, I guess."

"Jesus Christ. You've never even let a guy feel you up?"

Aubrey shut her eyes again. "Please," she said. "Can we talk about something else?"

Nadia laughed. "You're so cute," she said. "I was never like you. I lost my virginity and . . ." She shrugged. "I don't even talk to him anymore."

She'd never told Aubrey about Luke. She didn't know how to explain their time together and she'd feel embarrassed trying to, because everything that had happened between them could be traced back to one of her own stupid choices. She was the one who'd gone to Fat Charlie's day after day to see Luke. She had fallen in love with a boy who didn't want anyone to know he was dating her. She'd started sleeping with him months before she was leaving for college and she hadn't even insisted he wear a condom every time. She had been the type of foolish woman her mother had cautioned her never to be and she hated the idea of Aubrey knowing this about her.

Aubrey opened her eyes again. They were watering, and Nadia dabbed a tissue, careful not to smear her eyeliner.

"I wish I could be more like you," Aubrey said.

"Trust me," Nadia said. "You don't want to be like me."

That night, the beach was empty aside from the flicker of a bonfire past the lifeguard tower. Almost deserted, like their own private island. She reached for Aubrey's hand, Aubrey lagging behind her, tugging at the black minidress.

"Don't let me drink too much," she said.

"That's the point—we're gonna loosen you up."

"Nadia, seriously. I'm such a lightweight."

"Oh, you can't be that bad."

"That's what you think."

Cody Richardson's kitchen was more crowded than usual. Tall skaters in ripped skinny jeans howled over beer pong while beside them, three fat blondes counted out loud before downing tequila shots. On the floor, a pale, freckled girl passed a joint to two skinny boys who were too busy making out to notice. Nadia mixed Aubrey a drink, but she shook her head.

"That's too much," she said, pushing the cup back.

"It's only two shots!"

"You didn't even measure it."

"I poured for two seconds. Same thing."

After her first cup, Aubrey started to relax.

After her second, she was smiling, no longer caring that her dress almost showed her ass. After her third, she was dancing with a boy who certainly cared that her dress almost showed her ass, so Nadia pulled her away before he got too handsy. Aubrey was an adorable drunk. She clung to Nadia, throwing her arms around her, toying with her hair. She plopped into her lap, an arm around her shoulder. She told Nadia she loved her, twice. Both times, Nadia laughed it off.

"No," Aubrey said, "I really do love you."

When was the last time anyone had told her that? She felt embarrassed that she couldn't remember, so she pretended not to hear. She twisted open a bottle of water and handed it to Aubrey.

"Have some," she said, "before you puke."

Partying at Cody's sober was a strange experience. She felt like she was in a museum, sneaking under the guardrails for a closer look at the exhibits. She noticed the details, the sadness behind smiles, the tired faces, strained with pretend happiness. She was comforted, in a way, to know that she wasn't the only one who sometimes faked it. She finished her beer, barely buzzed, while Aubrey tried to goad her into drinking more.

"I can't," Nadia said. "I'm driving."

"But you're not even having fun!"

"I am . . ."

Aubrey pouted. "No, you're not."

"Yes, I am, and you're having fun. That's the point."

"But you're just sitting there."

"I'm having fun through you," she said.

And she was, oddly enough, even though she was sober, even though she was disappointed that she hadn't seen Luke. She felt grateful, almost, watching Aubrey party with the giddiness of someone who had just wrenched herself free of her body.

"JESUS, AUBREY." Nadia hooked an arm around her waist as she helped her up Monique and Kasey's driveway. "You are a lightweight."

"I'm not **that** drunk."

"Oh yes you are—"

"No . . ."

"Yes, you fucking are." She fumbled through Aubrey's purse for the gold house key. "Now, shut up, okay? Everyone's probably sleeping."

She clamped a hand over Aubrey's mouth as she shuttled her inside the dark house. Floorboards creaked underneath them and she stepped lightly, ushering Aubrey down the hall, her hand moist from her breathing. Inside her bedroom, Aubrey flopped onto the bed, stretching out like a starfish. Nadia wiggled out of her dress. She glanced into the mirror. Behind her, Aubrey propped herself up on her elbows, watching her undress.

"You're so pretty," she said.

Nadia laughed, rummaging through the drawer for a T-shirt to sleep in. She felt uncomfortable, knowing that Aubrey was looking. She'd never liked anyone watching her undress, not even Luke. She pulled on a faded Chargers T-shirt, piling her hair into a sloppy bun.

"You are," Aubrey said. "You are so pretty, it's not even fair."

"Come on. Let's go to bed."

"But I'm not tired."

"Want to change into shorts? You're not sleeping in that, are you?"

"We'll talk, right?" Aubrey said. "When you're in college."

Nadia's throat tightened, but she didn't say anything, shielded by the dark and the quiet. "Of course," she finally said, unsure if she was trying to comfort Aubrey or herself.

Down the hall, the air conditioner hummed loudly, but her mind refused to settle, not even after Aubrey grew quiet and still beside her. She slept on her stomach, like a baby, and in the darkness, Nadia rested a hand on her back, feeling it rise and fall.

"Remember the trampoline?" Aubrey said. "That I told you about? The one in my neighbor's yard?"

"What about it?"

Aubrey clenched her eyes shut, her voice dropping to a whisper. "That was the first secret I ever kept."

IN THE MORNING, Luke's bum leg burned. An unusual type of pain. He knew other types well, a side effect from a reckless youth. A broken arm after accepting a dare to swing across the monkey bars blindfolded, sprained ankles and jammed fingers from pickup basketball games taken too seriously, cracked ribs from drunk fights with friends. In college, he learned pain intimately, the tautness of sore muscles, the feverous push beyond all points of reason, the weight of a hundred pounds on your back, digging into your shoulders, cutting off your breath. The pain of too-tired, can't-get-up, no-thinking, just-surviving. After football, he didn't think he could ever unlearn pain. He felt violence still in his body, echoing against his bones.

The leg hurt differently, not the sting or swell he knew, just a dull, seasoned pain that felt hot when he stepped, especially in the morning after hours of not moving it. So when his mother banged on his door early one Sunday morning, he took a minute to untangle himself from his covers and shuffle barefoot across the room. Golden shards of light slanted through the slats of the blinds and across his carpet. He eased toward the door, gingerly opening it and poking his head out. In the hallway, his mother stood in a peach skirt suit, her purse clutched under her arm. He squinted into the sunlight, clearing his throat.

"What you need, Mama?" he said.

"Hi Mama," she said. "Good morning, Mama. It's so good to see you, Mama . . ."

"Sorry, I just woke up."

"Let me give you a hug since I don't do nothin' but work and hole up in my room all day . . ."

He stepped forward lightly, putting an arm briefly around her shoulders.

"What'd I tell you about going to see that doctor?" she said.

"It don't hurt that bad."

"Can't hardly walk and still won't listen to nobody." She shook her head. "Why you standing like that in front of the door?"

"You don't wanna go in. It's messy."

"You think I don't know that already?"

"C'mon, Mama, what you need?"

"I don't need anything. I just want to see my son."

"I been busy," he said.

She scoffed. "Busy. I know you're still thinkin' about that Turner girl. You just like your daddy. Can't let the past be the past." She touched his cheek. "Look, what's done is done. You got yourself in this mess and you should be on your knees thanking God for getting you out of it. Don't everybody get another chance, you know that?"

"Yes," he said.

"What you need to do is come to church," she said. "If you'd listened to the Word a little more, maybe none of this would've happened."

Luke leaned against the doorframe. He hadn't meant to get his parents involved but he needed the money quickly, and part of him had hoped that they would scold him for even considering aborting the baby and refuse to give him a dollar. Then he would've returned to Nadia, hangdog, his hands thrown up, and told her that he'd tried his best but couldn't find the money and maybe they should take a moment and think this over. But his parents, who didn't drink or swear or even watch rated-R movies, had helped Nadia kill his baby. He had asked them to.

"Okay," he said. "I'll try to make it."

In Oceanside, seasons blended together into year-round sunshine, but fall came regardless: cheerful welcome messages now flashed on Oceanside High's electronic marquee, and backpacks and binders had been pushed to the front of Walmart. Nadia had received e-mails from the University of Michigan informing her of orientation. She tried to swallow her nervousness each time she passed those generic back-to-school images framed in red and orange leaves. In Oceanside, leaves didn't burst into red and orange; they withered and faded into a pale green that filled the gutters and lined the streets. But for the first time in her life, by the time the trees hung empty, she would be living somewhere else.

The Sunday before she left for Michigan, Upper Room took up a love offering to send her on her way. She was the first one in the congregation to earn an academic scholarship to a big university, but it didn't cover everything. She would need little things—like a real winter coat—so the pastor asked Nadia and her father to stand at the altar with an empty paint bucket by their feet. Second John tossed in his cigarette money; he'd promised his wife he'd cut back anyway. Sister Willis gave the cash she'd set aside for her Powerball ticket and whispered to Magdalena Price that her numbers better not win that week. Even the Mothers tossed in a few dollars, long used to stretching Social Security checks like watered-down dish soap. Nadia had been so distracted by member after member who rose to give that she almost didn't notice Luke at first, sitting in the back pew. He wore a gray suit that dug into his shoulders and when her eyes flicked to his, her father's arm around her shoulders felt tighter.

After service, while her father stood in the receiving line to thank the pastor, she felt Luke sidle up behind her in the lobby.

"Can we talk?" Luke asked.

She nodded, following him past the congregation gathering in the lobby, out the front door, and around the church to the garden in the back. Violet African daisies bunched around the fountain and a bitter-leafed acacia spread over the stone bench where Luke sat, stretching out his bad leg. She lowered herself beside him.

"Heard you got in a wreck," he said.

"Months ago," she said.

"You okay?"

She hated his fake concern. She pushed herself to her feet.

"I don't have the money," she said.

"What?"

"The offering. My dad has it. But I'll pay you back."

"Nadia—"

"Six hundred, right? I'd hate for you to feel like you ever did me any favors."

"I'm sorry." Luke glanced over his shoulder, then leaned toward her, lowering his voice. "I couldn't go to that clinic. If someone had seen me—"

"So you didn't give a shit if someone saw me?"

"It's different. You're not the pastor's kid."

"I needed you," she said. "And you left me."

"I'm sorry," he said, softer. "I didn't want to."

"Well, you did—"

"No," he said. "I didn't want to kill our baby."

She would later imagine their baby growing up. Baby takes his first steps. Baby throws his bottle across the room. Baby learns to jump. Always

Baby, although sometimes she wondered what she would've named him. Luke, after his father, or Robert, after her own. She even thought of more distant family names, like her mother's father, Israel, but she couldn't imagine a baby bearing the heaviness of that name, its biblical sternness. So Baby he remained, even though in her mind, he grew into a boy, a teenager, a man. After Luke had said, for the first time, "our baby"—not the baby, not it—she couldn't help wondering who Baby would've become.

That night, the Flying Bridge was mostly empty, except for fishermen sharing a round at the bar, their thick backs hunched in flannel. She pushed through the front door, toward the booth in the back where Aubrey was waiting. Sometimes she thought about telling Aubrey everything, about Luke, about the abortion. She imagined the two of them in a dark room, how she would take a shaky breath and confess, how Aubrey would tell her that she had been forgiven. Sometimes she wondered if this was what had drawn her to Aubrey. If some small part of her thought that by gathering near to Aubrey—with her purity ring and her good heart—she would somehow be absolved. She would close her eyes and feel Aubrey's hand on her forehead, all of her sins lifting out of her body.

"What's wrong?" Aubrey said, as soon as Nadia sat.

Maybe Nadia could tell her how she hadn't been ready to be a mother, to forfeit her future, how she couldn't imagine how she could live any longer trapped in a house that only reminded her of her mother. How she'd thought she and Luke had both agreed it would be for the best, but how she hadn't really cared because she was granted the right to be selfish this one time, wasn't she? She would be the one sharing her body with a whole new person, so she should get to decide, right? But then Luke's face today when he'd told her that he'd wanted the baby—not the baby, **our** baby—which had gutted her, since she'd never imagined that he might. What young man did? He was supposed to be relieved that he'd been freed of his responsibilities, that she had handled the difficult part and resolved their problem. But maybe Luke was horrified by what she'd done. Maybe he'd left her at the clinic because he couldn't even stand to look at her after.

She could tell Aubrey all of this, and Aubrey would understand. Or she wouldn't. Her face would fall the way Luke's had—in horror, in disgust—and she would back away from the booth, unable to conceive of how anyone could kill a poor, defenseless baby. Or she would say she understood, but her smiles would tighten, never quite reaching her eyes, and she would call less and less until they stopped talking altogether. She would disappear, like everyone eventually did.

Nadia pushed away from the booth, suddenly feeling trapped. She wandered to the pool table, tracing her hand along the green felt. Her father had taught her how to shoot pool when she was young. He'd brought her to his commanding officer's house for a Christmas party, and while his friends drank spiked eggnog, he'd spent the evening in the back with her, teaching her how to shoot pool. After, they'd driven home slowly, circling through neighborhoods to look at the Christmas lights. Despite her pleading, her father never bothered to put up Christmas lights at their house, but he still drove her around to show her the beautiful designs other people had created.

"Do you play?" Aubrey asked. When Nadia shook her head, she said, "Wanna learn?"

"You play pool?"

"Kasey taught me." She grabbed a cue stick,

handing Nadia the other one. "Don't worry. I'll show you."

She patiently guided her through the basics, then stood behind her to correct her stance. Aubrey's hair tickled the back of her neck as she guided her hand back for her first stroke. Nadia wanted to feel the soft, constant pressure of another person's touch. She wanted Aubrey to hold her, even if it was a fake embrace.

"Can you show me again?" she said.

SIX

We left the world.

Each in her own time and way. Betty left when her husband died. On a business trip, he fell asleep one night and never woke up. Didn't seem right to her for anyone to die in a Motel 6, alone until a maid pushed in carts of clean towels. She thought of that moment often, how the maid must've shrieked, backing into the metal cart until it tipped, laundry flapping into the air; Betty imagined herself wrapping her husband in one of those fluffy white towels and holding him in her lap. But he had already left the world, so she left with him. Flora left the world when her children fought over who would care for her.

She had wet herself again, and listened to them argue while she sat in her own mess. Agnes left the world long ago, when she'd gone to the store with her children and the white man behind the counter said, let's see how much money you got there, gal. He made her empty her pocketbook on the counter, her few coins spiraling out, while he laughed and her children watched.

Chile, she says, this world ain't got nothin' good for me. Nothin' that I want, that's for sure.

We tried to love the world. We cleaned after this world, scrubbed its hospital floors and ironed its shirts, sweated in its kitchens and spooned school lunches, cared for its sick and nursed its babies. But the world didn't want us, so we left and gave our love to Upper Room. Now we're afraid of this world. A boy snatched Hattie's purse one night and now none of us go out after dark. We hardly go anywhere at all, besides Upper Room. We've seen what this world has to offer. We're scared of what it wants.

IN MICHIGAN, Nadia Turner learned how to be cold.

To wear gloves, even though she couldn't text with them on. To never text and walk because you might slip on a patch of ice. She learned to wear a scarf, to always wear a scarf, they weren't just decorative like the ones she wore in California with her tank tops. To always get her free flu shot at the student health clinic. She started taking cod-liver oil pills that her boyfriend Shadi swore by, or at least his Sudanese mother did, sending them to him by the boxful. He'd grown up in Minneapolis, so he knew how to be cold. He told her about stuffing heat warming packs in her pockets, how it was better to melt ice with sand instead of salt, how she should start taking a vitamin D supplement because she was black.

"You think I'm joking," he said. "But it's unnatural, being colored in all this cold. We need more sunlight than these white people."

She looked it up on her phone. He was right, people with darker skin did need more vitamin D, but he was also right about feeling unnatural in Ann Arbor. She had never lived in a place so white. She had been the only black girl before—in restaurants, in advanced-placement classes—but even then, she was surrounded by Filipinos and Samoans and Mexicans. Now she looked out into lecture halls filled with white kids from rural Michigan towns; in discussion sections, she listened to white classmates champion the diversity of their school, how progressive and accepting it was, and maybe if you had come from some farm town, it seemed that way. She felt the sly type of racism here, longer waits for tables, white girls who expected her to walk on the slushy part of the sidewalk, a drunk boy outside a salsa club yelling that she was pretty for a black girl. In a way, subtle racism was worse because it made you feel crazy. You were always left wondering, was that actually racist? Had you just imagined it?

She'd met Shadi at a Black Student Union meeting her friend Ekua dragged her to in the fall of her freshman year. Barack Obama had just been elected president and the BSU and Gay-Straight Alliance were cohosting a forum to discuss whether high black voter turnout also caused the gay marriage ban to pass in California. By then, Nadia had already grown tired of town hall meetings, but she'd gone because she was homesick. She stood in the back, piling her plate with free Boston Market, when she noticed Shadi on the panel. He had deep brown skin and a smile that broke his face in half, turning his already slanted eyes into crescents. He was nerdy in black horn-rimmed glasses, but his body seemed lean and athletic even under his sweater. He had boxed growing up, she would later learn, which seemed so unlike him, so needlessly dangerous for a man who still swallowed cod-liver oil pills because his mother told him to. He was nothing like the boys she usually liked—brash and showy boys who didn't even carry book bags to school, only tucking the thinnest binder under an arm as if to advertise how little they cared. Shadi was, she could already tell, About Something. He out-debated everyone on the panel, even though he raced through so many different points, she often couldn't tell which side he was on. He challenged the idea of there even being sides.

"What's with this black versus gay bullshit?" he asked at one point, leaning into the table. "There are black gay people, you know."

For a second, her heart sank. Was he talking about himself? But after the meeting ended, he wandered over to the back and asked what she thought. He stuck his hands in his pockets, head bowed as she spoke, and she realized that he had noticed her in the back the whole evening, that he had been showing off for her. Maybe he was like the boys she normally liked, at least a little.

Shadi was passionate about human rights, and their sophomore year he started a campus newspaper dedicated to reporting news about political movements in Palestine and Sudan and North

Korea. She found herself reading about places that had always seemed vague and distant to her. When she told him she'd received an e-mail about studying abroad, he urged her to apply, and the winter of their sophomore year, he went to Beijing and she went to Oxford.

"Is it safe?" her father said, when she'd called to tell him she'd been accepted.

"It's England, not Afghanistan."

"How much does it cost?"

"My scholarship covers it," she said, not mentioning that she'd picked up a job at Noodles & Co. in addition to her work-study to pay for it.

"And you have all your documents?" he said. "Your passport and stuff?"

Shadi had driven her to the passport office to get her picture taken. He already had stamps in his from visits to France, South Africa, and Kenya, and she realized, waiting in the tiny office, that her mother had never even left the country. This would be her life, accomplishing the things her mother had never done. She never celebrated this, unlike her friends who were proud to be the first in their family to go to college or the first to earn a prestigious internship. How could she be proud of lapping her mother, when she had been the one to slow her down in the first place?

Winter in England was gray and dreary, but it was better than a Michigan winter. Anything was better than a Michigan winter. She felt like every winter would kill her, and when she reached the skyless Februarys and bleak Marches, she promised herself she would book the soonest flight back to California. Then spring broke, always unexpectedly, and Ann Arbor slipped into its quiet, humid summers and she felt normal again, sunning her legs at restaurant patios, lounging on rooftops, and willing the sun to hang above her longer. This had surprised her most about Ann Arbor—she could feel normal here. In Ann Arbor, she was not the girl whose mother had shot herself in the head. She was just a girl from California, a girlfriend to an ambitious boy, a student who loved to party but somehow always made it to class. At home, loss was everywhere; she could barely see past it, like trying to look out a windowpane covered in fingerprints. She would always feel trapped behind that window, between her and the rest of the world, but at least in Ann Arbor, the glass was clearer.

Whenever they Skyped or texted or talked on the phone, Aubrey asked when she would come home. "Soon," Nadia always said, although she found countless reasons not to return: summer internships in Wisconsin and Minnesota, service-learning trips in Detroit for Thanksgiving, Christmas at Shadi's, where there was no baby Jesus or manger but his mother set up a tree and sled and reindeer, their whole house as American and wintry as a Coca-Cola commercial. Nadia wondered if it was only for her benefit, if they thought this would make her feel comfortable, like if she had cancelled last minute, they would've just rolled away all the decorations like a play set and ordered Chinese food. She tried not to think about her father, alone on another holiday, and she turned in Shadi's bed, toward the window and the houses blanketed in snow.

TWO YEARS AFTER Nadia Turner vanished, Luke Sheppard began walking to Martin Luther King Jr. Park to watch the Cobras. He'd never even known the semiprofessional football team existed until he'd gotten hurt. Then he'd started looking for football everywhere: downloading NFL podcasts, watching Pop Warner games out the window of his truck, listening to the cheerful bleat of the whistle as little boys, tottering under pads and helmets, knocked into each other. Parents in lawn chairs cheered, when the boys tackled, when they fell, when the ball squirted out of their arms, when they did anything at all. Luke had stumbled upon the Cobras that winter, a month after he moved into his apartment. He'd gone to MLK Park to do pull-ups because he couldn't afford rent and a gym membership, and halfway through his workout, a bus pulled up, black and copper with a snake, flicking its tongue, coiled on the side. He pretended to do push-ups while the team climbed out and split into their practice formations. The receivers—lanky, lean, and cocky, he could always spot them—bunched up before practicing their routes. He eased close to the ground, then away. The grass rose and fell, and he felt his hamstrings tighten, his fingertips missing the stubbly firmness of a football.

That was three months ago. Now he searched online for any mention of the team. He'd learned the names of the starting offensive players, their day jobs, and their nicknames, and when he saw them around town, waiting for an oil change or pushing a cart through Walmart, he mumbled them to himself. (Right tackle Jim Fenson, plumber, Fender-Bender.) He went to the park early on Saturday mornings to watch the team practice. He missed falling into those neat lines. He wanted to get back into football shape, stop eating fried food between shifts, stop drinking beer and smoking weed, and start treating his body like a machine again, an unfeeling, unwanting thing. He'd lowered to the ground for another push-up when he noticed the coach heading toward him.

"Thought you looked familiar," Coach Wagner said. He grinned, sticking out his hand. "I remember you. San Diego State. Speedy wide-out. But that leg—"

"It's better now," Luke said.

"Yeah?"

He ran a hitch route. His right leg felt gummy from the lack of exercise, his left burning as soon as he cut inside. When he trotted back over, Coach Wagner was frowning.

"Getting there," he said. "Look, call me when it's healed up all the way. We could use you."

The Cobras did not pay their players—any money the team made went toward equipment and transportation—but Luke didn't care. He slid the business card into his pocket. Beside the coach's phone number, there was a glossy emblem of a snake and he ran his thumb across it his whole walk home.

"Don't you think you should focus on your career?" his mother asked the next night.

He hunched over the kitchen table, stirring his

dirty rice. He hated going to Sunday dinner at his parents' house but not enough to turn down free food and free laundry. When he walked in, his father cleared his throat and said, "Didn't see you at church this morning," and since Luke had stopped coming up with creative excuses, he just shrugged. He daydreamed during his father's endless grace and while his parents discussed Upper Room, he ate, imagining how long the leftovers he would take with him might last. He normally survived Sunday dinner without saying much, but he'd brushed the business card in his pocket and felt an unusual excitement. For the first time, he'd felt like he had news worth sharing. But his mother just raised an eyebrow and his father sighed, slipping his glasses off his face.

"Get a job, Luke," his father said.

"I have one," Luke said.

"I mean a real one. Not that restaurant crap."

"And what about your leg?" his mother said. "What happens when you get hit again?"

"It don't hurt that bad."

His mother shook her head. "Listen, I know you love football but you got to be realistic now."

"When are you gonna take some responsibility, Luke?" his father said. "When?"

Maybe he was being irresponsible, but he didn't

care. He just wanted to be good at something again. By June, he was going to the park every day to run drills. CJ couldn't throw a tight spiral but he learned the routes, the sharp angle of a post, the soft curl of a buttonhook. He knew where to put the ball and he joked that if Luke could catch balls thrown by him, he'd be able to grab the ones thrown by a real quarterback. CJ wasn't as bad as he thought, which annoyed Luke; he envied CJ, even with his mediocre talent, because he had a body that worked right, that followed orders without complaint, not one that had splintered apart.

"I'm slow as shit, man," he said, huffing.

"I mean, you fucked up your leg." CJ plopped on the grass in his gray gym shorts from high school, which still had his name written on the thigh in marker. "It's gonna take some time."

"Ain't got time," Luke said. "Let's go again."

After evening workouts, he bought CJ a beer and they drank outside Hosie's, watching girls in bikinis trail in from the beach, sand clinging to their legs.

"You still talk to your girl?" CJ asked one night.

Luke took a sip of lukewarm beer, always slow, tiny sips, wanting to make it last.

"Who?" he said.

"That high school chick you was fuckin' with."

"She's not my girl," Luke said.

"I heard she's living in, like, Russia right now."

"Russia?"

"Or some shit like that. She's living in Russia and fucking with some African nigga."

Luke sipped his beer again, swishing it around his mouth. When she'd first left, he used to obsess over the college boys Nadia was touching. He imagined them, never athletic boys like him, but preppy boys in Michigan sweaters, who scurried around campus, stacks of books clutched against their chests. Now he had a name. Shadi Waleed, some Arab-sounding motherfucker. At Fat Charlie's, he searched him on the computer in the staff room and found pages of articles Shadi had written for some newspaper called **The Blue Review**. A blog post—of course he blogged—about, Luke was surprised to discover, football. Football as in soccer, but he was shocked that Shadi was interested in regular things like sports, although the blog post was about how France's World Cup hopes rested on their Muslim forward and wasn't that ironic? Luke didn't understand what was so ironic, but it must've been another thing that Shadi Waleed knew that he didn't.

He finally landed on Shadi's Facebook—his

breath caught when he saw the profile picture. Shadi lounging on a black chair outside a restaurant, Nadia Turner on his lap in a long, floral sundress, smiling behind sunglasses, her hand gently draped across Shadi's shoulder. She looked older now, her face more angular, her cheekbones sharpened. She looked happy. Luke flipped through the other photos—mostly posters for campus events, a few of Shadi hunching over a woman in a headscarf who must've been his mother—but he always returned to the one of Nadia in Shadi's lap. Her life had gone on like nothing had happened, but Luke was stuck, wedged in the past, always wondering what would've happened if they'd kept the baby. Their baby.

"Who the fuck is that?" a busboy asked Luke, pointing at Shadi's smiling face. "Your boyfriend?"

He cackled, but Luke shoved away from the computer so hard, the desk shook.

WHEN HE JOINED THE COBRAS, Luke thought his anger might finally subside, but instead, he felt it growing. Football was a safe place to be angry. Every time he laced up, he cupped his anger, keeping it safe. The first time he got hit in

practice, he saw a white flash, his mind washed
over with pain, then he pushed himself off the
ground and hobbled back to the huddle. That hit
made him feel like himself again. He started shit-
talking, taunting men double his size, who could
cripple him with another blow.

"That's all you got, bitch? Come on, mother-
fucker, try me again!"

The next play, the same linebacker came loping
toward him and Luke cut inside, breezing past
him as the ball smacked into his hands and he
sprinted into the end zone. He felt almost disappointed he hadn't been hit again. His anger
belonged here. Hell, all of the Cobras were angry.
Everyone had a story of near fame and missed
chances: the coach who'd fucked them over, the
family debt that forced them to drop out and
get a job, the recruiter who never saw their full
potential. No one's anger was more welcomed
than his because the team pitied him the most.
He was the youngest, the one most robbed of
his future, so the other players were kind to him.
Roy Tabbot invited him on fishing trips. Edgar
Harris changed his oil for free. Jeremy Fincher
loaned him a tux so he didn't have to rent one for
a friend's wedding.

"Don't fuck it up either, dickbreath," Finch said,

handing over the garment bag. It was the nicest thing anyone had done for Luke in months.

When there was no practice, Luke went to team barbecues. He stretched on white lawn chairs as the Cobras crowded around grills, arguing about the best way to marinate a steak. Finch said that steaks didn't need marinade at all, none of that foo-foo pussy shit, just eat the goddamn meat like you're meant to. Ritter said sorry, he didn't want to eat the steak straight off the cow, it meant he wasn't a fucking Neanderthal, not that he was a pussy, and Gorman said of course Finch knew a lot about eating meat. The wives carried out bowls of potato salad and macaroni and cheese, sometimes joining in the group and jibing the men, and Luke thought, I could have a life like this.

He sat by the kiddie pool, watching the Cobras' children splash, and when they climbed out, they jumped on him, their bodies slick and cold as they tried to tackle him. He pulled himself out of a dog pile and found one of the wives—Gorman's or Ritter's, he could never remember—standing over him, blocking the sun from her eyes. She was smiling.

"You're so good with kids," she said.

"Thanks," he said, embarrassed by how good that made him feel.

Late after one barbecue, when the party had died down and he sat under the fading tiki torch, finishing off his beer, he told Finch that he had been a father once, long ago.

"Fucking bullshit is what it is," Finch said. "She wants to get rid of your kid? You got no say in that. But say she wanted to keep it. Guess who she's hitting up for money? Guess whose ass is getting hauled off to jail if he can't pay? A man's got no rights anymore."

Luke drained his beer, watching the flame above them flicker and dance. He felt pitiful, but if a man couldn't feel pitiful late at night after drinking too much, when could he?

"She left me," he said. "She went to Europe and shit and now she's fucking some Arab mother-fucker."

Finch hooked an arm around his neck. "I'm sorry, brother," he said. "That's some bullshit and we both know it. I love my wife more than any-thing, but I'd kill her if she got rid of my baby."

His eyes bulged a little, and Luke could tell he meant it. He suddenly felt sick. He stood too fast, the ground beneath him tilting and he felt dizzy, like when he used to put on his mother's reading glasses and run around the house. Finch refused to let him walk home and pulled him inside. His wife put sheets on the couch for him, even though Luke told her he was fine with just a blanket. He felt touched by her extra effort, until he realized that maybe she just didn't want him to puke on her couch. He hoped he wouldn't. He stretched out, feeling the bumps in the cushion, his body taut with pain. He was grateful for how much he felt everything now. The wife brought a blanket from the hall and he closed his eyes as it fluttered on top of him.

MRS. FINCHER'S NAME WAS CHERRY. First name like the fruit, last name like the bird.

"Not Sherry," she said. "Everyone wants to call me Sherry. Why would I want to be named after liquor?"

"I went to high school with a girl named Chardonnay," Luke said.

"Well, you're a baby," she said. "You probably went to school with a girl named Grapefruit."

She was always doing that, calling him a baby. He didn't mind it. She wouldn't tell him her age but he figured she was around thirty-five, not old but at the age where women start to think they are. If he ever got married, he decided, he would find a woman older than him. Too much pressure, being the older one in the relationship. When you were the baby, a woman didn't expect much from you. She wanted to take care of you and he felt comforted by it all, her attention and her low expectations. If an actor over fifty appeared on TV, Cherry would say, "I bet you don't even know who that is," and he would shrug, even if he did, because it made her laugh. He'd sit at the counter while she made her kids sandwiches and although he never asked, she always made him one too.

He wasn't attracted to her, not the way he usually was to women he chose to spend time with. She was fat. She had a too-wide smile and a strong chin. She was Filipina and she'd grown up poor in Hawaii. Luke had never even thought about there being poor people in Hawaii.

"Don't y'all just surf and roast pigs and wear grass skirts and shit?" he asked. Cherry didn't talk to him for two days.

"You got to shut off that TV and fucking go somewhere, Luke," she said later. "Paradise ain't paradise for everyone."

She'd met Finch when he was stationed at Kaneohe Bay. She'd waited tables nearby at a tourist trap called Aloha Café, where the menu featured items with names like Surfside Steak and

Luau Lamb Chops. Finch ordered the Beach Bum Brownies, but he kept calling them Butt Brownies, which made her laugh. She was eighteen. By the time she reached Luke's age, she had married, moved to the mainland, and birthed three kids. Luke liked her children but he wondered if they were the only reason Cherry and Finch were still together. When he came over to watch a game with Finch, he studied the two of them, expecting to spot some invisible bond between them. But Finch rarely acknowledged Cherry and she was quiet around him, as if they had parceled out space in the house, carved it up like warring countries fighting over territory. Cherry behind the kitchen counter, passing through the living room like a tourist, Finch awkward anywhere near a stove, instead sprawling across the couch.

At Cobras parties, Cherry sipped pinot grigio with the other wives, always seeming a bit bored. Once Luke had heard the other wives call her stuck-up and he thought about her stories about eating sugar sandwiches for dinner, how she rarely saw her parents, who worked at the Dole cannery, how she'd grown up thinking that everyone knew their parents vaguely, by shadows cast in late nights or half-remembered forehead kisses at dawn. How she'd gotten married and grown fat and still felt the need to hoard—stashing candy bars in end drawers, packing old clothes in garbage bags at the back of her closet—because what if there wasn't enough? Poorness never left you, she told him. It was a hunger that embedded itself into your bones. It starved you, even when you were full.

"I'm starting a new diet tomorrow," she said, unwrapping a Reese's cup she'd tucked in her coupon drawer.

"Which one?" he said.

"The one where you can only eat what the dinosaurs ate."

"Didn't they all die off?"

She laughed. "That's why I like you, Luke."

"Why?"

"Because you're honest," she said. "Because you don't say, 'Oh Cherry, you don't need to go on a diet.' What bullshit. The people who tell you that are the same ones calling you a fat ass once you leave the room."

He liked that she thought of him like that—honest, shrewd, unsentimental. He found himself spending more time around her, even though he knew he shouldn't. He wasn't used to having friends with wives but he understood that there were boundaries you ought to respect. And even though he knew he shouldn't visit when Finch wasn't home, he still swung by the house sometimes before his afternoon shift. He usually made up some excuse—he wanted to return a socket wrench Finch had lent him, he lost his playbook, he thought he'd left his water bottle on the coffee table. In reality, he just wanted to talk to Cherry, who always seemed interested in his life. She told him where he should look for a better-paying job, how he should consider going back to school, how he should stop stalking Nadia's Facebook.

"That's your first mistake," she said. "You never go sniffing around an ex. Why would you want to see how happy she is without you?"

Cherry was right. She was right about many things, and he liked asking her for advice. He couldn't ask his own mother, not anymore, not since the morning he'd told her about the pregnancy and she'd returned with cash. He didn't blame her for helping him but he knew something had shifted between them in that moment—his mother had done something he'd thought her incapable of, and the boundaries of their relationship had suddenly moved, leaving him disoriented, like stepping into a room and feeling for where the walls had once been but instead only touching air.

"What're you two hens jabbering about?" Finch said, when he came into the kitchen and caught them in mid-conversation. Cherry always said "Nothing" and went back to being her silent self. It amazed Luke, how quickly she could shift. Maybe all women were shapeshifters, changing instantly depending on who was around. Who was Nadia, then, around Shadi Waleed?

"I saw your video," Cherry said one day when Luke came by to return a book he'd borrowed called **Blu's Hanging**. Here, she'd said, handing it to him. Here's your poor Hawaiians. He'd almost told her that he didn't have to read about it to believe her but he read the book anyway because he could tell it mattered to her. He liked it enough, even though he'd read online that the treatment of Filipino characters might be a little racist. Was that true, he'd planned to ask her. Was it true that in Hawaii, Filipinos are treated like blacks?

"What video?" he said, half listening as he tried to find the spot on the shelf where the book had been.

"What do you mean?" she said. "What other video is there?"

"Oh," he said. "That one."

"Finch had some of the guys over," she said.

"They kept watching it again and again and again."

He had a sudden, clear image of the Cobras hunched around Finch's computer, replaying the video of his injury and laughing. Jesus Christ, look at Sheppard! One more time, okay, wait for it, wait for—oh shit! The bone and everything! He'd thought he was a Cobra but he wasn't. He was just a gruesome joke.

"Can I see it?" Cherry asked.

"You already did," he said. He felt strangely betrayed by her, as if she, of all people, should've known better than to watch the video.

"No," she said. "Your leg."

She'd spoken so casually, it took him a moment to even realize what she'd asked. "Why?" he said.

"Just want to," she said. "I can't even understand how you walk on that thing half normal, let alone play."

She was curious, but not like he'd imagined the Cobras, searching for a laugh. She looked like a person climbing out of a wrecked car, eager to inspect the damage to convince herself it wasn't worse than what she imagined. He sat on the La-Z-Boy near the bookshelf, quietly rolling the leg of his sweatpants up to his knee. His mother had cried when she'd seen him in the hospital bed, his shattered leg propped up in front of him, and not wanting to worry her, he had smiled and said, "It's fine, it don't even hurt." His father had called later that afternoon from Atlanta—he was delivering a keynote address at a pastors' conference that night but he'd sent a prayer cloth in his stead. When his mother had placed it on his busted leg, Luke hadn't felt the healing power of God. He'd felt nothing, and maybe, that was the same thing.

He shivered as Cherry's hand traced down his leg to the ugly brown scar stretching down to his ankle. She bent and kissed his scar, and he closed his eyes, believing, like a child, that her kiss might stop his hurting. How easily he had believed then, how simple it had seemed, a kiss from his mother and a body that always, somehow, healed.

THE NEXT EVENING, he hauled the trash out to the alley behind Fat Charlie's, still thinking about Cherry's kiss. He had left right after—her youngest daughter had appeared in the hallway, demanding juice, and Cherry had pushed herself to her feet, not looking at Luke. She was embarrassed, and why wouldn't she be? She was spare with her affection, even to Finch, as if the two were in a competition fighting to be the one who seemed to care the least. But Luke was grateful for her kindness. He wanted to call her when he got off work. Maybe he could ask her to get a drink. Not a drink, maybe coffee. He didn't even like coffee, but coffee seemed like the thing you invited a girl to do to show that you weren't just trying to fuck her. He dragged a bulging garbage bag, lugging it into the green dumpster. The sun was setting over the pier, the sky blazing orange. Sometimes Oceanside could be beautiful, even from a dirty alley.

He was heading back inside when he saw the Cobras. Finch and Ritter and Gorman and five others, all coming down the alley.

"Yo assholes," he said, "I can't get all of you free beer, so don't even ask."

He knew something was wrong when no one laughed or insulted him back.

Years ago, Luke would've been fast enough to duck inside the restaurant. But before he could even turn, he caught Finch's right hook. He blacked out before the Cobras started stomping on his leg.

SEVEN

In rehab, Luke learned to walk again.

Not all at once, but slowly. He spent his first two weeks pushing a walker down the four halls of his floor. He learned the halls intimately, like a policeman memorizing his beat: the mint green checkered linoleum, the nurses' station, the corner where old women knitted and gossiped. He dragged himself down the halls, stunned each morning by how difficult a simple action could be, the placing of one foot in front of the other. He now had a titanium rod screwed in his leg, from his knee to his ankle, which would remain there for the rest of his life. He would set off plenty of metal detectors, the surgeon had told him, but someday, he'd be able to walk again. For now, he had to work on strengthening his ankle, bending his swollen knee, developing his quad and hamstring. He slid his foot forward, straining to place the heel down, then the toe, while his rehabilitation aide Carlos followed, just in case he fell. Carlos's father was Colombian, his mother Nicaraguan, but everyone called him a Mexican.

"Always a Mexican," he said. "They ask me, 'Ay Carlos, why don't you fix us up some tacos?' I don't know nothing about no fucking tacos. Go fix me some tacos, you like the goddamn things so much."

It was true. When Luke had first checked in, a nurse told him that the aide assigned to him was Carlos, the Mexican guy.

"You'll like him," she said, "he's real funny. Little guy but he's strong. Those are always the strongest ones, the little guys."

Carlos was barely five-five, broad-shouldered and stout. He used to be a personal trainer at a gym. Luke had always thought of trainers as yoked men with muscles bulging out of their tank tops, but Carlos looked more like the type you might trust if you were a fat housewife looking to lose a few pounds. He was tough but encouraging. He lectured Luke about taking his pills,

all of them, even if he didn't feel like it, the anti-
biotics to prevent infection, the aspirin to stop
blood-clotting, the pain medicine. He helped
Luke stretch on the table, massaging his leg first
with aloe vera lotion. Luke was used to trainers
rubbing down sore muscles, easing out cramps, or
taping sprained ankles, but that was in the locker
room. He felt awkward, splayed on a table in an
exercise room, another man rubbing lotion onto
his skin. Maybe Carlos was gay. Why else would a
guy take a job where he had to lotion other guys?
But Luke never said anything because Carlos's
massages felt good. The tissue damage went deep.

"Christ, those guys really hated your guts,"
Carlos said. "They didn't want you to ever walk
again."

Luke had never told his parents that the Cobras
had jumped him. It'd be one thing if he had slept
with Cherry—he would've accepted his punish-
ment then like a man—but to be jumped for seek-
ing her friendship seemed too shameful to admit.
Besides, his parents would only tell him that they
had been right about the team all along. So he'd
told them that some guys had tried to mug him,
and no, he hadn't seen their faces.

On the overhead television, Carlos played
fútbol matches while Luke did his daily exer-

185

cises; panting, leaning against the wall, Luke followed the tiny ball across the ocean of grass. He'd always found soccer boring, but he grew to like the nonstop pace, the constant movement, the flashy celebrations. Maybe he would've been good at soccer. Maybe he could've found a sport to love that wouldn't have destroyed his body.

"You used to be a big man," Carlos said. "You ain't anymore. Gotta accept that. It's okay to not be a big man. It's enough to be a good one."

It didn't matter who you'd been out in the world. In rehab, you were just like everyone else, struggling to gain control of your body. Luke was the youngest person in the center. Most of the patients were elderly; in wheelchairs, they scooted down the hall with their feet, like children who'd outgrown their strollers. Between therapy sessions, Luke liked to sit in the hallway and play cards with the old men. Stroke victims, most of them. His favorite was Bill, a retired jailer from Los Angeles.

"I grew up in Ladera Heights," Bill told him. "Back when it used to be black. You can't even go in there now. Got taken over by all those—" He dropped his voice, pointing at Carlos walking down the hall. Mexicans.

Bill had fought in the Korean War but he'd

ended up at the rehab center after tripping on the sidewalk and breaking his hip. The man had survived war and prisoner riots, only to be brought down by upraised pavement. He wasn't married. He had been—three times before—so he was the marrying type, just not the stay-married type. He'd always been a ladies' man—Luke spotted him flirting with the nurses, holding their hands as they wheeled him down the hall, sweet-talking them for an extra cookie after dinner. Luke used to think he might be that type of man, the kind who never settled down, but what good did that do you when you were eighty and alone at a rehab center?

"You sweet on anyone?" Bill asked him once. "Big football guy. I know the girls got to be chasing you."

Luke shrugged, reshuffling the deck of cards. He'd thought about calling Nadia once or twice but what would he say? That the only thing he did every day was learn to walk? How simple exercises, like knee lifts or leg curls, made him groan? How he spent hours in a wheelchair, playing poker with old men to pass the time? One evening, he was in the middle of dealing out another hand when the elevator doors opened and out stepped Aubrey Evans.

"Hi," she said. "The Mothers asked me to drop this off."

She held up a knitted blanket, a bundle of pink and green and silver that was startlingly bright against the white walls. He led Aubrey to his room. She didn't say anything as he pushed his walker slowly down the hall, staggering with each step. He collapsed on his bed, embarrassed by how winded he was. Aubrey folded the blanket neatly and set it on the end of his bed. He'd never been alone with her before. He knew her from church, vaguely—she seemed nice and religious in a way that had always bored him. But people seemed to like her. His mother. Nadia, according to all the pictures he'd seen of them together on Facebook.

"I didn't know you were still in town," he said.

"I'm taking classes," she said. "At Palomar. And working."

"Where?"

"Donut Touch." She frowned when he snorted. "What?"

"Nothin'," he said. "It's just a dumb name."

She smiled. "If you really wanted a donut, you wouldn't care what it's called."

He couldn't remember the last time he'd eaten a donut. Even before he'd existed on plastic hospital food, he had converted back to a football diet, good, clean eating, grilled chicken and vegetables at every meal. A lot of good that'd done him. He pushed himself to his feet, holding on to the walker for balance.

"Do you still talk to Nadia Turner?" he asked.

"All the time," she said.

"Is she still in Russia?"

"What?" Aubrey laughed, her nose scrunching up. "She was never in Russia."

"Really?"

"England. France, for a little bit." She paused. "Wanna see pictures?"

He did but he shook his head, staring at the floor. "Nah," he said. "I just never knew anyone who went to Russia."

"Me either," Aubrey said. "But she goes everywhere. Anywhere she wants to be, she goes."

He felt stupid for the time he'd spent imagining Nadia in Russia, wearing furry hats in front of colorful buildings shaped like tops. But if anyone he knew went, it would be her. How had he ever thought she would stay in town with him and raise their baby?

Aubrey dug in her purse for her keys. She was leaving and he felt a sudden need to stop her.

"We pray for you every Sunday," she said. "Let me know if you need anything."

"You could bring me a donut," he said.

THE NEXT DAY, Aubrey brought him a red velvet donut moist and sweet enough, he could forgive the stupid name. Other things she later brought him: a new deck of playing cards, chewing gum, a book called **Why Do Christians Suffer?** that he didn't read but kept on the nightstand so she'd see it when she visited, a daily planner where he could keep track of his progress, a bundle of get well cards from Upper Room, and a tank top that said **Beast Mode** that he wore during his exercises. She was pretty in a quiet way he grew to like. Nadia's beauty bulldozed him but Aubrey's prettiness was like a tea candle, a warm flicker. When she visited him after work, she looked cute in her uniform, a black polo shirt with a pink donut on the front. She fiddled with the matching visor as she stepped off the elevator, her curly ponytail bobbing. She smelled sweet, like frosting.

"I used to have one of those joints," he said once, pointing at her purity ring.

"Really?"

"I was like thirteen. But my hand outgrew it, so my dad had to saw it off me."

"You're joking."

He held up his hand. On his right ring finger, a light brown scar.

"It's okay," he said. "I ended up fucking a girl later that year. I would've done it anyway, the ring just would've made me feel bad."

"It's not about feeling bad," she said. "At least not for me."

"Then what is it? Like a married-to-Jesus thing?"

"It just reminds me."

"Of what?"

"That I can be clean," she said.

She was a good woman. The more time he spent around her, the more he realized how rarely he thought anybody else was actually good. Nice, maybe, but niceness was something anyone could be, whether they meant it or not. But goodness was another thing altogether. He was wary, at first, disarmed by Aubrey's kindness. What could she want from him? Everyone wanted something, but what could she possibly hope to gain from a man whose whole world had constricted to four hallways? Sometimes they played cards in his room, dipping their hands into a paper bag filled with donut holes. Other times, she wheeled him outside and they sat, watching cars come and go in the parking lot. He never asked her about Nadia although he wanted to—he would feel exposed even mentioning her again. Besides, like Cherry said, why would he want to keep hearing how happy Nadia was? How big and exciting and fulfilling a life she led. He wasn't a big man anymore. He wouldn't be famous, like he'd dreamed as a kid, teaching himself to sign his name in all curved letters so he would be prepared to autograph a football. He would live a small life, and instead of depressing him, the thought became comforting. For the first time, he no longer felt trapped. Instead, he felt safe.

He taught Aubrey to play poker, then blackjack. She picked up both games surprisingly quickly, and he told her that they should go to Vegas someday and play in a real casino. She laughed. She'd never been before.

"Why would I go to Vegas?" she said. "I don't party. Or gamble."

"Because it's fun," he said. "There's food. And shows. You like plays, don't you? We could go. When I get out."

She smiled a little, plucking a card from the middle of her hand.

"Sure," she said. "That sounds good."

She was just being nice, but he still clung to her words, marking them in his planner that night.

"WHAT YOU GONNA DO when you get out of here?" Bill asked.

Luke had just graduated to crutches and he was hobbling around the hallway, giddy and awkward. He'd progressed faster than anyone had expected, Carlos told him. He'd given Luke a tiny pedometer to wear when he walked down the hall, and within a month, he had already logged 50,000 steps. Carlos printed him a certificate that said **MVP: Most Valuable Pacer.** Aubrey helped him hang it on his wall.

"I don't know," he said. Fat Charlie's didn't offer sick leave—they'd replaced him weeks ago. He needed to find a job or he would have to move back home with his parents, who had already spent their own money paying for his last month at the rehab center. He hobbled down the hallway, calculating how much it must have cost, and felt overwhelmed by the thought of it. Just another thing he owed them. He would have to find work soon, maybe another restaurant on the pier. What else did he know how to do?

"Nah, nah," Bill said. "You got to want more than that."

Luke laughed. "Like what? I'm supposed to wanna be president or some shit?"

"That's the problem with you brothas," Bill said. "You got lazy. You know why? Because you know these young sistas will pick up the slack. Grown men living with their mamas, whole mess of kids running around, ain't got a job. Somewhere along the way we became a race of men happy to let women take care of us."

Luke had grown up listening to old folks at Upper Room make similar speeches, about how they'd fought so hard just to watch his generation throw any progress away. As if he owed them somehow for being young and ought to personally repay them for their humiliations. Still, he liked hanging out with the old men in the hallway, listening to their stories and imagining their lives. Bill never listened to the trainers when they tried to guide him through his exercises. He was too stubborn, too softened, over the years, to pain. Who could blame him? He was old with no one waiting for him on the outside. He just wanted to talk shit with his buddies and look at pretty nurses. Luke was the only one who could get Bill out of his wheelchair.

"You're pretty good at this," Carlos told him.

Luke had convinced Bill to finish his quad stretches, cheering him on until the old man plopped back in his wheelchair with a huff. In the doorway, Carlos looked impressed.

"You should look into physical training," Carlos said. "Shit, you been here long enough."

Luke told Aubrey, and the next day, she printed out a list of qualifications he needed to become a physical therapy assistant. Two years of school, which discouraged him, but Aubrey said the time would pass anyway—why not spend it chasing after something he wanted? She'd squeezed his shoulder and he felt himself relaxing. She was right, and besides, if he had learned nothing else in rehab, he'd learned how to be patient. He'd spent the past few months relearning how to walk. He felt that he could wait for anything.

When he was finally released from the rehab center, strong enough to lean on a cane alone, time seemed to rush at him. He missed the soft seconds in the center, days that blurred into one another, time marked only by mealtimes and exercise routines and Aubrey's visits. Out in the world, he felt time racing past him and he could never catch up. In the center, he'd been a fast learner, nimble compared to the others, but at his parents' house, he felt like he was moving in slow motion, like every effort to get out of bed and shower, to dress himself and cook breakfast, took three times as long. During the day, he worked on his applications to physical therapy programs and tried to find a job. But he didn't have any real skills and most unskilled jobs required that you at least be able to lift fifty pounds. Finally, he asked his father if there was any work he could do at Upper Room.

"Maybe I can do something around the grounds," he said. "Pick up trash. I don't know. Something."

Luke felt embarrassed, begging for pocket change, but his father placed a warm hand on his shoulder and smiled. He had probably been waiting for this moment for years. When his only son would return home, humbled, and ask to help out the ministry. Maybe he'd imagined this moment when Luke was born—a son who would inherit the church someday. A son standing beside him at the altar, leading teen Bible studies, following him through the halls of Upper Room. How disappointed his father must've been, given instead a son who worshipped pigskin, who spent his Sunday praise in front of the television, who hadn't been called by God to do anything but run and catch.

"The church is growing," his father said. "Getting older. We could use someone to visit the sick and shut-in."

"I can do that," Luke said.

He understood sickness better than anything else. Sickness burrowed deep inside you, and even if you were cured, even if you could be cured, you would never forget how it felt to be betrayed by your own body. So when he knocked on doors, carrying donated meals, he did not tell the sick to get well. He just came to sit with them while they weren't.

He still saw Aubrey around Upper Room. He'd been worried at first that she wouldn't talk to him now that he was out of rehab, that maybe their friendship had been restricted to that space. But she always seemed glad to see him. She never came by the house, although he hinted that that would be okay. But on Sunday mornings, she sat beside him, not in the front pew where he'd sat with his parents as a boy, but in a back pew near the aisle so he could stretch out his bad leg. Each Sunday, when his father laid hands on the sick, she glanced at him, and each Sunday, he looked away, studying the fringes on the rug. One week, she leaned in toward his ear.

"Do you want to go up?" she asked. "I'll go with you."

How could anyone believe healing was that easy, only a matter of asking for it? What about those who remained sick? Did they just not ask hard enough? But she reached for his hand, her fingers wedged against his purity scar. Their palms kissed and he felt, for the first time, that he could be whole.

ON A BRISK MAY NIGHT, Luke pushed through the concession stand crowd with his plastic cup of overpriced stadium beer. CJ trampled after him, carrying a cup of beer that sloshed against his hand. He didn't like baseball but he'd agreed to the Padres game because they rarely hung out now that they no longer worked together. CJ had wanted to check out a football game—in the springtime, you could always find an arena game or even a spring practice—but Luke told him he wanted to watch baseball. He didn't, really, but he couldn't put himself through more football.

He'd already given football too much. He would find something new to love.

During the seventh-inning stretch, the crowd began to sing as an animated Friar Fred danced on the scoreboard. CJ moved his lips, the way Luke mouthed along to church hymns. When they sat, CJ took a sip of his tepid beer before setting it back on the ground.

"I gotta get out of fuckin' Fat Charlie's, man," CJ said.

"And do what?"

"I don't know. Anything else. Maybe join up."

"Marines?"

"Shit, maybe. What else I know how to do?"

He couldn't imagine CJ in camp or huffing through the desert with a gun strapped to his back. Could CJ even pass the fitness test? He was strong enough, sure, but you had to run three miles and he had never seen CJ run thirty yards.

"What if they send you out somewhere?" Luke said.

CJ shrugged. "At least it's something. I gotta be on my shit like you. You got a future. What I got?"

An old black vendor climbed the metal stairs, hollering, "Peanuts! Who wants a big bag of salty nuts?" The crowd laughed and Luke sipped his beer, wiping his mouth with a grease-splotched napkin. He wasn't used to anyone else envying his life. He lived at home and collected fifty dollars each week from his father that felt more like an allowance than a paycheck. He leaned on a cane when he had to walk a long distance and at the stadium, he'd been patted down and wanded three times after the metal rod in his leg had set off the detectors. But he was building something, at least. He was starting his physical therapy classes in the fall. He spent his weekends with a girl who calmed him, who pieced him together. A pretty brunette in a retro Tony Gwynn jersey passed and he wondered if he could bring Aubrey to a game. She'd look cute in his cap, and maybe they'd get caught on the Kiss Cam and she would lean toward him, not embarrassed by the cheers of the crowd. He would hope for the Padres to hit a home run just to see her face when fireworks shot across the sky.

At the top of the eighth, a small black boy in an Angels jersey three times too big for him hopped on the seat, yelling for the cotton candy man. The vendor didn't notice, starting down the aluminum steps.

"Ay man!" Luke stood, wincing at the sudden movement. "Right here!"

He pointed at the boy. The vendor stopped and the boy stumbled down the row, climbing over legs as he waved his dollars in the air. The man stooped with the carousel of pink and blue swaths of cotton candy and the boy jumped, pointing to the baby blue. He wiggled impatiently as the vendor gave him his change, then he smiled, triumphant, holding the cotton candy in his hands. Everyone ushered the boy down the row, hands against his back so he didn't trip. Luke's finger brushed against the smooth inside of his thin arm as he passed.

"Tell me a secret," Aubrey said later.

Luke stretched out on his bed. His room was warm from the late spring heat but he couldn't open a window or Aubrey would be cold. She was always cold and he liked that about her, how he felt responsible for warming her. She was curled against his chest and he bent to kiss her forehead. His parents were gone for the evening but he knew she hadn't come over to do more than cuddle. When they'd first started dating, he'd tried to find times to spend with her alone. He knew she was waiting to have sex but she wouldn't want to wait forever. Just a matter of time, he figured, until she felt ready. But months later, they still hadn't had sex yet. Often, when Aubrey visited, they didn't even go near his bedroom, eating dinner with his parents instead or sitting together on the porch swing. Maybe it was weird for her, hooking up in her pastor's house, so he started visiting her at her sister's house instead, even though he felt awkward in a house full of women. He stepped inside a bathroom with a counter covered in girly products—bottles of all shapes and sizes, moisturizers, facial cream, serum, leave-in conditioner—and washed his hands with pink soap that left his skin feeling soft and smelling like powder. It made him feel unmanly, so he started washing his hands with the orange dishwashing soap in the kitchen instead.

No matter where they went, they didn't have sex. Kissing was fine and sometimes touching was okay, but always over the clothes and always above the waist. He'd never dated a girl before who he hadn't seen naked and he burned, imagining what it would be like to really touch her. When they spoke on the phone at night, he pictured her in bed, lying against the sheets in tiny shorts and a tank top with no bra. He touched himself sometimes as she talked about her day, thinking about how her nipples would look poking against white cotton. He always felt guilty afterward for defiling her image. Dirty.

Under her thin T-shirt, he could make out the swell of her breasts and he wanted to touch her but he stopped himself. She wanted a secret. She was trying to be serious. He thought about mentioning the boy at the baseball game. He hadn't stopped thinking about the smoothness of the boy's skin but that sounded creepy, even in his own head. She wouldn't understand. He barely understood it himself.

"I got a girl pregnant once," he said. "She didn't keep it."

Aubrey was quiet a minute. "Who is she?" she finally said.

"A girl I used to know," he said. "I loved her, but she didn't want the baby."

"What happened to her? The girl, I mean."

"It was a long time ago," he said. "We haven't really talked since."

She reached for his hand. He felt relieved, even though he still couldn't bring himself to tell her the whole truth.

"Tell me something," he said. "Something you never told anyone."

She stared up at the ceiling. Then she said,

"When I was little, I used to think I had super-powers."

He laughed. "What?"

"Super senses," she said. "Not powers, because they didn't make me feel stronger. But you know how in biology class, they used to talk about how animals adapt? Like how over time, fish at the bottom of the ocean started doing weird things like glowing in the dark so they can lure prey and survive? It was like that."

"What type of superpower?" he said.

"Like I could smell if a man was good or bad. Or I could jump out of my skin when he touched me."

"Who?"

"And I could hear really good," she said. "I could hear him moving throughout the apartment, like a rat clicking through the pipes. I could hear him before he got to my room. And I always wondered why my mom never heard but I told myself she couldn't. Because she didn't have super senses."

She started to cry. His clumsy hands cupped her face and he kissed her wet cheeks, her jaw, her forehead. He buried his face in her neck, wanting to keep her in her skin.

EIGHT

We forgot about Nadia Turner, the way any unseen person is unthought of. She was a pretty, unmothered girl who'd wrecked her daddy's truck, and after, she fell out of our minds. Except for the few moments she popped up, like when someone asked Robert Turner how his daughter was doing and he said fine, just fine, finishing up her sophomore year. Or working an internship in Wisconsin this summer, yeah, some government thing, who knows. Robert continued to lend his truck. The first lady did not hire another assistant. But we didn't see Nadia Turner again. Not Thanksgiving. Not Christmas. Not long patches of summer while we were sweating in our prayer room, cycling through cards filled with requests. In hot months, wanting always reaches its peak.

Only years later, years after we heard the rumor, have we collected the signs. Betty says weren't it peculiar that she'd never wanted to volunteer in the children's church room, not even when she was flitting and following Aubrey Evans around? Agnes, the most attuned to spiritual things, says she passed the girl in the church lobby once and saw a baby trailing behind her. A little boy in knee socks, and when Agnes glanced back, he was gone. Oh I knew, she says, when we bring up Nadia Turner. I knew right away, just as soon as I seen her. I can always tell an unpregnant girl.

After a secret's been told, everyone becomes a prophet.

A WINTER, AND THEN ANOTHER, and then another. Soon, Nadia had been gone so long, she felt guilty about returning home at all. By senior year, she thought of Oceanside as a tiny beach setting trapped inside a snow globe; occasionally, she might take it down from her bookshelf and gaze at it, but she could never fit inside. As graduation neared, she took the LSAT and applied to law school at NYU and Duke and Georgetown, any program that might keep her away from home, finally accepting an offer from the University of Chicago. She had planned to work throughout the summer in Ann Arbor, then move to Chicago in the upcoming fall. But home tugged her back in the form of a breathless phone call from Aubrey: Luke had proposed that night, they were getting married, she wanted Nadia to hear it first.

"What's the matter?" Shadi asked, when she hung up the phone. He perched on the edge of the couch. "I thought she's your friend."

"She is."

"So why aren't you happy?"

"Because her fiancé's a dick."

"Then why's she marrying him?"

"She doesn't know it."

A different man, a more perceptive one, might have asked how Nadia knew. But Shadi just pushed off the couch and went to boil noodles for dinner. He didn't ask certain questions about her life before him because he didn't want to know the answers. She was happy to oblige him, avoiding any mention of the summer before college altogether. She couldn't tell him about Luke and the baby. Shadi was a good, progressive boy but maybe he wouldn't understand why she'd gone to the abortion clinic. Maybe abortion seemed different when it was just an interesting topic to write a paper about or debate over drinks, when you never imagined it might affect you. And since she couldn't tell him about the baby, she couldn't explain why she'd been so devastated when Aubrey visited two years ago and announced that she'd been spending time with Luke. At first, Nadia didn't even hear her. She was so excited to see her, she could hardly believe that Aubrey was actually here, in the passenger's seat of Shadi's Corolla, which he'd graciously lent her so she could pick Aubrey up from Detroit Metro Airport. On the ride back to Ann Arbor, Nadia kept glancing at Aubrey and grinning, already imagining the dive bars she would bring her to, the frat parties that would make Cody Richardson's house seem as quiet and peaceful as a library. She would be introducing her college boyfriend and her college friends to her back-home friend, those two disparate parts of her life blending in a way that felt sophisticated and mature. Then she realized that Aubrey had mentioned Luke.

"What?" she'd said.

"I said, me and Luke have been spending time together."

"What?" Nadia said again.

"I know," Aubrey said. "Don't you think it's weird?"

"Why would it be weird?"

"I don't know. We just never really spent time together before but now . . ."

She'd trailed off cryptically. Spending time, what did that even mean? Fucking? No, Aubrey would've said something if she'd broken her virginity pledge, wouldn't she? So if they weren't having sex, what were they doing together? That had bothered Nadia the most. Luke courted Aubrey. He took her on trips to the zoo, where he'd bought nectar so they could feed the birds. Aubrey sent Nadia pictures of them posing in front of the birdcage, Luke dripping with tropical birds on his arms, or the two of them celebrating their first anniversary at Disneyland, Luke wearing a Goofy baseball cap with dog ear flaps. Nadia couldn't imagine Luke ever wearing a cutesy hat in public, let alone planning a date that took more effort than sending a text message a few hours in advance. He was different now. Or maybe he was different with someone other than her.

She'd never thought their relationship would last. How could it? What could they possibly have in common? What could possibly bind them together? Instead, she'd scrolled incessantly past photographs of the two of them sitting together on the edge of a dock or sharing dinner downtown or posing in the kitchen with Pastor and Mrs. Sheppard on Thanksgiving. Mrs. Sheppard beaming, an arm around Aubrey's waist, as if she had actually selected her perfect daughter-in-law years ago. She must have felt relieved that Luke had finally realized it.

"So are you going?" Shadi asked. "To the wedding?"

"I guess I have to," she said.

"I can always go with you," he said.

She heard the smile in his voice even though his back was to her. He hinted about this often, visiting home with her and meeting her father. Their friends teased them about marriage but she always avoided the topic of a deeper commitment. Besides, his mother liked her but she wanted Shadi to marry a Muslim girl.

"Okay," Nadia said when he'd announced it. "What do you expect me to do about that?"

"Nothing," he said. "I just think it's funny."

"My dad wants me to marry a Christian boy," she said. "It matters to some people."

She felt annoyed by the way Shadi hinted about the future. He'd just received a job offer from Google but, he'd mentioned once, almost slyly, that if she wanted to move back to California after graduation, he could transfer to the Mountain View office. She'd laughed at his underestimation of the expansiveness of California. Didn't he know that Mountain View was an eight-hour drive from San Diego? Still, it scared her, his willingness to pick up his life and follow her. She'd fallen for him when he wanted to become an international reporter, flying on choppers into war-torn countries. His independence liberated her. But now he was going to work in an office and she felt crushed already by his hopes for her. As graduation approached, she found herself picking fights with him more, like when she told him she didn't plan to walk at commencement. Shadi told her she was being selfish.

"Graduation's not about you," he said. "It's about everyone who cares about you. Don't you think your dad wants to see you walk?"

"Don't you think it's none of your fucking business?" she said.

She didn't want to walk if her mother couldn't be there to watch her. Her mother had never gone to college but said she would someday, always someday. When the Palomar College catalogue came in the mail, she would lean against the countertop, scanning the bold titles of courses she would never take. Once, Nadia's father had thrown out the catalogue with the rest of the junk mail and her mother had almost rooted through the trash can for it before her father said he'd already taken it to the dumpster.

"I thought it was trash," he'd said.

"No, Robert, no," her mother said. "No, it's not trash."

She'd seemed desperate, like she'd lost more than a catalogue that arrived in their mailbox every six months. By then, her mother was too busy with work and family to return to school, but she'd always told Nadia that she expected her to go to college. She reminded her of this when she checked over her math homework or chided her for her sloppy handwriting or quizzed her on reading assignments. Nadia knew she was the reason her mother had never gone to college and she'd wondered if, after she left home, her mother might finally go. Now graduation seemed silly. Why should she dress in a cap and gown and sweat in the sun, when her mother was not there to pose in pictures with her and cheer when her name was called? In her mind, she only saw pictures they would never take, arms around each other, her mother gaining little wrinkles around her eyes from smiling so much.

Nadia apologized to Shadi that night. She slipped inside his bed naked and he groaned, rolling toward her, stiff before she even touched him. She tasted the salt off his skin, the ticklish spot on his neck, as he fumbled in the nightstand drawer. She was on the pill but she always made him wear a condom too.

"What're you thinking about?" he asked after.

"I hate when you do that," she said.

"Do what?"

"Ask what I'm thinking. As soon as you ask, my mind just goes blank."

"It's not a test," he said. "I just want to know you."

Later in the night, she shrugged his arm off her. She felt sweaty with him hugging her all night. Sometimes she wondered if she only loved him when it was cold, in the middle of winter when everything was dead.

Aubrey Evans's entire life boiled down to the places she'd slept.

Her girlhood bed with its pink princess headboard, pullout couches in relatives' living rooms when her father left, the backseat of her mother's car when hospitality ran out, the trundle of Mo's daybed when they'd moved into a new apartment, her mother's bed because she hated to sleep alone, her own bed after her mother's boyfriend moved in, her own bed where her mother's boyfriend touched her, the bed in her sister's guest room where she'd escaped, and now Luke's bed, where they had never made love. His non-making-love bed was her favorite. The department store normalcy of his blue plaid bedspread, always a little mussed as if it'd just been sat on. There wasn't much else in his studio apartment: a wicker basket from his mother, now filled with free weights, a crumpled pizza box jutting out of the trash can, Nikes lined up near the door, wooden cane propped against the wall. The first time she'd visited him in his apartment, she'd frozen in his doorway, unsure of what to do. They had never been this alone before—in a place that belonged to no one else, where no one else had a key and might interrupt. Luke had gestured toward his bed.

"Sorry," he'd said. "There's nowhere else to sit."

So they'd sat on his bed and watched a movie. Other things they did in his bed: ate pizza on paper plates, played cards, played Madden with the injury setting turned off, watched the Super Bowl, listened to music from her tinny laptop speakers, held hands, kissed, argued, and prayed. They had slept together, as in beside each other. She'd fallen asleep on pillows smelling faintly of his cologne and he'd curled against her, kissing the back of her neck as she drifted off. But she hadn't felt afraid. All beds told stories, and Luke's told a different one. She pressed her ear against his pillow and heard no rage. Just the rustling of his covers as he scooted close to her and her own thudding heart.

"Are you okay?" he asked. "All that stuff about the party."

"It's fine," she said.

"Tell her to stop if it's too much. My mama's like a runaway train once she gets going."

"She's just trying to help."

"Still," he said. "Once she gets going."

They'd just returned from his parents' house, where his mother had hooked an arm around Aubrey's waist and ushered her around the back-yard, explaining the layout for the bridal shower.

"Now, the waiters will be right there," Mrs. Sheppard had said, pointing toward the center of the yard. "Not too close, though, we don't want them hoverin' over folks while they eat. Lou's Catering wasn't my first choice but you know John wanted to support Deacon Lou's business.

Of course, he had nothing to say the whole time I was planning things but he's got all the opinions right before I book the catering. I hope Lou's boys paid attention. I told them cranberry tablecloths but I just know they'll bring red."

If it was exhausting to worry about tiny details, it was even more exhausting to pretend to. Aubrey felt guilty for not caring about whether the tablecloths were cranberry or red. Mrs. Sheppard was working so hard to plan a beautiful shower for her, she should at least share in her concerns. But she had other worries. Months before her wedding, she had stopped sleeping. Like any big life change, it happened both gradually and all at once. At first, she shaved off minutes, falling asleep later, waking up before her alarm. Then an hour here and there as night fell and she lay under her covers, her laptop toasting her stomach, another episode of television reflecting off her glasses. Then big chunks of time, scoops of it, patches in the middle of the night when she woke to get water and tossed in bed and sat by the window and read her Bible until light cracked through the blinds. By April, she was only sleeping a few hours a night and those few hours made her feel more tired than if she hadn't slept at all. She was unsleeping, and it wasn't the wedding jitters like everyone tried to tell her. She had decided to invite her mother and she hadn't heard back from her yet. She was both worried that she would and would not come.

"Are you fucking kidding me?" Monique had said. The two of them were sitting around the kitchen table, which had been covered for the past few months in wedding books Mrs. Sheppard sent over. The war room, Kasey called it.

"Mo, relax," Aubrey said. "She probably wouldn't come anyway. Mrs. Sheppard said I might regret it if I don't at least invite her—"

"So you want her to come."

"I don't know," she said, although she had already imagined the reunion: her mother stepping off the train, carrying a small green suitcase, as the flaps of the past began to lift. Her hair would be shorter now, whipping around her head in curls tinted with silver. She would wear a coral cardigan buttoned all the way to her neck because the coastal breeze would chill her and she'd glance around the station, shielding her eyes from the sun, until she spotted Aubrey. Then she'd smile, and at breakfast, Aubrey would notice all the little things her mother did, the way she sliced her muffin diagonally, how she folded her arms when she was listening, the way she always chatted with the waiter when he checked on them. She would feel like a little girl again, enraptured by her mother's face.

"Who cares what Mrs. Sheppard thinks?" Mo said. "She's not your mother."

"Neither are you," Aubrey said. She'd felt gratified at first, but later, she felt sick, picturing the way her sister's dark eyes had widened and filled. Her eyes weren't one of the features they shared, inherited from their mother. Aubrey's eyes were her father's, a man neither of them knew. When she was young, Aubrey had cried when she first learned that they were only half sisters. It's okay, her sister had told her, because I love you twice as much.

"Whose wedding is it?" Nadia had said over the phone that night.

"Mine."

"And who gets to be the wedding dictator?"

"Me."

"Thank you. If Mo doesn't want to talk to her, she doesn't have to. But it's your wedding and you should invite whoever the hell you want. Life is short and if you want to see your mom again, you should."

Aubrey dug her fingernails into her palm. She used to do this often when she first moved in with her sister. A bad thought appeared, and she made a fist, squeezing as hard as she could. Her sister would always grab her hands and rub them between hers, like they were just cold. On the edge of her bed, she opened her palm, watching the tiny, clear crescents turn red.

"You there?" Nadia said. Her voice sounded farther away.

"I'm sorry," Aubrey said. She hadn't even realized how insensitive it was to ask Nadia whether she should invite her mother.

"Why're you apologizing? You didn't kill her."

"Still."

"Don't, okay?"

"Don't what?"

"Treat me like some poor sad girl."

"I'm not." Aubrey paused. "I wish I could've known your mom."

"Me too," Nadia said.

Aubrey wondered if they were the only ones who felt they didn't know their mothers. Maybe mothers were inherently vast and unknowable.

"How's Michigan?" she asked.

"Cold as fuck. It's still snowing. Can you believe that?"

"That's what you get for wanting seasons."

"Fuck that. Seasons are overrated."

She liked listening to Nadia's adventures in Michigan, how that first winter, her friends from Chicago had taken her to a Von Maur to find a coat and boots, how they'd laughed at her for being so fascinated with the Midwestern department store where a live pianist played as she slipped her feet into fuzzy boots. She had only fallen on ice once, her sophomore year on the way to a party, and she was proud that she'd caught herself with the hand that wasn't holding the beer. Nadia had lived in other places too. Her summer internship in Madison at the state capitol, her semester abroad at Oxford, where she took weekend trips to Edinburgh and Berlin, how in Paris, she'd gotten caught by the Metro doors slamming shut on her backpack and a crowd of annoyed Parisians had to yank her free. Aubrey loved that story, the idea that the unflinchingly cool Nadia Turner would be so awkward in one of the most sophisticated cities on the planet. Maybe you didn't know who you would be in the world. Maybe you were a different person everywhere you lived.

"Tell me your England story again," she said, "about the boat."

A punt, Nadia had explained when she'd e-mailed her. She and some friends had gone punting on the River Cherwell. She had been the only one brave enough to steer the punt because the other girls were intimidated by stories of the pole getting stuck in the mud along the riverbank and the boat overturning. So Nadia had steered while everyone drank Pimm's and champagne, herself drinking more than she probably should have because it was so hot. She was tipsy and tired from pushing the pole, but she'd steered the punt the entire time, passing under the leafy trees. She did not flip the boat once. It was, Nadia had written, one of the best days of her life.

Over the phone, Nadia let out a low laugh. Aubrey imagined her in her Michigan apartment, sitting by a window, watching the snow fall.

A WEEK BEFORE her best friend's wedding, Nadia came home.

She leaned toward the window as the plane descended through the springtime fog. Spiky tops of palm trees emerged, then the red Spanish rooftops that covered every home. The houses had been the first thing she noticed when she landed in Michigan—white with slate roofs, like the homes she'd only seen in movies, not tan stucco topped with wavy red. In the San Diego Airport bathroom, she fixed her hair while two women spoke Spanish beside her, and even though she could only understand snatches of words, she felt grateful for the familiar foreign sound.

When she stepped outside the terminal, her father waved from the curb. He was hard to miss—the only man nearby in a truck. She didn't wave back but she started toward him, dragging her suitcase and balancing her coffee. She was wearing huge sunglasses, even though the sky was cloudy, and she felt cheated by the overcast sky, as if the city had known the sunshine was one thing she was looking forward to and had denied her of it anyway. As she neared, her father climbed out of his truck to help her with her bag. They smiled at each other, tentatively, as if both were afraid the other might not smile back.

"Well, look who it is," he said.

"Hi Dad."

He reached out to hug her and she hugged him back, an awkward, one-armed hug so she didn't spill her coffee. He looked the same but a little older, his skin more wrinkled, his hair sprinkled with more gray. She wondered who cut his hair now.

"It's funny," he said, pulling onto the 5. "You drink coffee now."

He smiled a little, nodding at her cup. She'd never drunk coffee before college. She'd tried a sip of her mother's once but nearly spit it out. She'd expected it to be sweet, like hot chocolate, but it tasted bitter and gross. Now she couldn't even drink hot chocolate anymore—she'd bought a box of it last winter to lift her spirits but it was so sweet, she threw it out. Airport Starbucks was barely coffee, and she already missed the French press at Shadi's apartment, even though the first time he showed her how to use it, she'd rolled her eyes and said she wanted a cup of coffee, not a science experiment. But she didn't tell her father this. She didn't need him to know how many mornings she woke up at Shadi's.

"Your friend," her father said, "he's flying in later?"

"On Friday," she said. "I hope that's okay."

At the Detroit Metro Airport, Shadi had kissed her good-bye. "I know you hate going home," he'd said, rubbing the back of her neck where her hair met her skin. "You're a good friend." She'd kissed him again because she wasn't a good friend, not even close. A good friend would not have to muster joy for her best friend's wedding, a good friend felt it naturally. She felt anxious about this whole trip and she couldn't decide if Shadi flying in to stay with her and her father made her feel better or worse.

"And your term?" her father said. "It went well?"

"It was fine," she said.

"And you'll get your diploma and everything?"

"They're sending it here."

"Okay. That's good."

"You're not mad about that, right?"

He shrugged. "I would've liked to see you graduate," he said. "But you gotta do what you think is best."

She leaned against the warm windowpane as they passed the Del Mar lagoon. Shadi had called her selfish, but her father wouldn't even admit that he was upset, and somehow, that was even more frustrating.

When they pulled up to the house, she followed her father, who insisted on carrying her suitcase, to the front door. She stepped inside after him and suddenly stopped. The house felt different, smelled different even, as if it were a living organism whose basic chemistry had changed. Could a house change its smell in a few years? Or had she just forgotten what it was like to be home? She glanced around the living room and realized what had actually changed. Her father had taken down the photographs. Not all of the photographs—she inched forward and spotted one of her on the coffee table, her high school graduation picture on the mantel. Just the photographs of her mother. Light rectangles marked the walls where she had been.

"How could he do that?" she asked Shadi later. "She's my mother."

She had never cried in front of him and crying into the phone felt as embarrassing as if he'd been watching. She crouched on the carpet by her bed, dabbing her eyes with her tank top.

"Maybe it hurts him to look at her," Shadi said.

"It's like she was never here. Like he never loved her."

"I think he still loves her. That's why it hurts so much."

"I'm sorry," she said.

"Why? You didn't do anything wrong."

"Still. You didn't call to hear all this shit."

"It's your life," he said, "I want to hear it."

She closed her eyes, trying to remember the photos that had hung on the walls. She had passed these pictures every day, but now she only remembered them vaguely—her parents on their wedding day, her mother in a garden, her family at Knott's Berry Farm. How had she not memorized them? Or maybe she had once but she was beginning to forget. Did the house smell different because her mother's scent was gone? Or had she just forgotten how her mother smelled?

THE SHEPPARDS LIVED in a sleepy, sedate neighborhood, one home in a row of identical houses with wavy roofs and canopies of arching palm trees. On the front porch, a brown welcome mat read **God Bless This Home**—a prayer or an order, anybody's guess. In the front entrance, tan walls were covered in paintings (two women playing lawn croquet, a funeral procession painting they had seen on **The Cosby Show**). A mahogany piano that looked too pristine to be played rested against the staircase, and on top of it were carefully arranged family portraits. Pastor and Mrs. Sheppard smiling in front of a chapel on their wedding day, the proud parents posing with their newborn son, and toward the end of the piano, teenage Luke in a cap and gown, glowering at the camera, too cocky to smile.

The afternoon of the wedding shower, Nadia followed voices into the backyard, where round tables, covered in deep red tablecloths, clustered on the Sheppards' lawn. The catering crew, a passel of black teenagers in starched white shirts and aprons, ushered around the yard, pouring ice water and lemonade into glass goblets. She spotted Aubrey across the lawn, under a leafy tree surrounded by a circle of women. She wore a white dress swirled with gold that flowed to her knees, her curly black hair hanging to her shoulders, and she was laughing, her hand covering her mouth. It was striking, how perfectly she belonged here.

Aubrey beamed when she saw Nadia pick her way across the grass. She skipped over to her, throwing her arms around her neck, and their bodies collided, knees knocking.

"I can't believe you're back!" Aubrey said. "I missed you so much."

"Me too." Nadia laughed, feeling silly for hugging in the middle of the yard but unwilling to let go first.

Aubrey looped an arm through hers and guided her around the party, past women from Upper Room who seemed as shocked to see her again as if she'd floated out to space. Well, look who it is, they said. Others pulled her into hugs and said, more pointedly, well, look who finally decided to come back home. In their eyes, she was a prodigal daughter, worse than that even, because she hadn't returned home penniless and humbled. A prodigal daughter, you could pity. But she'd abandoned her home and returned better off, with stories of her fascinating college courses, her impressive internships, her cosmopolitan boyfriend, and her world travels. ("Paris?" Sister Willis said, when she'd shared the story. "Well, **la-di-da**.") Was she pretentious now? Or had leaving caused an irreparable tear between her and the other women at Upper Room? Or maybe that fissure had always been there and leaving had allowed her to see it. Halfway through the conversation, Mrs. Sheppard wandered over to the circle. She wore a pink skirt suit and heels that sank into the grass as she walked.

"Welcome back, honey," she said, patting Nadia's shoulder.

Nadia wanted to tell Mrs. Sheppard about all that she'd done in the past four years. Her residence on the dean's list, her internships, her trips abroad. She'd gone away and made something of herself and she wanted Mrs. Sheppard to know. But just as quickly as she'd said hello, the first lady was gone, bustling around the yard, chatting with the other guests. She didn't care about anything Nadia had accomplished. Any interest she might have held in her had faded years ago, as soon as Nadia ceased working for her. So Nadia swallowed her stories. She allowed Aubrey to drag her to another group of women, and when the tour ended, she made her way to a table where Monique and Kasey were seated. She hugged both of them, grateful for their familiarity.

"Enjoying the spectacle?" Monique said.

"Don't do that," Kasey said.

"What? Is it not? I mean, waiters? Who is she trying to impress, really?"

But who did Mrs. Sheppard need to impress? No, Mrs. Sheppard had thrown Aubrey this bridal shower out of love. Nadia imagined Mrs. Sheppard and Aubrey poring over wedding catalogues together, Mrs. Sheppard at the dress fitting, watching Aubrey twirl in the mirror, how the first lady might have teared up a little at the vision, how proud she felt that her son had found a good girl—the right girl. How happy she must be, now that she had finally won the daughter she'd always wanted. At lunch, Nadia picked at her food before scraping the remains into the trash can. She felt claustrophobic in the sweeping backyard and went inside to the bathroom upstairs, where she sat on the fuzzy toilet seat cover and texted Shadi. **Miss you, stinky.** He should be getting off work soon, and she wished she were back in Ann Arbor, lounging on his beat love seat or drinking coffee at a sidewalk table on Main Street, watching people pass by. She didn't belong here anymore, not the way Aubrey did.

She had started back downstairs when she spotted Luke's bedroom. From the hallway, it looked different, and as she eased closer, she saw that it had been converted into a guest room. No longer Luke's room, the walls covered in football posters, a twin bed pushed against the window. She remembered sneaking into that room, how she'd always felt strange undressing in his childhood bedroom, tossing her bra atop a desk papered with red and blue footballs, slipping out of her jeans near a shelf that held Pop Warner trophies, kissing him while Jerry Rice, plastered above his bed, watched.

"I don't live here anymore."

Behind her, Luke Sheppard appeared in the doorway. He looked cleaned up, his stubbly cheeks shaven, and he even wore his glasses, a rectangular pair he'd bought from the drugstore. "I only wear them when I need to look smart," he'd told her once, carefully folding them into his breast pocket. She hadn't understood. Didn't he always want to look smart?

"I moved out," he said. "Got a place by the river."

"I don't care," she said, embarrassed that he knew she did. "I have a boyfriend."

"I know. The African guy."

"He's American," she said. "His parents are from Sudan."

He shrugged. She hated how casual he seemed, how freely he commented on her life when they hadn't spoken in years. Anything he knew, he'd learned from Aubrey, and she felt betrayed, imagining the two of them in bed together, chatting about her. He stepped inside the room, leaning on a wooden cane, and she looked away as he hobbled past her, plopping on a bed that squeaked under his weight.

"You wanna know something?" he said.

"What?"

"I used to steal shit from church," he said. "When I was little."

"Liar."

"Dead ass."

"Like what, then?"

"Anything. Just to see if I could."

To prove it, he reached under the bed and pulled out a maroon prayer book with a cracked leather cover. He'd stolen it from Mother Betty's piano bench in the sixth grade. Sister Willis had sentenced him to thirty minutes of prayer in the sanctuary for talking in class, and he'd explored the church instead, lying on his belly to peek under pews, toeing at the fringes in the carpet, stomping around the altar. The piano bench had fascinated him—a seat that stored things? There must be something important and secretive inside, like the fake books where movie villains stored guns. Instead of the weapon arsenal he'd hoped for, there were only loose sheets of music, ballpoint pens, and the prayer book.

"That's my mother's," she stammered.

She hadn't seen the book in years. Her mother used to keep it on her nightstand, but one day, it'd gone missing. She'd searched for it all over the house for weeks.

"I know," Luke said.

"She thought she lost it."

"I'm sorry," he said.

"Why the fuck didn't you give it back?"

"I felt bad."

"So you just kept it?"

"I forgot all about it," he said. "I found it when I was moving. I had to get it to you."

He handed the book to her. She sat next to him, flipping through the silvery, thin pages. Hymn names floated past her eyes and when she leaned closer, the book smelled like dust and leather and, faintly, her mother's perfume. She felt her eyes water, and Luke's hand, warm on her back.

THE WEEKEND BEFORE THE WEDDING, a reply from Aubrey's mother finally arrived, written on the back of the invitation she'd sent: **We can't make it. But congratulations!** She stood in front of the mailbox, reading the message once, twice, then three times, before she slid the card back into the envelope and threw it in the trash can. When she stepped inside, her sister was sitting on the couch, watching the news. Aubrey slipped off her shoes and climbed on the couch beside her, laying her head in Monique's lap.

"She's not coming," she said.

"Okay."

"That's it?"

"What do you want me to say?"

"I don't know." She chewed her lip, watching as a blonde reporter interviewed a firefighter in front of a smoldering house. "Is it so stupid that I wanted her at my wedding?"

"No," her sister said. "Who wants to say they hate their mother?"

She closed her eyes, feeling her sister brush her hair back from her forehead. The summer before her senior year of high school, Aubrey had visited her sister in Oceanside for the first time. At the airport, Mo had met her at the baggage claim, waving wildly as if Aubrey wouldn't recognize her otherwise. She looked the same—petite, her hair cut short the way their mother hated—but she'd beamed as she pulled Aubrey in close and said, "Look at you. You're all grown up now." Behind Mo, a white woman stood with her hands in her pockets. Late twenties, dirty-blonde hair that looked wet, a smile that looked too much like a smirk. She wore a gray tank top and baggy jeans cuffed at the ankles and she stepped forward, jutting out her hand.

"Great to finally meet you," she'd said. "Hope your flight was good."

Aubrey said that it was, thank you, and they'd all stood there awkwardly until Mo said, shouldn't they be going now? She grabbed the rolling suitcase and Kasey lifted the duffel bag off Aubrey's shoulder. She pretended to struggle under the weight.

"Oof," she told Mo. "She **is** your sister."

She seemed like the type who tried to be funny when she felt uncomfortable, and Aubrey vaguely felt like she should laugh, just to relieve everyone. On the drive to their house, they asked her harmless questions about school and her friends, and she offered soft, monosyllabic answers. From the backseat, she could see them exchanging worried glances and at a stoplight, she heard Mo say quietly, "She's just sleepy." Like when they were younger and she'd always speak to their mother on Aubrey's behalf, as if she weren't actually there.

She wasn't, not really. All week, she'd wandered around her sister's house like a ghost. She felt like she'd left her body behind in her bedroom, under Paul's hands, his breath hot against her neck, and she was floating around outside of it, always feeling its pull. Her last day in town, her sister had taken her to the beach, where they'd fallen behind a tour group. A bespectacled old man with a fanny pack strapped around his waist told the small crowd about the glory of the Oceanside pier, the longest wooden pier on the West Coast, which had been rebuilt six different times. A storm destroyed the first pier over two hundred years ago, and during low tide, you could still see the remnant woodpiles under the water. The second and third piers were damaged by storms, and when the fourth pier opened in the 1920s, the town threw a three-day-long celebration. Twenty years later, it was leveled by another rainstorm.

"This pier," he had said, stomping his foot, "this

very pier was dedicated in 1987. A few blinks ago! And in your lifetimes, there'll be another pier and maybe even another. The storms will come and we'll keep on building."

Later, once they'd reached the end of the pier, she'd asked her sister if she could live with her. She'd squeezed Mo's hand and whispered, please don't make me go back. But during that slow walk behind the tour group, she'd stared down at the wood beneath her feet, exhausted just imagining the city continually rebuilding a pier that would eventually fall into the ocean. There was nothing special about the pier aside from its length, no boardwalk or Ferris wheel, just a tackle shop marking the midway point and at the end, a diner. The pier was nothing but a long piece of wood that kept crumbling until it was rebuilt, and years later, she wondered if that was the point, if sometimes the glory was in rebuilding the broken thing, not the result but the process of trying.

The day after her mother's reply had arrived, Aubrey met Nadia at the beach. She lay in the sand, propping herself up by her elbows, while beside her on the blanket, Nadia rolled over onto her back. She wore a tiny black bikini that made every man stare, but she seemed indifferent to the attention, as if she were so accustomed to captivating strangers that it hardly registered. Of course she was used to it, just look at her. Since high school, she had grown leaner, her clothes simpler and her makeup less dramatic in a way that only seemed to highlight how naturally beautiful she was. Aubrey felt so pudgy beside her, she couldn't even bring herself to take off the baggy T-shirt and shorts she'd worn over her swimsuit. Had she always felt like the ugly friend? Or was this new? Was she just feeling insecure because of what she'd accidentally witnessed at her bridal shower? She'd tried to tell herself it was nothing, but she still couldn't get the image of Nadia and Luke talking in bed out of her mind. Not in bed, really, but on his bed, as casual and intimate as if they were old pals. She'd left her guests in the yard to search for him, and when she saw the two of them in his room, she froze in the hallway, as if she were the one interrupting their party. She'd felt terrified every time she'd grown closer to Luke— the first time he held her hand, or kissed her, or invited her to cuddle in his bed. But Nadia looked comfortable. This closeness wasn't new to them. They shared some sort of past together, and the fact that neither had mentioned it hurt the most. An unspeakable past was the worst kind.

"What happened with you and Luke?" she said.

Nadia shifted. Her eyes were hidden behind big sunglasses, her arm draped across her forehead.

"What?" she said.

"I know you guys were involved."

She didn't actually know this, but if she pretended she did, it would give Nadia less room to deny it.

"A long time ago," Nadia said. "It was nothing. We hooked up a few times and— You're not mad, are you?"

"Why would I be mad? It was nothing, right?"

She sounded jealous and ugly but she didn't care. Why had neither of them told her anything? Did they think she was so fragile, she'd crumble at the news?

"Look, I swear it was nothing," Nadia said. "I mean, fuck. I haven't talked to him in years. We just hooked up in high school. Do you know how many guys I hooked up with in high school?"

She laughed a little at herself, then sat up from the blanket, brushing sand off her stomach. Aubrey saw herself reflected in the black sunglasses—her face almost a pout, her hair smushed from where she'd been lying on it. She felt silly for being upset. Of course Luke had been with other girls. She'd known about his reputation before she'd begun dating him. And high school seemed so far away.

She'd had crushes on boys in high school whose names she couldn't even remember now. To Luke, Nadia had probably just been another conquest. Or maybe she'd been memorable to him. How could she not be? She was beautiful and confident and strong. She wouldn't feel scared just sitting in a man's bed. She probably wore the types of nighties and lingerie that Aubrey had received from the more brazen of her bridal shower guests, things she knew she would never put on. She would feel like an idiot, standing in front of Luke in some tiny, strappy thing. She didn't know how to titillate a man. How was she supposed to know what he liked? What if she still felt like jumping out of her skin when he touched her? She clenched her fist again, feeling the sharp relief of her own fingernails.

THE SUN BEGAN to lower in the sky when two Marines wandered over and tried to goad them into joining a game of volleyball. Both men wore dark swim trunks but their identical buzz cuts gave them away as military. Not just their haircuts but their eagerness. The stocky Latino smiling at Nadia looked too friendly, like all of the young Marines who lingered by the movie theater and the bowling alley, hoping to talk to girls. He bounced on his heels in the sand like a hyper child, his face still dotted with acne scars.

"Come on, ladies," the tall black one said. "We need two more players."

He was looking at her, Aubrey realized, a direct gaze, the way most men looked at Nadia. She looked away. She always felt nervous around strange men, even though she'd known the man who'd hurt her. If a man who knew you could hurt you, who knew what a man who didn't might do?

"I'm not really sporty," Nadia said.

"You can be on my team," the young one said. "I'll teach you how to play."

She smiled. "I know how to play. I'm just not good."

"That's okay too," he said, smiling back. "I'll teach you how to play better."

His name was JT, which stood for Jonathan Torres. He told them they could call him whichever they liked. He wasn't exactly handsome but he had an easy smile that seemed to break Nadia down. She toed Aubrey, who was still firmly planted on her blanket.

"Come on, Aubrey," she said. "Let's play."

"That's okay. I'll just watch."

The tall one, who went by Miller, refused, resting his hands on the waist of his gray swim trunks.

"Nope," he said, "can't go on without you."

He reminded her of Mr. Turner, the quiet way he spoke, his constant alertness, but most of all, his smiles, which always looked deliberate. He seemed steady. The volleyball net was only a hundred feet away. She could always leave if she wanted to.

"Oh, what the heck," she said, letting Miller help her up. His rough palm was gritty with sand.

She had made an impulsive decision, the type of thing she never did. Suddenly the night crackled with promise. She could be a different girl tonight, the type who could talk to strange men and not feel scared. She could only be that girl because she was with Nadia Turner. When JT returned with a volleyball, they walked together to the nearest net. He chatted with Nadia the whole time, carrying their blanket under his arm.

"How old are you really?" she said.

He grinned. "I told you. Twenty."

She turned to Miller. "Is he lying?"

"No comment," he said.

JT was eighteen, they found out later. After their match, they squeezed into a booth at Wienerschnitzel, sharing the chili fries and hot dogs the Marines had bought them. Both men had jostled at the cash register, arguing over who was going to pay. They'd only been buddies for six months, Miller told them, but in the Marines, that felt like a lifetime.

"You shoulda seen this kid." Miller pointed his fork at JT, dripping a string of cheese on the table. "Comes out here with nothin'. Don't know nothin'. Can't even wash his own socks."

Miller was twenty-eight, wiser and shrewder. He'd joined the Marines fresh out of high school and had already been to Iraq twice. He'd lost partial hearing in his right ear from a mortar that exploded near his head.

"I can't hear you for shit," he told Aubrey during dinner. "You talk so soft."

She scooted a couple of inches closer. Her thigh pressed against his.

"Better?" she said.

He was just flirting with her, she thought, until his head dropped, his brow furrowed as he concentrated on hearing her. He wasn't the type to play flirty games. JT had spent half the volleyball game joking around and the other half missing the ball flying past because he was too busy watching Nadia in her bikini. Miller had dominated. He seemed like the type who played to win everything, who yelled at the TV screen when he lost in a video game or slammed his paddle on the Ping-Pong table after a bad hit. He'd never yelled at Aubrey when she messed up, though, and after she did the smallest thing right, he trotted up the court to give her a high-five. Had he always been this serious or had his seriousness come from fighting overseas? JT had never been deployed, but he knew his time was coming. He wasn't scared. That was the reason he'd enlisted in the first place, to complete missions.

"And to learn things and travel," he said, through a mouthful of fries. "And to go to California to eat hot dogs with pretty girls."

The beach was dark by the time they returned. The boys tossed the ripped cardboard from their two six-packs onto the fire they'd made, which burned steadily in the pit, crackling over driftwood and crumpled newspaper. Miller had wanted to start the fire without lighter fluid.

"It's cheating," he'd said, kneeling by the stone circle with his cigarette lighter. He tried to coax the burning embers into a flame, stacking the wood in complicated geometric shapes. You had to let air in, he explained, but not too much or the fire would blow out. You had to find a perfect symmetry, because the same air that gave life had the capacity to destroy it. JT grew tired of waiting. He borrowed a can of lighter fluid from a few pits over.

"Just a little bit," Miller said before JT doused the wood. The flames leapt and the girls screamed. JT just laughed.

"Fuck!" he kept saying. "You see how high that went?"

Miller eased off the ground, brushing sand from his knees. He looked disappointed.

"It's okay," Aubrey said. "You almost had it."

He smiled at her but with all lips, no teeth. She'd put her engagement ring back on after she'd taken it off to play volleyball and Miller had noticed it. She sat next to Nadia on a big log, both wrapped in their blanket. The night air was chilly and they scooted close together, sharing a bottle of Heineken. She rested her head against Nadia's shoulder, suddenly nostalgic for the summer they'd spent together, the car rides and movies, the hours swinging in Mr. Turner's hammock. She was getting married and Nadia was returning to the Midwest. Would they ever spend time like that together again? Could you be nostalgic for a friendship that wasn't over yet or did the fact that you were nostalgic mean that it already was?

Across the fire pit, JT plopped onto the sand. "Sure wish someone would cuddle with me," he said.

"Don't look at me," Miller said.

They shoved each other and the girls laughed. Later, the Marines would return to the barracks or maybe patrol the movie theater, looking for new girls. But for now, it was enough to pretend that they were all friends, that they would all see each other again. Miller gave Aubrey a pained smile.

"Enjoying the end of your freedom?" he said, nodding at her ring.

She didn't say anything, but she felt like she hadn't entered into her freedom yet.

"The end," JT scoffed. "Hell, I'm just waiting for something to happen."

He was quiet for a moment. The fire was dying, and Miller tossed another handful of cardboard scraps to feed the flames. Then JT grinned, hopping to his feet.

"I'm tired of just sittin' here," he said. "Let's go for a swim."

JT peeled off his shirt, tossing it into the sand, and shucked his flip-flops into his hands. He took off for the pier, yelping as he sprinted toward the water.

"Come on," Aubrey said.

"Are you crazy?" Nadia said. "That water's freezing."

"I don't care."

She pulled Nadia off the log, their blanket falling into the sand. She dragged her past the fire, then they were running, half laughing, half screaming through the damp sand to the pier. Once she'd leapt off, crashing into the cold water, she thought about how her sister would kill her if she knew. She would lecture her about quadriplegics who'd landed in shallow water and shattered their vertebrae. But she'd jumped and nothing bad had happened. Another cold wave hit her, soaking the shorts she hadn't bothered to take off. JT floated around them in circles. Nadia laughed, her hair turning curly, and Aubrey threw her head back, floating under the moonlight. On the shore, Miller stood alone, leaning against the concrete restroom, his shirt in his hand. She stumbled out of the water.

"Why're you standing out here by yourself?" she said.

"Because you're all crazy," he said. "I'm not jumping off that thing."

"Why? You scared?"

"Of dying?" he said. "Yes."

He had fought in a war. He had killed people,

or if not, he had been trained how to. He had lived with death, so he knew there was nothing brave in not fearing it. The only people who didn't were those stupid enough to not know the reality of it.

"I'm not scared," she said.

"Of what?" he said.

"Of you."

They were both still for a minute, then Miller reached an arm around her waist. She didn't move. He kissed her, soft at first, then harder, and when his lips trailed down her neck, she froze and burned at the same time. Before she knew what she was doing, she pulled him in the darkened bathroom, onto the grimy floor still covered in damp sand. She could barely see him in front of her, she could only feel him, his large hands squeezing her. He could kill her. He could bash her head against the floor. He could strangle her with those large hands and crush her throat. But she didn't feel paralyzed by the danger, only excited. She climbed on top of him, and he moaned into her mouth.

"I don't have anything," he whispered.

A condom, he meant. She pulled away. Outside, the moon shone brightly over the waves, and through the bathroom door, she could see Nadia and JT bobbing in the water, still laughing and

247

splashing each other. She climbed off of Miller and waded out to join them, soaked again, unable to tell what was the ocean and what was herself.

"I THINK HE LIKED YOU," Nadia said. "The old one."

They were parked, watching the sun rise over the San Luis Rey River, or what was left of it. In the summertime, the river dried up, cracked earth snaking through the trees. Aubrey leaned against the truck window, the glass warming her face. She swore she could still smell Miller on her. She wanted to tell Nadia about what had happened in the bathroom, how she had taken charge, how she hadn't felt afraid, but she didn't, for the same reason she'd refused Miller's number at the end of the night. She knew she would never see him again and she wanted to keep the memory to herself. She didn't feel unburdened by sharing hard truths. Hard truths never lightened.

"Why didn't you tell me?" she said.

"Tell you what?"

"About you and Luke. You were never gonna tell me."

"Why would I? We hooked up in high school. It's not a big deal!"

"It is to me!"

She had never yelled at Nadia before and for a second, she felt proud watching her flinch. Then Nadia pulled her into a hug.

"I'm sorry," she whispered. "I'm sorry, okay? I won't keep secrets from you."

She kissed her forehead, and Aubrey felt too exhausted to fight her. She sank into Nadia's side, amazed that after everything, she could still feel something as gentle as Nadia's fingers in her hair.

NINE

The wedding was all any of us could talk about once the invitations had arrived. Shiny gold squares of paper with cursive so fancy you had to squint just to read it, tucked inside a white envelope with gold trim, closed with a seal that bore the first lady's initials, a slanting **L** propped against a curvy **S**. The bright invitations bounced light and when we held ours close at coffee hour, the card made our faces glow. We'd all heard secret details about the wedding; Deacon Ray's wife, Judy, told Flora the cake was from Heaven Sent Desserts, three levels high and rich enough to lose a tooth. Third John told Agnes there would be over a thousand guests at the wedding. At bingo, Cordelia, the church organist, whispered to Betty that the reception would be in the pastor's own house, servants ushering glass flutes on silver trays to and fro.

You can't blame us. At our age, we'd seen plenty of weddings, far too many of them, really. Weddings so boring we nearly slipped to sleep before the minister even spoke, weddings between people who had no business even thinking about marrying, who couldn't bring themselves to share a sandwich, let alone a life. But this wedding, it got us feeling hopeful again. We were generally unimpressed with the stock of young people in our congregation. The boys were sullen and slow, slouching in the pews, tight-mouthed when you tried to speak to them. When we were girls, we knew boys who were Spirit-filled, Bible-quoting believers. (We also knew pool-shooting, cigarette-smoking gamblers, but at least they had enough sense to wear a belt.) Now the girls were even worse. Our mamas would've whooped our legs if we'd dared to come to church like these girls, bubblegum-popping and hair-twirling and hip-switching. Anyone knows a church is only as good as its women, and when we all passed on to glory, who would hold this church up? Serve on the auxiliaries board? Organize the Women of Worth conferences? Hand out food baskets during Christmas? We looked into the future and saw the long banquet tables growing dusty in the basement, the women's Bible studies emptied, assuming these girls didn't turn the meeting room into a disco hall.

But Aubrey Evans was different. When we'd seen her crying at the altar all those years ago, she'd reminded us of ourselves. Back when we were just girls piling into camp meetings wearing starched calico dresses and white gloves; girls who sang solos and baked sweet potato pies for the church picnic; girls who kneeled in segregated churches, forced to sit off to the side so the white preacher didn't have to look at us. In her, we saw us, or us as we used to be. Girls who had felt that first spark of a slow love. A pastor's hand on our forehead and we had fallen, hands back and arms wide and crying out, for the first time, a man's name. Jesus! And when we'd cried out a man's name for the second time, it felt like a shadow of that first moment. So even though we hadn't known where she'd come from, we'd understood why Aubrey Evans couldn't stop crying when the pastor asked what gift she'd come forward to receive and she whispered, salvation.

THE NIGHT SHADI ARRIVED, Nadia's father took them out to eat at a restaurant at the harbor called Dominic's. She'd spent all morning searching through her mother's prayer book. She turned each page slowly, pausing when she spotted her mother's loopy handwriting scribbled in the margins. Most times, her mother's blue pen had underlined a word or phrase in the prayer, random, abstract words like **peace** or **refuge**. Occasionally, her mother had written notes but those were impossible to understand—under one psalm, she'd jotted down what looked like a grocery list. Nadia wasn't exactly sure what she was looking for—a clue, maybe, but a clue that indicated what? Why her mother had wanted to die? What did she expect to find in the prayer book? A suicide note?

"It makes sense," Shadi had said, on the ride home from the airport. "Don't most people leave notes?"

Part of her had always felt relieved that her mother had never left one. In Nadia's mind, her mother's suicide had always been impulsive and urgent, a need to die that had blinded her until she could see nothing else. If she'd had time to sit down and write a note, then she would have had enough time to realize that she shouldn't shoot herself. A note would seem selfish, a desire to justify what she'd already known was a hurtful choice. Still, Nadia had searched the prayer book, hoping to find anything that would help her understand her mother.

At dinner, her father ordered shrimp scampi and bought a bottle of merlot for the table. She didn't tell him that he'd paired his wine wrong. Her father didn't drink wine and he went out to nice restaurants like Dominic's even less. He wanted to impress Shadi, and their chumminess only annoyed her. When she'd brought Shadi home, her father had given him a slow tour around the house, the two men standing almost identically, hands in their jeans pockets. They talked easily about things she didn't care about—golf, Michigan football—and she stood by awkwardly, listening, as if she were the guest meeting the parent for the first time. Worse, at one point during his tour, her father had gestured to the blank walls.

"Sorry," he told Shadi. "As you can see, we need to do some redecorating around here."

Both men had laughed. She'd excused herself from the room. But the more she thought about it, the more incensed she grew, until she was silent and surly at dinner.

"You had no right to do that, you know," she finally said.

Shadi glanced at her. Her father paused, pasta flopping over the prongs of his fork.

"What?" he said.

"Take her pictures down."

Her father's jaw clenched. He set his fork on the edge of his plate.

"Nadia," he said, "it's been four years—"

"I don't care. She's my mother! How do you think that makes me feel? To walk in and she's just gone?"

"She **is** gone," her father said. "And you've been gone too but now you want to tell me how to live in my own house? You think everyone's life just stands still while you're away?"

He slowly wiped his mouth with a napkin, then pushed away from the table. She watched him disappear around the corner to the bathroom, hating herself for not keeping her mouth shut. She held her head in her hands and felt Shadi massaging her neck. Later that night, he tiptoed into her bedroom, slipping under the covers. She felt crowded with him squeezed onto her twin bed, but she was too miserable to refuse his company.

"I'm such a bitch," she said.

"You're not," he said. "It's okay to be angry."

She felt suddenly annoyed by his patience. He was endlessly reasonable in a way she could never be. Just once, she wished he would get upset at her. Just once, she wished he would see her for who she truly was.

"I fucked the groom," she said.

He was silent so long, she wondered if he'd fallen asleep.

"When?" he finally said.

"Four years ago."

"Well," he said evenly, "then that was four years ago."

"He's marrying my best friend," she said. "You wouldn't give a shit if your best friend had fucked me?"

"Not if you were seventeen then. When you're seventeen, you fuck everybody."

He tightened his grip around her waist. Once he'd fallen asleep, she slipped out from under his heavy arm. She sat by the window, falling asleep in the moonlight, cradling the stolen prayer book.

NADIA CRIED THREE TIMES at the wedding.

Once, when Aubrey walked down the aisle,

smiling and clasping a bouquet of lilies, her white train trailing past like a gulf Nadia would never be able to cross. She'd dabbed her eyes a second time during Luke's vows. He'd written them himself and his hands shook as he read them aloud. She'd watched his trembling hands, wanting to calm them with her own. Her eyes watered a third time at the reception during the first dance, while Luke and Aubrey swayed to a Brian McKnight song. He was probably singing in her ear, his voice scratchy and out of tune. At the table beside her, her father watched the two spin, Luke's dancing a little jerky because of his leg. Was her father thinking about her mother, their own wedding day? She'd heard the story, how they'd married with only two hundred dollars between them. Her mother's friend had sewn the dress, another baked the cake, and they'd served fried chicken and sandwiches for their guests. A cheap wedding for sure, her mother had said, laughing, but people told them for years it had been the most fun wedding they'd attended. She'd never imagined her parents as fun people, but maybe they had been then. Or was her father thinking about her own wedding someday? She glanced at Shadi, who smiled and squeezed her hand. She dabbed her eyes again, aware of a new way she would disappoint her father.

There was no alcohol at the reception. She hadn't expected the Sheppards to fund an open bar but she'd hoped for at least champagne. After an hour, she excused herself to the bathroom and stepped outside the reception hall for a breath of air. She slipped out the back door, surprised to see Luke outside, leaning against a planter, the silver tie around his neck already loosened.

"What're you doing out here?" she said.

"I needed a break," he said.

"From your own wedding?"

He shrugged. She hated when he did that, shrugged instead of actually responding. At least Shadi wanted to talk about things.

"Want a drink?" Luke said. He pulled a flask out of his pocket.

She laughed. "Here? Are you crazy?"

He grinned, shrugging again as he unscrewed the flask and tipped it to her. She felt like they were kids, sneaking out to meet up in the park while their parents were sleeping. She took a small sip and then another, the whiskey burning her throat.

"I met your dude," Luke said. "He's nice."

"I like nice boys now," she said.

He smirked. "He don't seem like your type."

"I don't have a type."

"Bullshit. Everyone does."

"And Aubrey's your type?"

It came out meaner than she'd meant. She just didn't understand the attraction, and maybe she never would understand all the things that had changed since she'd been gone. He took the flask from her, tilting it back.

"No," he said. "But that's why I love her."

She had hoped for a release. She would go to this wedding and when she watched the two of them kiss at the altar, the part of her that was still hooked into Luke would finally give. A click, then the latch would open and she would finally be free. Instead, she felt him burrowing deeper into her. She felt the dull burn of an old hunger, all the times she had wanted him, the times she had hoped he might hold her hand in public, the nights she had dreamed about when he might finally tell her he loved her. He'd made her feel like love was something she had to claw her way into, but look at how easily he loved Aubrey. Well, of course he did. Aubrey was easy to love.

He passed the flask back to her. Behind the reception hall, near pipes and silver towers, away from the romance and lights, the crowds of well-wishers snapping photographs and dancing to oldies, they drank together, growing tipsy and warm, passing the flask until it lightened and emptied. Luke tucked the flask back into his pocket, and silently, as if following some unspoken cue, they both headed back into the hall. In the lobby, Mrs. Sheppard was standing in the doorway, her hands on her hips. She wore a pink skirt suit with a floral brooch that made her look like she'd been plucked off a rosebush, thorns and all.

"There you are!" she said. "Everyone's looking for you."

"Sorry," he said. "I just needed a minute."

"Well, come on. You can't just go running off."

She grabbed his arm, tugging him back into the hall. Nadia began to follow but Mrs. Sheppard blocked the doorway.

"This," she said in a low voice, "needs to stop."

Nadia felt twelve again, caught kissing and shamed behind the church building, and in her surprise, she said what she wished she would have said then.

"I didn't do anything wrong," she said.

"Girl, who you think you're fooling? You know how many girls like you I've seen? Always hungry for what's not yours. Well, I'm telling you now this needs to stop. You already caused enough trouble."

"What's that supposed to mean?"

"You know what I mean," Mrs. Sheppard said. "Who you think gave you that money? You think Luke just had six hundred dollars laying around? I helped you do that vile thing and now you need to leave my son alone."

Mrs. Sheppard shook her head a little, daring Nadia to say something, and when she didn't, the first lady straightened her brooch and returned inside the reception hall. Nadia stood alone in the lobby so long that Shadi came looking for her, and she nodded when he asked if she was okay. But later she would wonder how she hadn't questioned where Luke had found the money so quickly. She'd been so desperate, she'd imagined him capable of anything. Now she knew that he was.

IN THE MORNING, the newlyweds would be on a plane to France, two days in Nice, two in Paris. Luke's parents had paid for their honeymoon as a wedding gift with help from the congregation. One of their biggest collections ever, his father had told him, and Luke felt honored by the well-

wishers, the members who could not even pro-
nounce Nice and still donated to send them there.
He would've been happy with a more local honeymoon. A Mexican cruise, a trip to Hawaii—he
imagined spotting Cherry at the Aloha Café and
ordering the Strawberry Sunrise—but Aubrey
had her heart set on France. And even though he
knew she only wanted to go there because Nadia
Turner had been, he'd agreed.

But that was tomorrow. Tonight, in their hotel
room, he eased up behind her, tugging the zipper
on her dress, amazed, as always, by how delicately
women's clothes were made, the tiny hooks, the
slender buttons. The first time he unhooked a
girl's bra, he'd fumbled around the clasps and he
felt a similar nervousness now, giddiness even. He
was scared he'd be disappointed and even more,
he worried that he'd somehow disappoint her. But
maybe it was the soft hotel lighting or the champagne room service had brought or the romance
of the wedding, the silk flowers, the music, the
decorations his mother had obsessed over. He'd
always separated sex and love but now the two
were intertwining and he felt as blustery as he had
when he was fourteen. He slowly pulled down
Aubrey's zipper until he saw skin and more skin.
But she reached back and stopped his hand.

"I know about you and Nadia," she said. "I know you slept with her."

He couldn't see her face. She was still bent away, one hand holding her hair out of the zipper's track. He froze, unsure whether to deny it or apologize.

"It's okay," she said. "I just want you to know that I know."

How did she know? What had Nadia told her? Or maybe Aubrey had sensed it on her own, like spotting paint clinging to their fingertips that neither had been careful enough to wash off. Only hours into their marriage and he'd already hurt her. But he would be smarter now. He ran his hands along the smooth cups of Aubrey's shoulders and kissed the back of her neck. She was better than him but that would make him better. He would be good to her.

ON THE FLIGHT back to Detroit, Nadia dreamed about Baby. Baby, no longer a baby, now a toddler, reaching and grabbing. Pulling at her earrings until she unhooks his chubby fingers. Baby hungry always for her face. Baby growing into a child, learning words, rhyming -at words from a car seat on the way to school, writing his name in green crayon in the front of all his picture books. Baby running with friends at the park, pushing girls he likes on the swing. Baby digging for Indian clay in the sandbox and coming home smelling like pressed grass. Baby flying planes in the backyard with Grandpa. Baby searching for hidden photos of Grandma. Baby learning how to fight. Baby learning how to kiss. Baby, now a man, stepping on an airplane and slinging his bag into the overhead bin. He helps an older woman with hers. When he lands, wherever he's headed, he gets his shoes shined and stares into the black mirror, sees his face, sees his father's, sees hers.

TEN

Scripps Mercy Hospital called at midnight, and Nadia knew before answering the phone that her father was dead.

She had been half dreaming and she might have slept through the shrill ringing altogether if Zach hadn't jabbed her in the back. As soon as she'd cracked open an eye and seen her phone screen light up with an unknown number, she knew that something terrible had happened to her father. A car wreck. A heart attack. He'd left the earth while she was sleeping, slipped away as silently as her mother had. But when she'd answered, a nurse told her that her father had dropped a bar-bell on his chest while lifting weights in the backyard. A crushed diaphragm, two broken ribs, and a punctured lung. He was in critical but stable condition.

She hung up. Beside her, Zach groaned into his pillow. She'd met him in Civil Procedure I when they were both 1Ls. He was the golden boy from Maine, skin tanned from summers spent boating, blond hair ruffled like a Kennedy. His father, grandfather, and great-grandfather had all been attorneys. She was the first-generation student who checked out textbooks from the library because she couldn't afford to buy them, whose stress about her mounting student loans only offset her fear of flunking. When he'd first asked her out at a party after their first-semester finals, she told him she doubted they had anything in common.

"Why?" he said. "Because I'm white?"

He liked to refer to his whiteness the way all white liberals did: only acknowledging it when he felt oppressed by it, otherwise pretending it didn't exist. She had been wrong after all—they did have a few things in common. They both wanted to practice civil rights law. They both knew what it was like to grow up in towns hugged by the ocean. And they both liked to text each other at the end of long nights studying, inevitably ending up together in bed. She didn't expect much from him, which was liberating. He was a good time and she needed one. Breaking up with Shadi had drained her and law school had turned her into a stressed-out wreck. She drank so many pots of coffee while she studied that the smell of coffee made her feel anxious. Zach's good humor, his easy looks, his expectation that life open itself to him were a comfort. She'd never asked him for emotional support before, but later, she felt grateful that she hadn't been alone when she received the phone call about her father. Zach drove to her apartment and helped her pack a bag. She was moving numbly, grabbing handfuls of clothes out of drawers and stuffing them in a suitcase.

"You know I haven't visited my dad in three years?" she said.

She hadn't flown home since Aubrey and Luke's wedding, since Mrs. Sheppard had cornered her in the lobby of the reception hall. In the years that followed, she'd reexamined everything about that summer before college: the pastor's tentative visit, when he'd seemed unusually invested in her well-being, as if surveying damage he'd caused; Mrs. Sheppard's coldness at work, how surprisingly kind she'd seemed right before Nadia left. Had she thought that Nadia might tell? Was that the real reason she gave Luke the money for the abortion? Not to help a girl in need but to make her go away? Nadia imagined the pastor's wife in line at the bank sliding her withdrawal slip to the teller, how quickly she must have stuffed the cash in an envelope, paranoid that she might encounter a congregation member who would see the stack of money and somehow know what it would purchase. For years, Mrs. Sheppard had known her secret. For years, Nadia had thought she was hiding, when hiding had been impossible all along.

Her secret had unraveled, and Luke had never planned to tell her that his parents knew. He could've warned her when he'd brought her the money. She would've been upset with him for telling them, of course, but she had been too desperate to complain about where the money had come from. Now she only felt angry. She imagined her father settling in his pew each Sunday, sedate and unaware as the Sheppards eyed him. Poor Robert, too busy carting loads in his truck to know what had happened in his own household, blind to everything but his grief. And when was the last time she'd even spoken to her father? Really talked to him, not just called on Christmas or left a voice mail for his birthday. He didn't like talking on the phone much and she'd been so wrapped up in her own life. She sat on the edge of her bed, suddenly exhausted. She hated hospitals and didn't want to see her father in one.

Zach peeked out of her bathroom, where he was packing her toothbrush inside a ziplock bag. He looked strange in her apartment. She always slept over at his place.

"We should hurry if you wanna catch your flight," he said.

"Three years," she said. "Jesus, what did I think was gonna happen?"

"Look, I'm sorry about all this but we gotta get to the airport. And I have work in the morning."

He fidgeted a little, her toothbrush still in his hand. Of course he wanted to leave. He was helping her pack in the middle of the night, which was already more kindness than she could expect from a man who wasn't her boyfriend. Or even, really, her friend. She nodded, zipping her suitcase shut. Not until she glanced out the airplane window at the neon lights outlining O'Hare Airport did she realize that she had no idea when she would be back.

HER FATHER CRIED when she stepped inside his hospital room. Because of the pain or because he was glad to see her, or maybe even because he was ashamed for her to see him like this, in the hospital bed, his side bandaged, a tube sprouting out of his chest. She paused in the doorway, rocked by the sight of him. She hadn't seen him cry since her mother's funeral but that was different. Hunched over a church pew in his black suit, he had seemed dignified. Stately, even. But in a mint green hospital gown, plugged into beeping machines, he just looked fragile.

"I'm sorry," he said. "Got you flying all the way out here—"

"Daddy, it's fine," she said. "It's fine. I wanted to see you."

She hadn't called him Daddy in years. She'd tried it out when he first came home from overseas, rolling the word around in her mouth, wondering how he might react to it. She'd been so desperate for him then, following him around the kitchen, climbing on his lap while he watched television, patting his face as soon as he'd shaved to feel his smooth cheeks. But then he'd settled back home and she'd grown up and found Dad fit him better—a curt word, a little removed. The nurse rolled in a cot but she stayed in her chair, holding his hand while he slept. His palm felt rough and worn. She couldn't remember the last time she'd done something as simple as hold her father's hand and she was afraid to let go.

She fell into a fitful sleep, and when she awoke in the morning, she found Aubrey sleeping on the cot, covered in a thin hospital blanket. She suddenly remembered calling Aubrey from the airport—she was frantic and needed someone to talk to before the four-hour flight. Aubrey hadn't answered. Even in California, it was late. But Nadia had left a long, rambling voice mail. She'd felt comforted hearing Aubrey's voice, even if it was just her outgoing message.

She knelt by the cot and stroked Aubrey's hair.

"What're you doing here?" she whispered.

Aubrey's eyes fluttered open. She always woke slowly, returning to the world in waves. How many mornings had her face been the first thing Nadia saw?

"I got your message," Aubrey said. "Of course I'm here."

They hadn't seen each other since the wedding. Every time they talked on the phone, Nadia tried to convince Aubrey to visit her in Chicago. It would be easier seeing her that way. She couldn't imagine spending the night in Aubrey and Luke's guest room, surrounded by all the pictures from their new life. But Aubrey always gave an excuse for why she couldn't make the trip: she was too busy, she had just started at KinderCare and couldn't ask for time off yet, she had promised Mrs. Sheppard she would help her with the Women Who Care conference, the children's church play, the annual picnic. Maybe she was too busy or maybe she didn't want to leave Luke behind. Maybe she had become that type of wife, the ones who couldn't go anywhere apart from their husband, who kept calling him to check in and spent the whole time feeling guilty and displaced, like an organ that had managed to exist outside of the body. Who wanted to be that type of wife? Afraid to leave her married home, like if she left her life for a few days, it might not remain once she returned. Or maybe it wasn't fear, but something else. A deep satisfaction. Maybe she just didn't want to be apart from Luke. Maybe he just made her that happy.

"I'm sorry," Nadia said. "I didn't mean—"

"Shh." Aubrey pulled her into a hug. "How is he?"

"Stable. That's what they're saying. I don't know, the doctor hasn't been by yet. How long have you been here?"

"Don't worry about me. Do you want coffee? Let me get you coffee."

Aubrey returned ten minutes later holding cups from a café that Nadia didn't recognize. She accepted it anyway, even though the smell, wafting through the lid, reminded her of libraries and textbooks and exams. She was already anxious, a cup of coffee couldn't make her feel worse. She and Aubrey sat in the waiting room, while the doctor examined her father's chest for any sign of infection. Her father couldn't sit up by himself yet. He was still struggling to breathe.

"They said—" Nadia paused. "If he hadn't been in such good shape, he probably wouldn't have made it."

"Don't think about that," Aubrey said. "He made it. That's all that matters."

But Nadia couldn't stop imagining her father pinned under his barbell in the backyard, trapped and alone. If one of the neighbors hadn't been grilling in his yard, if he hadn't heard a scream, her father might have died there. And she, so concerned with studying for the bar exam and having noncommittal sex with white boys, might not have called home for weeks. She wouldn't even have known that her father was gone. Would anyone have? She rested her head on Aubrey's shoulder. She smelled like Luke, like she had unwrapped herself from his arms and driven straight to the hospital, and Nadia closed her eyes, breathing in his familiar scent.

AFTER A WEEK, her father was finally released from the hospital. Nadia was relieved to go home after a week of living out of her haphazardly packed suitcase, a week of barely sleeping on the hard cot, a week of sipping watery coffee while her father underwent chest scans and breathing tests. A week in which an endless parade of Upper Room members filtered in and out of her father's room: Sister Marjorie, carrying a slice of her homemade pound cake; First John, bringing a Miles Davis biography that he'd just finished; the Mothers, fussing and fawning with the socks they'd knitted because hospitals just got so cold and you could never have too many pairs of thick socks; even the pastor, who'd come by one morning to pray, laying a palm on her father's forehead. Everyone seemed a bit surprised to see Nadia there, like Third John, who'd jolted when he saw her in the doorway.

"Look who's here," he said, with a grin, as if he had fully expected her not to be.

Of course she was there. Of course she had flown home to visit her father in the hospital.

How could anyone think that she wouldn't? Was that why the congregation had flocked to see him? Everyone had been so convinced that she wouldn't visit her sick father, that she would leave him there all alone, so they'd all made sure to visit him themselves. She could imagine them already, whispering about her after Sunday service. How they would pity her father with his dead wife and his daughter too busy to visit home. How they would feel noble, honorable even, for standing in the gap and serving as the family he ought to have.

On the cab ride home, her father turned toward the window, like he was grateful to see sunshine again. He still couldn't walk on his own, so she helped him into the house, grabbing him the way the nurse had taught her. She realized, lowering him into bed, that she hadn't been in her father's room since it had become his room only. He still slept on the left side of bed like he used to, the other half untouched as if her mother had just rolled out of bed to get a glass of water.

"Go rest," he said. "I'll be fine."

She hesitated before finally slipping out his door. What good could she do him half asleep? She showered and crawled into her bed, drifting off to sleep, when she heard the doorbell ring. When

277

she opened the door, she found Luke Sheppard on her steps. He held a red Tupperware container under one arm, his other arm leaning against his wooden cane.

"I'm with the sick and shut-in ministry," he said. "Can I come in?"

Marriage hung on Luke's body. He looked older and fuller now, not fat, just satisfied. He filled out a baby blue sweater that Aubrey had obviously bought him—the soft color he never would have chosen, the careful stitching he wouldn't have noticed—with the satisfaction of a man who no longer had big decisions to make, who relied on a woman to buy his sweaters. He slowly wandered into her kitchen, leaning on his cane, and asked where he should put the food.

"I don't need your food," she said.

"It's not from me," he said. "It's from Upper Room."

He'd stopped shaving too. She imagined him abandoning his razor in front of the bathroom sink—he was satisfied, why groom?—and Aubrey teasing him when she passed to brush her teeth. Maybe she loved his beard, the way his hair tickled her when they kissed. Maybe he only did things that she loved.

"You told your parents," she said.

"What?"

He looked confused, then his face washed over and his shoulders slumped. He stared at her tiled floor.

"I needed the money," he said.

"Then make up a reason!"

"They would've said no." He stepped toward her. "It had to be a really good reason."

"So that's the best reason," she said. "That I was having your baby."

"It's not like that—"

"I bet your mother skipped all the way to the bank—"

"You needed the money," he said. "I'm sorry I didn't tell you, I just thought—it seemed easier that way. You would've worried."

"Just go," she said.

He let himself out, not meeting her eyes. He wouldn't care that he'd hurt her. He had a good life now and she'd done nothing but drag him back into the past. During long lulls in the afternoon, she thought about him, how peaceful he seemed. This had always frightened her about marriage: how satisfied married people seemed, how unable they were to ask for more. She couldn't imagine feeling satisfied. She was always searching for the next challenge, the next job, the next city. In law school, she'd become prickly and analytical, gaining a sharpness while Luke had rounded and filled. She felt hungry all the time—always wanting, needing more—but Luke had pushed away from the table already, patting his full stomach.

I MADE AN appointment with the doctor, Aubrey typed. She waited a moment, then a reply arrived from rmiller86:

Baby?

For a second, she thought he'd forgotten their rules. No sweet-talking, no flirting, just plain, friendly conversation. Miller had first e-mailed her a year ago. **Don't know if you remember me,** his e-mail began, but as soon as his name appeared in her in-box, she returned to their sweaty kiss on the dirty bathroom floor and felt her whole body burning. Of course she remembered him. Did he think she rolled around with so many strangers in beach bathrooms that she might forget him in particular? She'd called Nadia, angry that she had given him her e-mail address.

"Jesus, Aubrey," Nadia said, "that was, like, years ago. I just thought it'd be funny. How was I supposed to know he'd actually write you?"

Aubrey wouldn't have written him back if he

hadn't mentioned that he was currently stationed in Iraq. He couldn't tell her where—security reasons—but she imagined him somewhere hot and horrible, covered in dust and dodging bombs. A soldier all alone in the desert—it wouldn't hurt to write him back. Writing him was the good thing to do. The patriotic thing. Besides, he was halfway around the world. There would be no bathroom floor. Just nice, friendly conversation.

His first name was Russell. She imagined his family and friends calling him Russ, maybe even Russy when he was small. She began sending care packages addressed to Lt. Russell Miller, boxes filled with the things he asked for—soap, jelly beans, car magazines—and things he hadn't asked for—homemade cookies or novels or even a photograph, like the one from last Mother's Day, when she'd skipped church and gone for a ride with Mo and Kasey up Pacific Coast Highway. In the photo, she was nestled in the crook of her sister's arm and her pink tank top strap had slipped partway down her shoulder. She'd sent the photo to Russell because she looked more natural in it than in any other picture she'd ever taken. The picture was innocent enough—her sister was in it, for god's sakes—but she sometimes wondered if he'd noticed the tank top strap, if he'd imagined himself beside her, slipping a finger underneath it. If he did, he never said. He thanked her for the picture. **I feel like I know your sister,** he wrote. **Like she's my mother too.**

He was lonely. She was lonely too, in her own way. Luke had just been promoted to floor head at the rehab center, so he worked longer hours. He'd also started spending his evenings at Upper Room, helping his father. Between church and work, he couldn't even find the time to go with her to the doctor about her trouble getting pregnant.

"I can't," he said, popping a green bean into his mouth. "Carlos got me training a couple of new guys." He ate like that often now, leaning against the counter. If you went through the trouble cooking a man a meal, the least he could do was sit to eat it.

"Can't you move something around?" she said.

"Like what?"

"I don't know. It'd make me feel better if you came with me."

"It'd make me feel better if everyone stopped obsessing about babies," he said. "We're young. We got time."

They had been trying to get pregnant for a year. She hated that word, **trying**. Why did it take such effort, such drudgery, for them to accomplish what millions of people did effortlessly every year? She bought pregnancy tests by the armload from the 99 cents store and she took them every two weeks, even when she had no reason to think she might be pregnant, like tossing pennies into a wishing well. When she visited Mrs. Sheppard for tea, she felt her mother-in-law gazing at her with pity, the way you look at a child who is adorably failing at some simple task. She listened to Luke's mother offer advice, about pregnancy superfoods she should try, about vitamins some doctor on **Oprah** recommended. Now she'd finally made an appointment with her doctor but Luke wouldn't even go with her.

"I don't get it," she told Nadia. "Why does he act like it's no big deal?"

She was sitting at Nadia's kitchen table, watching her sort her father's medicine into a daily pill organizer.

"I don't know," Nadia said. "Maybe you should. Just relax, I mean."

"I am relaxed. Do I not seem relaxed?"

"I know, I just mean—you have time, that's all."

Nadia opened a new vial of pills, counting the tablets in her palm. She sounded harried and distracted, too worried about her father to care about anything else, and Aubrey wished she hadn't even mentioned the appointment. Luke always said the same thing—they had plenty of time to have a baby—but she still felt like she'd already failed him. She couldn't get pregnant and she knew it was her fault because Luke had made a baby before, accidentally, with some name- less girl. That girl hadn't even wanted his baby, yet Aubrey was incapable of forming a child she prayed for every night. She didn't say this aloud, though. She already felt selfish enough, going on about her doctor's appointment while her friend was frowning and counting pills. Besides, she'd never told Nadia about Luke's aborted baby. She hadn't told anyone, except for Russell, but that was different. Russell wasn't anyone. He was a phantom who ghosted across her computer screen. She shut her laptop at night and with a click, he disappeared.

IN LAW SCHOOL, Nadia had lived by detailed schedules, her days planned down to the hour. But in the hospital, where long periods of wait- ing were only punctuated by brief visits from doc- tors, she had felt like she was floating in time, unhinged from it completely. Now that she was back home, she created a new schedule. She didn't write it down, the way she'd kept a calendar on the dry-erase board back in her apartment, but she memorized it, and soon her father did too. She woke at six, checked his breathing, and showered. Her father slept in his easy chair in the living room now—lying down was too painful—so she rubbed his shoulders each morning, working out the kink in his neck. She helped him to the bathroom, only as far as the door. He still had too much pride to allow her to help him bathe, although she was increasingly aware that that day was nearing, if not during this injury, then someday in the future, the way all people grew old and infantile. Maybe that was what her mother had tried to avoid. Maybe it was easier to exit while she was still young and capable than wait for her own eventual decline.

The doctor had told Nadia that the biggest concern about her father's injury was infection, but she knew there were other things to worry about too. Pneumonia. Lung collapse. Fluids filling his chest. And pain. Even if nothing further went wrong, the pain alone could prevent her father from breathing deeply. Each morning, she checked him for fever and guided him through his breathing exercises, ten deep breaths every hour. She packed frozen peas inside his shirt for fifteen minutes to decrease the swelling. She encouraged him to cough, always afraid she might see blood. Three weeks in, she found herself looking at the phlegm her father had coughed into a wad of tissue and realized she didn't feel disgusted at all. She was too worried to feel anything else.

She was starting to think like a nurse, Monique said. When her father was discharged, Monique had come by and talked her through all of the medicine bottles lined up on his dresser. She showed Nadia how to support him when he coughed to minimize the pain, how to listen to his chest for fluids, how to help him take little walks around the living room to keep his blood circulating. Nadia fell into her routine, most days not even leaving the house.

"You gotta go back to school," her father finally told her. "You can't just sit around here all day."

She was helping him change for bed, pulling his navy USMC shirt over his head. She tried not to look at his scars, the parts of his chest that still looked bruised.

"I'm not," she said. "I'm studying for the bar. That's what I'd be doing in Chicago, anyway."

She never wanted him to think she'd halted her

life for him. Other fathers might have felt touched, but hers would only feel ashamed. She had inherited this from him, an inability to ask for help, as if needing something was an inconvenience. She always made sure to study in front of him, even though she could hardly concentrate. Every few minutes, she glanced up at him and swore she heard a hitch in his breathing. A snag in his throat or the swish of fluids filling his chest. She heard imaginary ailments. She felt herself falling apart. One night, when the pain was too bad for her father to sleep, she sat up with him, her hand clenched in his. She wanted to take him back to the hospital but he refused.

"What're they gonna do?" he wheezed. "Give me medicine? I got some right here. I don't need no hospital."

He told her war stories, about growing up in Louisiana with parents who hated each other. His mother had cared for him and his five siblings, while his father worked long hours at the oil refinery and spent his week's earnings at gambling houses and brothels. He'd return from work, sweaty and covered in soot, and his wife would draw his bathwater and iron his shirt so he could go back out to spend his day's pay on liquor and women. Her father had never understood why his mother would do that. She'd sit on the edge of the claw-foot tub—she had a long braid down her back that whipped up at the end—and pour warm water. She sometimes added a drop of cologne and the house, which usually smelled like food and dust, filled with a sweet fragrance. At catechism, when the priest talked about the woman who had poured expensive perfume on Jesus' feet, her father had thought of his own mother's devotion. At least Jesus had been grateful. His father never thanked his wife for anything.

One cloudy day, she was in the front yard, washing clothes in a basin, while her children were shooting marbles on the porch. Her husband came down the steps, bathed and cologned and wearing a shirt she'd starched and pressed. He was heading to the pool hall to gamble away his week's earnings and he would return in the early hours in that beautiful white shirt she'd scrubbed, now crumpled and musky with the smell of a cheap woman. And after standing in the welfare line all day, she would scrub it clean again. She stared down into the basin, at her fingers wrinkling in the warm water, at the pounds of shirts and coveralls and drawers waiting for her in the basket. As she would later say, she felt a heaviness on her chest, as if those shirts had all wrapped themselves tight around her heart. She didn't think. Her fingers wrapped around an ice pick that had been lying near the pump and she shoved it into her husband's back. He bled out on the laundry tub.

"The water was red, red," her father said. "I never seen anything redder."

He bore his father's name but he wanted to be nothing like him. When he'd enlisted in the Marines, his superiors noted that he was calm-headed and quiet, the type who kept to himself. He was called Altar Boy because of the rosary he wore under his uniform. After he was transferred to Camp Pendleton, he had a bunkmate called Clarence who was loud and charming, the exact opposite of himself, so of course, they became friends.

"He wanted me to meet his sister," her father said. "I thought she'd be ugly. Guy wants you to meet his sister, she usually is. Guys with pretty sisters don't want their friends sniffing around. But he said we'd be good for each other." He turned his head toward the glass door, where the morning sky lit pink. "I couldn't believe how pretty she was. And young. Guess I was young too. I watched my daddy bleed out over a laundry tub and I never felt young after that. But your mom, she had light. She smiled at me and my whole chest cracked open."

Her father finally fell asleep by noon, his head slumped toward the window. By the time the doorbell rang that afternoon, Nadia had been awake for twenty-four hours. She stumbled to the door, expecting Aubrey, but instead, Luke paused in the doorway, clutching a plastic container of food to his stomach. She knew she looked horrible—scrawny and mean, eyes dark and puffy, her T-shirt hanging off her shoulders, her hair in a tangled ponytail. She hadn't showered or slept or eaten in hours. In his startled eyes, she felt like a sliver of herself, like an ice cube passed around inside a mouth until it hollowed into a slender crescent.

He guided her to the kitchen table and microwaved a plate of chicken and rice. She hugged herself, watching him move quietly around her kitchen, catching the microwave before it beeped, quietly shutting the utensil drawer. He set the steaming plate in front of her.

"Eat," he said.

"I should've visited," she said.

"You gotta eat something."

"I should've come home more."

"How would that change anything? Even if

you'd been there, what was you gonna do? Lift a hundred pounds off him?" He slid the plate toward her. "You gotta eat now. You gotta stay strong so you can help him too."

"I left him," she said.

"You went to school. He wanted you to."

"I left him like she did."

He touched her cheek and she closed her eyes, melting into the softness of his fingers.

"No," he said. "It's not the same."

"It is," she said. "I feel like I have to be her for the both of us."

She started to cry. Luke pressed her head against his shoulder, then he guided her away from the kitchen table. In the bathroom, he knelt on his good leg and ran water into the tub.

"Why are you doing this?" she said.

"Because," he said evenly, "I want to take care of you."

Later, he would set a glass of water on her night-stand and tuck her in bed. She would fall into a heavy sleep, relaxing for the first time in weeks because Luke was in the living room watching over her father. Before drifting off, she would think about how much she had wanted this when she was waking up in the abortion clinic. For Luke to be there, taking care of her. She was exhausted from taking care of herself. But for now, Luke stepped out as she undressed, as if he hadn't seen her naked before, as if he didn't already know the contours of her body, down to the dimple on her stomach where, her mother used to say, God had kissed her. Luke had kissed that same dimple before, fitting his lips against the divine's. She sank into the warm bubble bath and closed her eyes.

IN THE MORNING, Luke brought her father's medicine and Nadia kissed him in the kitchen. The paper drugstore bag crinkled in his hands as he hooked an arm around her waist. In her bedroom, the curtains whipped open in the breeze and Luke lowered her onto her childhood bed, which squeaked under their weight. Quiet, quiet. Not the rushed motions of their youth, a dress shoved up to her stomach, jeans sagging to his knees. Now he unbuttoned his shirt and folded it on the back of her desk chair. He slipped her socks down her ankles. He loosened her freshly washed hair and buried his face in it. Now they were slow and deliberate, the way hurt people loved, stretching carefully just to see how far their damaged muscles could go.

ELEVEN

It wasn't an affair.

Affairs were for boozy, lonely housewives or horny businessmen, real adults doing real adult things, not sneaking her high school boyfriend into her childhood bed. Nadia felt layers of the past peeling away; she was slowly stepping backward into her old life. Luke on top of her, his familiar warmth and weight, every man since him melting away like the springtime fog. He visited each day during his lunch break and she snuck him into her room while her father took his afternoon nap. In her bed, Luke wasn't married anymore. He didn't know Aubrey. She was seventeen again and tiptoeing with Luke through her parents' house, except now they had to be extra quiet, hoping that his cane wouldn't drum too loudly against the floor.

In her bed, she believed the impossible. She felt herself growing younger, her skin softer and tighter, her mind unfilling with the textbooks she'd read. Luke uncrippled, unswallowing aspirin by the palmfuls. Unloving Aubrey. He kissed Nadia and she felt untouched, their baby unforming inside of her, their lives separating.

She unhinged from time, her days splintering into before and after. Before Luke visited, she cleaned the kitchen, helped her father to the bathroom, gave him his medicine, showered. She combed her hair but never put on makeup—too much effort would ruin the naturalness of their tryst—and helped her father to his armchair. After Luke, she showered again, closing her eyes into the steam, as if the hot water could rinse away what she'd just done.

Some days, they did not have sex. Some days, Luke sat at the kitchen table while she made him a sandwich. She felt him watching her as she cut it in half and imagined that this small moment was normal for them. She slid into the chair across from him and propped a leg onto his lap; he ate and under the table, stroked her calf. Affairs were

shadowy and secretive, not lunches shared in a
sunbathed kitchen while her father napped in the
living room. But these quiet, clothed days felt
the most treacherous, the most intimate.

"I love you," he whispered one afternoon, his
fingers stroking her stomach, and she wondered
if he was speaking to her at all or the ghost of the
child they'd made. Could you ever truly unlove
a child, even one you never knew? Or did that
love transform into something else? She wished
he hadn't said anything at all; he was tugging at
the edges of her fantasy. What was love to her
anyway? Her mother had told her she loved her
and then she'd left. There was nothing lonelier
than the moment you realized someone had abandoned you.

"You left me," she said. "You left me in that
clinic—"

"But I'm here," he said. "I came back."

THE MORNING OF HER APPOINTMENT, Aubrey
sat in the waiting room, watching an overhead
television play a video on heart disease. Cartoon
red blood cells slid down a chute, ramming into
each other like bumper cars. The leading cause
of death among women, the video reminded her,

as it looped for the third time. Was this cartoon supposed to make you feel better about the fact that your heart might be slowly killing you? She sighed, reaching for a magazine instead. She hated going to the doctor. When she'd first moved to Oceanside, her sister sent her to an endless stream of them. A doctor who gave her a physical where she'd tried not to cry when she unbuttoned her jeans and slipped into the thin paper gown. She felt sick, imagining Paul spreading inside of her like a virus. But there was nothing wrong with her, the doctor had said, and she refused to speak to her sister the whole ride home, ashamed that Mo had thought there might be. Then she'd been sent to a psychiatrist who prescribed her an anti-depressant that she never even opened, the orange vial gathering dust in her drawer. A therapist who asked banal questions about school—never Paul—but she'd still felt sick the whole hour, because she knew those questions were lurking. After, she'd climbed into Kasey's car, resting her head against the window until they made it back home. At night, she'd heard Mo and Kasey argu-ing in their room, the walls too thin to mask their angry whispers.

"All I'm saying is that she gets so stressed about

that doctor—now what?" Kasey had said. "We gonna send her to another doctor for that too?"

A moth fluttered into the waiting room, its brown wings as thin as a scab. She chewed her thumbnail—a nasty habit, her mother had always said—as the moth spiraled through the room, past the receptionist's desk, the window facing the street, two women sitting under the television, until it drifted onto a stack of magazines. She watched it land, its wings folded like an arrowhead. Her sister had called her earlier and asked for updates when she finished. She'd been trying for months to convince Aubrey to schedule this appointment. Didn't she want answers? Wouldn't a diagnosis—even a bad one—be better than wondering why she hadn't been able to get pregnant? Maybe, but Aubrey hated the idea of waiting for a doctor to tell her what was wrong with her body. She'd made the appointment anyway, which told her one thing: she was beginning to feel desperate.

In Dr. Toby's office, Aubrey lay on her back, staring up into Denzel Washington's eyes. Her doctor had tacked posters of handsome movie stars on the ceiling. "It helps my patients relax," he'd said during her first visit, offering her a wry smile. She clenched her fists as soon as the doctor's cold tools entered her. She still tensed up when anything was inside her, even Luke's finger. On their wedding night, she'd hurt so bad, she felt tears gather at the corner of her eyes. But she hadn't said anything and Luke kept pushing into her, slowly and insistently. How could he not tell that he was hurting her? Or worse, how could he not care? If he loved her, how could he enjoy something that caused her pain? But she soldiered through because this was what you were supposed to do. A girl's first time was supposed to hurt. Suffering pain is what made you a woman. Most of the milestones in a woman's life were accompanied by pain, like her first time having sex or birthing a child. For men, it was all orgasms and champagne.

She hadn't expected that her second time would hurt too, or her third, or even now, years later, that she would still dread the moment when Luke first entered her. He enjoyed it—she could tell from the way he closed his eyes or bit his lip—but she always clenched her fists until she grew used to him moving inside of her. It might be psychological, she'd read online. She felt disgusted at the idea of Paul still lingering in the back of her mind, as if when Luke touched her, Paul watched from the foot of the bed. Or maybe her troubles had nothing to do with Paul at all. Maybe she just wasn't turned on enough. The website said that women should verbalize their desires, but what were you supposed to say? Were you supposed to sound breathy and baby-like, the way sexy women spoke in the movies? Or crass and vulgar. Did men actually like that in bed? Once, Luke had told her that he wished she would initiate sex more.

"I feel like you don't really want me," he said.

She was stunned. Of course she wanted him, he was the only one she'd ever wanted. But she didn't know how to make him feel that way. She pulled out the teddies and nightgowns she'd been given at her bridal shower, examining them a moment before burying them back in her drawer. She bought whipped cream and chocolate syrup once, but could never figure out how to make the smooth transition from the bed to the refrigerator, so she brought them to Kasey's birthday party to eat with the cake and ice cream. Maybe nothing was wrong with her body. Maybe she was just bad at sex or her husband was bored. Maybe if she was sexier, more enticing, she would be pregnant already.

Dr. Toby told her not to worry.

"Everything looks fine," he said. "You're both young and healthy. Just relax. Have some wine."

Have some wine, as if that was all it would take. Dr. Toby had spent years in medical school just to arrive at that recommendation? She drove to Mrs. Sheppard's office, furious at the doctor for wasting her time, but Mrs. Sheppard told her to cheer up. After all, the doctor could have given her a bad report. He could've told her she was hopelessly barren, that there was no chance she would ever give birth. Instead, he'd told her that she was healthy. Her mother-in-law reached across the table and squeezed her hand.

"Don't worry, honey," she said. "Everything in its own time. You can't rush God."

That night, Luke came home late. Aubrey was sleeping when she heard him fumbling in the dark, shedding clothes. When they first married, she'd always jolted awake at the sound of him moving in the dark. He could be anybody, creeping through her apartment. But now she knew the cadence of his footsteps, how he tugged off his jeans and his shirt before climbing in bed beside her. She smelled his familiar scent, a little sweet but warm. Manly. Their bed smelled like him, and on the few nights they'd spent apart, she always slept with his pillow on top of her own. Like how when they were dating, she would always leave her sweater on the kitchen chair where he hung his jacket, so he would place his on top of hers and when he left, her sweater would smell like him.

She rolled toward him and placed her hand on his warm belly. A few inches lower and she could slip her hand inside his boxers. She could kiss him and climb on top of him, the way she'd climbed on top of Russell long ago in the beach bathroom. A stranger, yet she still couldn't bring herself to touch her husband first. But before she could move, Luke lifted her hand and kissed her palm. Then he rolled over and went to sleep.

IN THE FADING EVENING LIGHT, Luke huffed in Nadia's backyard, bench-pressing her father's weights. He was killing time, waiting for her to finish reheating dinner, waiting for her father to fall asleep in front of the television so he could spend an hour with Nadia in her bedroom. He usually didn't come over this late, but tonight had been a surprise gift: his schedule had been switched at the last minute, so when he told Aubrey earlier that he had to work late, he hadn't been lying for once. He was a better liar than he'd thought he could be. It scared him a bit, how easily he could convince even himself that what he was doing wasn't wrong. All because Nadia had been first. She had been his first love, so maybe, in a way, she had the rightful claim to his heart. Maybe it was like how when you stepped out of the grocery store line to grab bread, no one could really be mad when you returned to your spot. It wasn't cutting if you had been there before.

He groaned, pushing up the barbell. He'd begun doing this, playing around with her father's weights when he came over. He had put on weight and he suddenly felt aware of it every time he undressed in front of Nadia. The last time she'd seen him naked, he'd been in elite shape, 220 pounds, five percent body fat. Now he'd grown extra padding on his stomach, his taut calves and biceps softening. He was already turning fat like the alumni who used to visit team practice during homecoming; Luke and his teammates had secretly laughed at them, men who hadn't quit a football diet once the football stopped. That would be him someday, he'd known that, but he hadn't guessed how quickly someday would come.

Since he and Nadia had started sleeping together again, he'd begun eating better, avoiding dessert, doing push-ups on the bathroom floor.

He felt shy about it, like an insecure teenager, but maybe that was what she wanted. She had loved him then, when he was young and handsome and cruel. He didn't want to be cruel to her anymore, but he could at least be handsome again.

"Do you want those?"

He racked the weights and sat up, his arms burning. Nadia lingered behind the screen door.

"What?" he said.

"Take them," she said, pointing to the weights.

"But they're your dad's."

"He doesn't need them. They almost killed him."

She leaned against the doorway, her foot scratching the back of her calf. She was wearing sweatpants, her hair tied up in a bun, and she had never looked more beautiful. He had never seen this side of her before, not the first time. Then, she had gussied herself up every time they went out, wearing miniskirts and cute sundresses and lipstick. He'd loved that about her, how much effort she put into looking pretty for him, but he felt even more connected to this dressed-down side of her. This was the real her and she trusted him enough to let him see it. The same way he knew that she had seen the real him. Aubrey saw a version of him that was better than he had ever been. But

Nadia had seen him at his worst. He'd been self-ish and mean to her, but she still wanted him. He felt liberated, knowing that he was seeing Nadia at her worst too. She had betrayed her best friend to be with him. She felt guilty about their affair, he could tell, even though she wouldn't admit it. Admitting it meant that she would have to stop seeing him. It was easier to pretend she didn't feel guilty.

So he pretended too. In her bed that night, he traced his hand down her naked shoulder, misted by their sweat.

"Do you ever think about that summer?" he said.

"Which summer?" she asked.

"You know the one."

Sometimes he felt trapped in that summer before she'd left for college, wondering about all of the things he should've done differently. If he'd just picked her up from the clinic. If he'd convinced her not to go to the clinic in the first place. If they would have been exactly like this, lying in bed together talking, except with a six-year-old running around in the living room.

"Sometimes," she said.

"Do you think we—" He paused. "Maybe we should have—"

She tensed in his arms and he knew he'd crossed a line. He knew by now the topics he could never discuss with her. Aubrey. Their baby. He expected her to pull away from him, but instead, she rolled toward him.

"Shh." She kissed his neck, slipping her hand under the covers.

"Nadia . . ."

"I don't want to talk," she whispered.

He would have to stop doing this, wondering about the life they might have had together, the family they might have been. He would have to be grateful for everything she gave him.

BABY REACHES FOR Daddy's unshaven face. Baby loves Daddy's rough skin. Baby bounces in the window when Daddy pulls into the driveway. Baby throws a rattle, a pacifier, a ball. Baby's got a hell of a throwing arm, Daddy's friends say, but Daddy secretly hopes Baby has good catching hands. Baby swings at T-ball, Baby chases across soccer fields, Baby lines up for orange slices and water after basketball practice. Baby listens to Granddaddy preach. Baby watches football in Daddy's lap. Baby asks Daddy about his leg, Baby learns about the fragility of dreams. Baby straps on pads and learns pain. Baby stops crying when he is hit. Baby tosses the football in the front yard with Daddy, who always catches the ball perfectly. Baby can't understand why he still drops, but Daddy tells him his hands are too hard.

You need soft hands, Daddy says. You touch a girl the same way you catch a football. Soft hands.

WEEKS AFTER HER VISIT to Dr. Toby, Aubrey made an appointment with a fertility specialist. She'd first read about Dr. Yavari on Fertility-Friends.com, the forum where she'd been lurking for the past few months. On evenings when Luke worked late, she ate her dinner in front of her computer screen, slowly scrolling past the giant banner at the top of the lavender website that read, **There is no such thing as trying too hard to get pregnant.** She never told anyone about the website, not even Luke. She didn't want him to think that she was baby crazed and desperate. But there was something comforting about reading the message boards, about knowing that other women were struggling worse than her. They were, after all, the ones with screen names like MommytoBe75 or Waiting2Xpect82, the ones reporting their last menstrual periods or charting their days past ovulation to strangers on the Internet. She pitied these women, except for the ones who were trying for a second or third child. We all just want one, she always thought, angrily clicking out the website. On the forums, a rambling thread about California fertility specialists mentioned Dr. Yavari, based out of La Jolla, whom former patients referred to as "the babymaker." The nickname comforted and disturbed Aubrey. She didn't want to think of her baby as created by a doctor, like some science experiment, but she appreciated the confidence everyone seemed to have in Dr. Yavari. Maybe this was what she needed, to visit an expert. Maybe Dr. Yavari could save her from becoming one of those sad women on the message boards. She called Dr. Yavari's office and when Luke said he couldn't miss work, she called Nadia and asked her to come with her.

"I can't," Nadia said.

"Why not?"

"Because," she stammered. "It sounds personal. Why don't you bring Mo?"

"She's working too. And who cares if it's personal? You're not exactly a stranger."

She laughed a little, but Nadia was silent. A quiet distance had grown between them since

Nadia returned. They still talked occasionally, but not as often as Aubrey had hoped they might. She tried not to take the unanswered phone calls and ignored texts personally. Nadia had her father to worry about, and the last thing she needed was Aubrey burdening her with her own hurt feelings. Still, she felt that distance widening the longer Nadia went without answering.

"Please," Aubrey said. "I just get nervous. And it'd make me feel better if you were there."

"I'm sorry," Nadia finally said. "I'm being dumb. Of course I'll come with you."

The next afternoon, they drove to Dr. Yavari's office, a tan building with palm trees sprouting in front. In the waiting room, framed photos of mothers cradling babies hung over the reception-ist's desk like a promise, but Aubrey felt like the images were teasing, dangling right in front of her the things that she wanted. Beside her, Nadia played with her phone and Aubrey tried to flip through a **National Geographic**, but ended up twisting it in her hands into a glossy tube.

"Why are you nervous?" Nadia asked.

"Because. I know something's wrong with me."

She tensed, waiting for Nadia to ask how she knew. Instead, she felt Nadia's fingers stroke the back of her neck.

"There's nothing wrong with you," she said quietly, and for a second, Aubrey believed her.

Dr. Yavari was Iranian, olive-skinned with dark eyes, and thirtysomething, much younger than Aubrey had expected her to be. She welcomed both of them into her office with a smile, sweeping her arm toward a chair in the corner. "Your sister can sit there," she said, and neither corrected her. Strangers often mistook them for sisters or cousins or even, Aubrey assumed, girlfriends. She was amazed by their ability to resemble each other, to become family, to occupy, at once, different ways to love each other. Who were they to each other? Anything at all. While the doctor flipped through her charts, she sat on the metal table, her legs swinging off the edge. In the corner, Nadia leaned against a counter covered in tubs of purple plastic gloves while Dr. Yavari asked Aubrey a series of questions. How often does your period occur? Is it heavy, light? Any sexually transmitted infections? Have you ever been pregnant? Have you ever had an abortion?

"What?" Aubrey said.

"I have to ask," Dr. Yavari said, drumming her pen against her clipboard. "I usually try to wait until the men are gone—you know, it happened in college, she never told her husband, et cetera."

"No," she said. "None." But she appreciated Dr. Yavari's compassion. She hoped the doctor didn't just guess that Aubrey was the type of woman who might have hidden a secret like that from her husband. She would have, but she hated the idea of the doctor knowing this about her.

After the exam, Dr. Yavari scheduled her follow-up appointment. Next time, there would be an X-ray to determine whether her fallopian tubes were open, a pelvic ultrasound to test the thickness of her uterine lining and check for cysts in her ovaries, and blood tests to measure her hormone production. When the doctor left, Aubrey dressed, pulling on her clothes that Nadia had folded in a small pile.

"I can't believe she asked you that," Nadia said.

"Asked me what?"

"You know. The abortion thing. Why does it even matter?"

"I don't know. It must, if she asked about it."

"Still. I can't believe it follows you around like that."

Later, Aubrey would wonder what had exactly tipped her off. The statement itself, or the unusual softness in Nadia's voice, or even the way her face had looked under the fluorescent light, slightly stricken with grief. In the moment between when Nadia handed her her cardigan and she accepted it, she knew that Nadia was The Girl. Since Luke had confessed to her years ago, she had often thought about this nameless, faceless girl who had gotten rid of his child. A girl he'd loved but who had vanished, like the baby, both gone forever.

On the drive home, traffic in front of them slowed. She gripped the steering wheel tighter as the car inched forward. Beside her, Nadia fiddled with the radio dials until she reached an old Kanye West song they both used to love, one they'd listened to endlessly in her room and danced to together at Cody Richardson's party. She thought about that night, how sloppy drunk she'd been, how easily she'd forgotten everything she didn't want to remember. She could have been anyone that night, in that skintight dress, dancing at a crowded house party with Nadia Turner. Toward the end of the night, Nadia had looped an arm around her waist and said, in her ear, "Let's get you home," and she had nodded, realizing that she hadn't even thought about how she would get home. She had known, somehow, that Nadia would take care of her. In bed that night, before falling asleep, she'd felt Nadia's hand touch her back. It was a fleeting gesture—casual, like picking lint off someone's sweater—but in that moment, Aubrey had never felt so safe.

After she dropped Nadia off, she stopped at the liquor store around the corner. The tiny Indian man behind the counter waved at her as she walked in. The store was mostly empty, a washed-out blonde hauling a six-pack of Coors to the counter, two boys fighting over a bag of Hot Cheetos. She grabbed an Italian pinot noir because she liked the shiny silver label. At home, she drank half the bottle while she dressed, the other half after she'd already slipped into one of the frilly black teddies crumpled in the corner of her drawer. She shook out the wrinkles, then stood in front of the mirror, fighting with the straps and bows. After the wine, she wouldn't be able to unhook it herself. She imagined herself stuck in the teddy forever— would someone have to cut it off her, the way her father-in-law had sawed off Luke's purity ring?

She finished her wine on the couch, listening to the dull thud of the clock. By the time Luke came home, she was drunk and sleepy. She'd meant to answer the door in the teddy—she wanted to be the first thing he saw—but she was too slow and by the time he stepped inside, she was still splayed on the couch. He froze in front of her, still holding his keys.

"Are you okay?" he said.

She stood too quickly and lost her balance, grabbing the armrest to steady herself.

"Come here," she said.

"Are you drunk?"

She grabbed the teal drawstring on his scrubs and tugged him closer. She reached inside his pants and felt him staring at her in a way he never had before, pitying her desperation. When he pushed himself inside, she clenched her eyes and found sweetness in the pain.

THE NEXT DAY, Luke asked Nadia if he could take her on a date. His face, inches from hers on her pillow, looked shy; she'd forgotten how curly his eyelashes were. The afternoon sun filtered in through the blinds and she felt lazy, warm and stretching against her sheets.

"Maybe downtown?" he said. "Or the harbor? I don't know. Wherever you wanna go."

She traced his tattoos, the maze of interlocking images that covered his left arm. When she'd last undressed him, seven years ago, he'd had a few tattoos but now his full sleeve fascinated her: tribal markings stretched over his shoulder, and near his elbow, a skull gritted its teeth; a fanged demon's tongue transformed into flames that licked up around Luke's wrist. A cross on his biceps, and above it, the words **On my own.** A lion's head covered Luke's left pectoral, the mane flowing away like smoke. The other half of his chest was smooth, bare, his right arm untouched. His ink stopped abruptly, like he'd slipped one arm into a sweater and forgotten about the other.

"Why?" she said.

"Why what?"

"Why a date?"

He pressed her hand against his heart and rolled onto his side. She'd always heard that men hated to cuddle and it surprised her that Luke liked to be on the inside, cuddled by her. She had almost laughed the first time at the idea, but it made sense in a way, that everyone would want to be held. She wrapped her arms around him and kissed his muscled back.

"I don't know," he said. "I just want to take you somewhere nice."

"What if someone sees us?" she said.

"Let them," he said. "I don't care."

"You're married."

"What if I wasn't?"

For a moment, she allowed herself to imagine it, how simple he made it seem, like a gate stood between him and freedom and all he needed to do was slip a finger under the latch. Luke was good at this, always finding an escape. She remembered watching him on the football field, amazed by how his body seemed to know, down to the second, when to juke left or right, always aware of the direction danger appeared. He'd escaped her once before; she couldn't help him do the same to Aubrey. Aubrey sitting on that metal table inside the fertility doctor's office, how small she'd looked next to the size of her wanting.

"You can't," she said.

"Why not?"

"Because she loves you," she said. "We're just fucking around, but she loves you."

"It's not just fucking," he said. "Don't say that—"

"It is to me," she said.

He silently dressed but paused halfway, his pants hanging at his ankles. He looked like he might cry, and she turned away. He didn't love her. He felt guilty. He'd abandoned her once and now he was latching onto her, not out of affection but out of shame. She refused to let him bury his guilt in her. She would not be a burying place for any man again.

Luke forgot his watch on her nightstand, so the next morning, she brought it to Upper Room.

When she pulled into the parking lot, Mother Betty was shuffling across the street from the bus stop. The DMV had taken her license after she failed her last driving test.

"They got me on those questions," she said. "Who knows the answers to all those little questions anyway? I been driving sixty-six years and never hit nobody but these people gonna say I can't drive because of their little questions?"

She watched Mother Betty slowly sift through her ring of keys to unlock the front door, her hand shaking. It wasn't right, a woman her age waiting for the bus before daybreak.

"I can give you a ride," Nadia said. She fumbled through her purse for a piece of paper. "I'll give you my number and you just call me when you're ready to go to work. Okay?"

"Oh no, honey, I couldn't trouble you."

"It's no trouble at all. Really. Please."

She held out the scrap of notebook paper. Mother Betty hesitated, then accepted it.

"You got a caring spirit," she said. "I can sense it in you. Just like your mama."

Nadia left Luke's watch on Mother Betty's desk. She drove home, glancing at her reflection in the rearview mirror. She touched the image but did not see her mother's face, only smudged glass.

TWELVE

Years later, we realized the watch should have told us everything. Only two reasons a woman might have someone's husband's watch:

1. She's sleeping with him.
2. She repairs watches.

Nadia Turner didn't look like a watchmaker to us. But even though the truth hadn't dawned on us yet, we still pitied Aubrey. On Sunday mornings, when we gathered around her in the church lobby, we felt her sadness swell. Agnes peered into the life of a baby girl born to parents who distrust each other. A girl who distrusts the world too, for reasons she doesn't quite understand. She feels the coldness spreading between her parents and second-guesses everything: if her parents can pretend they are in love, what else could they be lying about to her? What else could the world keep from her, hold away in its hand?

She may hear this story, someday, and wonder what it has to do with her. A girl hiding her scared in her prettiness, an unwanted baby, a dead mother. These are not her heartbreaks. Every heart is fractured differently and she knows the pattern of her cracks, she traces them like lines across her palm. She has a living mother and besides, she was always wanted. Prayed for, even. Now she's grown, or at least she thinks she is. But she hasn't yet learned the mathematics of grief. The weight of what has been lost is always heavier than what remains. She's heard her granddaddy preach about the good shepherd who leaves the ninety-nine behind in search of the one lost sheep.

But what about the flock he abandons? she wonders. Aren't they lost now too?

THAT FALL, Nadia Turner mothered. In the gray mornings, while her father slept, she scraped his keys off the hallway table and pulled his truck out of the driveway. She rolled down the window, sticking an arm out into the damp air, and cruised through quiet streets, past coffee shops flipping "Closed" signs, women in bathrobes strapping backpacks on children at bus stops, surfers in wetsuits with boards racked on tops of trucks, until she reached a prim white house with blue trim. She began to feel like a valet, hopping out to help Mother Betty up the high truck stairs, especially once the other Mothers began to ask her for rides.

"Oh, I hope you don't mind," Mother Betty said, "but I told Agnes you could carry her to the drugstore."

No, no, she didn't mind. She learned the curves of the roads that led to the Mothers' homes. She'd never even thought of them having homes before—she wouldn't have been shocked to learn they stashed bedrolls in the choir closet and slept right on the pews. But Mother Agnes lived in a gray apartment building downtown, Mother Hattie in a rusty red house near the Back Gate. Mother Flora lived in an assisted-living home called Fairwinds, which was across the street from an elementary school and a child-care center. She was surrounded by death and children, children outside her window toddling to day care, children running around on playgrounds or biking home from school. Mother Flora was tall and willowy. She'd played basketball as a girl. Nadia learned other things, like Mother Clarice used to be a special-education teacher, and her friends called her Clara. Mother Hattie was the best cook. Mother Betty had been the prettiest.

Nadia wasn't quite sure how old the Mothers were but they must have been in their eighties or nineties by now. No surprise the DMV wanted them off the road. But she still felt sorry for them, especially Mother Betty, who for years had risen before everyone and arrived at Upper Room with her keys, so she made sure to pick her up early. She didn't feel guilty about sneaking out of the house anymore. Her father was getting stronger. In the afternoons, he walked in slow laps around the backyard, practicing his breathing exercises. She sometimes watched him through the glass while she read her bar exam books. She never wanted him to know she still worried about him, so when he took his medicine at night, she busied herself in his room, dusting the nightstand or putting his laundry away or idly straightening her mother's perfume bottles. She used to love playing with her mother's perfume, particularly one black bottle. Her mother only spritzed it on her neck when she and her father were going out for the night. So when Nadia held the bottle to her nose, she longed for a night when it'd been exciting to watch her parents disappear through the door because she'd known they would always come back.

She mothered as a penance, like sliding fingers along rosary beads. Each mile, its own prayer. If she gave her time selflessly, maybe she could forget the wrong she'd done. If she worked for no reward, if she was kind to people who could offer her nothing in return, maybe then her sins would be washed away. One afternoon, on the way to the drugstore, she mentioned that she'd recently found her mother's prayer book. Found, she'd said, because that was the simpler way to tell the story, editing out Luke's role altogether. The Mothers began to chatter, the way they often did, jumping in and interrupting and finishing each other's sentences.

"Oh, she used to love that thing. Always carryin' it under her arm."

"Didn't her mama give it to her?"

"Mhm, that's what she told me. She was a minister, y'know?"

"Not a minister, just a preachin' woman."

"Oh, what's the difference?"

"Minister needs a church."

"Fine, a preachin' woman. You knew that, girl? Your grandmama used to baptize folks in the river."

Nadia had always been curious about her grandmother but her mother did not like to talk about her much. "Oh, she was strict," her mother would say when Nadia had asked, or "She sure loved Jesus." Always broad, general statements, as if she were describing a character from a TV show she no longer followed. From the few photographs of her in the photo album, her grandmother seemed like a stern woman, but beyond that, she was a mystery. When she told the Mothers this, they nodded sagely.

"Well, they weren't much close."

"That's a nice way of puttin' it."

That night, when Nadia asked her father what the Mothers had meant, he told her that when her mother was pregnant with her, her own mother had thrown her out of the house.

"She said that no child of hers would be living in sin under her household, so I sent your mom a Greyhound ticket and she came out here to live with me." He sighed. "Your grandma wanted nothing to do with us and that was fine with me. But I never understood why she wouldn't meet you. Us, that's one thing. But a child? Your own grandchild? I don't know how anyone wouldn't want to know their grandchild."

She asked her father if her grandmother was still alive, and he shrugged. "As far as I know," he said. "Still down in Texas, I'm sure." As if he'd seen the wheels turning in her head, he added, "I'd leave all that alone. She made her choices. Chasing after her won't do no good." She found a brown Polaroid in a photo album of her mother posing with her brothers in front of their home. An address and date were scribbled across the back. She searched for more recent photos of the home online and tried to imagine her mother as a girl, dancing on the porch. Maybe her grandmother still lived there. She didn't seem like the type of woman who would move around. She wondered what her grandmother would say if she showed up on that porch someday. Would she blink away grateful tears, glad to finally meet her grand-daughter? Or would she shoo her off the steps like she had shooed her own daughter? Would she be angry that the source of their rift had material-ized right in front of her?

"Did Mom ever think about . . ." She paused, outlining the gold buttons on her purse with her finger. "Not having me?"

"What do you mean?" her father said. He

placed a white pill on his tongue and flung his head back.

"You know." She swirled around the buttons so she wouldn't have to look at her father when she said the word. "Abortion."

"Did someone tell you that?"

"No. No. I was just wondering."

"No," he said. "Never. She never would've done something like that. Did you think . . ." He paused, his eyes softening. "No, honey. We loved you. We always loved you."

She should've felt glad, but she didn't. She wished her mother had at least thought about it. A fleeting thought when she'd left the doctor and envisioned her own mother's face. During a hushed phone call with the man she loved. When she'd called a clinic to make her appointment and hung up in tears, when she'd sat in the waiting room, holding her own hand. She could've been seconds away from doing it—it didn't matter. She hated the thought of her mother not wanting her but it would've been better to look at her mother's face in the mirror and know that they were alike.

THREE WEEKS AFTER he'd seen Nadia last, Luke squatted over his back steps, striking a match against the railing. Dave's suggestion. Light a candle, he'd told Luke, the last time he called the helpline. Dave hadn't said what type of candle. A scented candle like the ones in Luke's mother's bathroom, a tiny tea candle placed on restaurant tables, a thick red candle emblazoned with the Virgin Mary you found in the Mexican food aisle. A birthday candle, rainbow-striped and slender. Any type of candle would do, Dave had said, so Luke bought a pack of slender white candles. He sat on the back steps of the house, cupping his hands against the flame. It was supposed to bring closure, Dave had said. Peace. But as soon as he'd lit the candle, Luke only felt stressed. A light evening breeze rustled through the trees, and he hunched behind a shrub, trying to shelter the flame, suddenly responsible for guarding the fragile thing.

Dave was a counselor at the Family Life Center in downtown San Diego. Luke had found their flyer stuck in his windshield outside a bar a few weeks ago. **Looking for real options?** the yellow flyer asked, above a picture of a pregnant woman holding her head and a man next to her, staring off into the distance. It was the first pregnancy center flyer Luke had ever seen with a picture of a man on it. The others only held sad, alone women. On pregnancy center flyers, men were as absent in the midst of a surprise pregnancy as they were in real life. As absent as he'd been. He called the number, just to see what it was about. He told himself he'd hang up. But the on-duty counselor, Dave, started talking to him about the myth that only women suffer after abortions.

"Men suffer a unique type of loss," Dave said. "Men struggle after losing their child to abortion because they've failed to perform the primary function of a father: protecting his family."

Luke had never thought of it like that. He and Nadia hadn't been a family—they were just two scared kids. But what if they had been? What if for a brief moment, they had been family, stitched together by the life they'd created? What did that make them now? Now Luke called the center every other evening. He hung up if anyone other than Dave answered. He'd told Dave about the boy at the baseball game, years ago. Dave didn't judge him. It was normal, he'd said, for post-abortive fathers to feel grief. Once you had created a life, you would always be a father, no matter what happened to the child.

Luke fished his phone out of his pocket and dialed, careful to keep the candle lit.

"This you, Luke?" Dave asked.

"Yeah."

"How're you, buddy?"

"Fine."

"Just 'fine'?"

"Yeah."

"Okay." Dave cleared his throat. "Thought any more about coming into the center?"

"I can't," Luke said.

"It'll help you, trust me, talking to someone face-to-face—it's a lot better than over the phone. Sometimes you just need to see someone, know what I mean?"

"Yeah."

"I don't bite. Promise." Dave laughed. "And I got some books I can give you, if you come down. This one—" His voice strained, like he was reaching for something. "Great one, called **A Father's Heart.** It's by this guy named—"

"I gotta go," Luke said.

"Hold on, pal. Don't run off. I'll just hold these for you when you're ready, okay?"

"Okay."

"So what's on your mind?"

"I bought the candles," Luke said.

"Great!" Dave said. "Light a candle. And close your eyes. Picture your child playing on a field at the feet of Jesus."

Luke closed his eyes, the candle's warmth flickering across his face. He tried to envision the scene Dave described, but he only saw Nadia, her smile, her hazel eyes—then he felt the burn. A glob of hot wax dripped onto his hand. He cringed, scraping the wax off against the step. Gravel and dirt clung to his skin. He should've put the candle inside something. Why hadn't he thought of that? Behind him, the back door swung open and his wife leaned against the doorway, frowning.

"What're you doing?" Aubrey said.

"Nothing."

"What's with the candle, then? You're dripping wax all over the place."

She toed the white blob on the steps. Luke leaned forward, blowing out the flame. He was only making a bigger mess.

"WHEN YOU GONNA settle down, girl?" Mother Betty asked Nadia one morning. "You always flittin' around, here and there. You think life is for wandering about, lookin' for what makes you happy? Those just white girl dreams and fantasies. You need to settle down, find a good man. Look at Aubrey Evans! When you gonna do the same?"

Luke no longer came by to visit her father, but she passed him in Upper Room sometimes. He always looked shy of speaking, but he never even mumbled a hello, his eyes tracing the worn carpet. That sliver of space between them when they passed in a narrow hallway felt electric. She told herself she could not think about him. She needed to be good. She began to meet Aubrey on her lunch break, when they sat at a table by the window and shared coffee. She thought about confessing, but every time, the words clung to the roof of her mouth. What good would come of telling the truth? She had ended things with Luke. What good would come of Aubrey knowing all the ways they had betrayed her?

She never went to Aubrey's house, but once a week, she met Aubrey for dinner at Monique and Kasey's. Returning to the little white house made her feel like a teenager again—she wanted to stay up late eating ice cream or lounge in the backyard until the light grew dim, her future awaiting her, unblemished and free. She and Aubrey walked to the corner store for snacks or sat in her old bedroom, painting their nails. She always propped Aubrey's feet into her lap and painted her toenails. It seemed like a small thing she could give.

By Halloween, Nadia had become such a fixture around Upper Room that the pastor had asked her to help chaperone the children's Halloween party. She said yes. She said yes to nearly everything anyone at Upper Room asked of her. At first, she'd only offered the Mothers rides, but now, while her father continued to heal, she began to loan his truck. She and Second John lifted dozens of folding chairs into the truck bed for the Men's Fellowship; she drove across town to pick up a new drum kit for the choir; she carried the food baskets from the homeless ministry to the shelter. She had grown up and found God, people thought, but she hadn't found anything. She was searching for her mother. She hadn't found her in any of the old places, but maybe she could find her at Upper Room, a place she'd loved, a place she'd visited right before dying. If she could not find her mother in the last place she'd been breathing, she would never find her at all.

The Halloween party did not require much hauling, besides the decorations, but she still agreed to help. Each year, the church handed out candy, the least offensive way to commemorate a holiday whose demonic origins worried them but whose popularity was too great to ignore. Costumes were allowed, but only positive characters. Superheroes but no villains and nobody dead.

Bible figures were preferred, but no one knew whether Bible characters skirted the death rule; each year, a smart aleck dressed in a mummy costume and called himself Lazarus. That evening, she barely recognized the children's church room. The lights were out, but the ceiling was covered in plastic glowing stars. If darkness was required for Halloween events, that didn't mean it couldn't be combatted by celestial light. The children crammed into the room and darted down the hallways with plastic sacks filled with candy. Bearded Noahs dragged stuffed animals behind them; Adams juggled half-bitten apples; Moseses carried paper tablets under their arms, and Marys rocked baby dolls.

In the doorway, Nadia perched on a chair with a bucket of candy between her legs. These were the moments when adulthood was formed, not a birthday but the realization that she was now the one pouring a handful of candy into children's bags, that she was now the one expected to give, not receive. Aubrey and Luke arrived later. When they'd texted, Aubrey hadn't mentioned that she would bring Luke, but why would she? He was her husband—wasn't it expected that he would always be with her? He wore a long brown bathrobe and whenever a kid asked who he was, he flexed and said that he was Samson. But his hair was short, so all evening the children beat him up and he had to take it.

"Who are you supposed to be?" Aubrey asked. She carried a pair of scissors. Delilah.

"Nobody," Nadia said. She hadn't known what to wear, so when children asked, she said that she was no one, a peasant.

All night, they sat in the children's church doorway listening to the laughter. She watched the ancient lovers give out sweets under the fake starlight, Samson lounging on the plastic chair, his bum leg stretched out into the hallway because it got stiff and painful if he folded it. He plucked pink Starbursts out of the bucket and gave a handful to Aubrey, because they were her favorite. Later in the night, Aubrey rested her head against his shoulder and the brief contact felt so intimate, Nadia looked away.

The night was brisk and dim, the sliver of moon barely illuminating the sky. When Aubrey went to the bathroom, Nadia stepped inside the children's church room to refill her bucket. She leaned against the window, listening to the faint yelping of coyotes, when Luke leaned closer to her.

"I've been talking to this guy named Dave," he said.

"Who's Dave?"

"He doesn't think it's good that we never talk about him." He swallowed. "Our baby."

A flock of angels skipped by in shimmery white dresses. This was a strange, lopsided universe, all saints but no sinners, angels but no demons. An off-kilter world where girls mothered old women and betrayed their best friends.

"We don't have to be sad anymore. Dave says he's in heaven right now." Luke smiled, reaching for her hand. "And your mom's holding him."

Luke gazed out the window, and under the faint moonlight, he looked almost peaceful when he talked about their baby, who, like their love, was miraculous and fleeting. She squeezed Luke's hand. If this was what he needed, she wanted him to believe it. She wanted him to believe it all.

THAT SUNDAY MORNING, Aubrey saw a Marine in the receiving line. She ordinarily didn't notice faces when she helped greet the congregation, still overwhelmed by the crowds who gathered to shake hands with the first family, a family she now belonged to, and she shuffled mechanically, repeating the same greeting, offering hugs, agreeing to coffee dates she would soon forget.

She wouldn't have noticed the Marine at all if not for his uniform: dress blues, hat tucked under his arm, gold buttons glinting in the light. When he stepped forward, she glanced up into his face and snatched her hand back.

"Oh," she said.

Russell Miller smiled, the same purposeful smile she'd seen on the beach years ago, the smile of a man who knew sadness and spent great energy warding it away. She knew that smile, because it was a smile she'd long practiced and perfected. She hid behind that smile, but no one saw it in her the way she saw it in Russell. He reached past her to shake Pastor Sheppard's hand.

"Great message, Reverend," he said.

She suddenly felt exposed, like the whole church would notice her standing beside Russell and know. Know what? That once upon a time, days before her wedding, she had kissed him in a beach bathroom stall? That after she'd gotten married, when Russell should've been banished to her memory, she still wrote him?

"Let's talk outside," she said.

Months ago, Russell had e-mailed her and announced that his tour overseas was ending. **Coming back to the States soon, wanna grab lunch?** She'd hated the fake casualness of it, as if he were an old high school friend in town who just wanted to catch up. Of course she wanted to see him again, but they both knew she couldn't. She was married. She was loved by one man and it was wrong—greedy, really—to ask for more.

"What're you doing here?" she said, once they'd stepped behind the church.

Russell shrugged. "You didn't answer my e-mail, so I figured I'd come by."

"Maybe I didn't answer for a reason."

"Which is?"

"I'm married."

"Married women can't eat lunch?"

"Not with strange men."

"I'm a strange man?"

She sighed. "You know what I mean."

"I don't," he said. "I been halfway around the world and back and all I want to do is take you to lunch. I don't mean nothin' funny by it. You just kept my spirits up while I was gone and I want to thank you. Your husband can even come if he wants."

She told Russell she would mention his invitation to Luke, but on their silent drive home from church, she stared out the window, imagining Russell beneath her on the bathroom floor, his large hands gripping her waist.

"What're you thinking about?" Luke said.

"Me?"

He smiled. "Of course you."

"I don't know. I'm not thinking anything."

He eased onto the brakes as he pulled up to a traffic light. Then he pried her hand from her lap, guided it to his mouth, and bit one of her fingers.

"What're you doing?" she said.

He grinned and bit another one.

"Ouch," she said, laughing. "Stop, you goof."

Then Luke kissed her hand and held it between his, and for the rest of the drive, she imagined her life caught between his teeth, her trusting him not to bite.

Two days later, she met Russell at Ruby's Diner on the pier. Even though he wore a blue gingham shirt with a tie and stood when she approached the booth, she reminded herself that this wasn't a date. Nothing intimate or romantic about lunch on the pier, where seagulls cawed and swooped overhead. Russell ordered a beer with his fish and chips. She ordered a Coke and a chicken salad, then later, a piece of lemon meringue pie to split, not because she was still hungry, but because she wanted their lunch to last longer. She'd worried at first that she'd feel awkward around him, but she was surprised by how natural she felt, chatting about mundane things, like the church picnic or her sister. Then Russell asked how her fertility appointment had gone.

"Fine," she said. She had received a message, weeks ago, from Dr. Yavari's office to confirm her follow-up appointment. She'd deleted the message. What would be the point of going back? Of consulting an expert to help make a baby that Luke didn't even want? No wonder he'd never cared while she'd obsessed over their inability to conceive. He only cared about the baby he'd lost years ago. He only cared about the baby he'd made with Nadia.

"You think your husband wants a boy?" Russell asked.

"I don't know. He never said." Had their baby been a boy or girl? Did it matter? The baby had probably been whatever Luke wanted.

"People always think men want boys," Russell said. "Like we couldn't imagine loving something that isn't exactly like ourselves."

"You wouldn't want a son?"

"Too dangerous," he said. "Black boys are target practice. At least black girls got a chance."

"I don't think that's true."

"What's not true? Why you think I enlisted? My pops told me, you better learn to shoot before these white men shoot you, and I did. I been all the way to Iraq and I could walk down the street here and get my head blown off. You don't know what that's like."

She scoffed. "I'm scared all the time," she said. "I never feel safe."

"Well, you got your husband to protect you."

"My husband's the one who hurts me," she said. "He thinks I don't know he's in love with someone else."

She had never said it out loud before. There was something freeing in admitting that you had been loved less. She might have gone her whole life not knowing, thinking that she was enjoying a feast when she had actually been picking at another's crumbs. Across the table, Russell slid his hand on top of hers. She stared at his rough skin, then the waiter came by with the bill and she forced herself to pull away.

FIRST JOHN TOLD LUKE about the pie. A slice of lemon meringue, shared between his wife and another man at a diner on the pier. The men were moving folding chairs into the meeting room before men's Bible study when the head usher broached the topic, a little bashfully, his eyes scraping the floor. First John's wife had been at lunch with one of her girlfriends earlier that week and she'd happened to see Aubrey sharing lunch with a man. A congregation member, she'd thought at first, but she'd never seen him around church before. The man had seemed hungry. His eyes never left Aubrey's face.

"I don't mean to stir up no mess," First John said, "but I'd want to know if it was my wife."

The pie had angered Luke the most. A lunch may have just been a meal, but splitting dessert was intimate. His wife and this strange man dipping forks into the soft cream, her fork, then his, then hers again, falling into an easy rhythm. This man must have watched her lift the fork to her mouth, his hungry eyes following as it disappeared between her lips. Maybe later, in a dark corner of the parking structure, he'd sucked the meringue off her tongue.

"How was your date?" he said, when he returned home.

Aubrey was sitting on the couch, folding laundry. She wore a brown shirt, a baggy gray cardigan that hung open to her waist, the type of drab outfit that made Luke feel, in that moment, that both of them were older than they had any right to be.

"It wasn't a date," she said.

"Then what was it?"

"Lunch."

"How come you didn't tell me about it, then?"

"I don't have to tell you about every lunch I go to."

"If you're out with some strange nigga, then yes, you fucking do!"

He never yelled at her. He snapped sometimes but he always felt horrible after, because she flinched when he raised his voice, which made him feel as guilty as if he'd actually hit her. He would never hit her but he felt that she believed it was always possible, so he'd forced himself to monitor his anger around her—to quiet his voice, to control his body, to never punch a wall or throw a glass, like he'd so badly wanted to. He never wanted her to feel scared of him, the way she felt around most men. But not this man she'd gone to lunch with. If Luke were married to another woman, he might have believed that lunch was just lunch. But he knew Aubrey. She didn't have male friends she went out with alone. If she'd gone to meet up with this man, lunch had to mean more.

She stared at him evenly. "I never ask where you

go," she said. "I never ask when you're sneaking off to see Nadia."

He swallowed. "That's different," he said.

"Why? Because you love her?" She laughed a little, shaking her head. "I'm not stupid. I'm not in law school but I'm not stupid."

"Please," he said.

"Stop. You don't have to lie to me anymore. You've always loved her—"

"Please."

"She's the one you want."

"Please," he said.

Her calmness scared him. He would understand if she had screamed and yelled or cried and cursed. He expected her to, but she was eerily calm and that was how he knew she would leave him. Maybe not right away but someday, he would return home and find her shelf cleared in the bathroom, her half of the closet empty. He'd be lonelier than he had been at the rehab center before she'd brought him a donut wrapped carefully in crinkly paper, a small gift he hadn't imagined himself capable of receiving. He stood in the doorway while she folded his sweaters across her chest, her arms holding his arms and crossing them into her heart.

THIRTEEN

I just don't know that girl's problem," Betty said.

We all peeked out the blinds, watching Nadia Turner pull out of the church parking lot. For weeks, she'd been silent and rude; she hardly spoke when she pulled up to our houses, answering in one word when we tried to be friendly. With that type of company, we would've been better off hiring a taxi. When she picked us up from church, she always paced outside of her truck, like she was late or something. Where she got to go? Who she got waiting for her but her daddy, and not like he was going anywhere.

"Maybe she worried about her friend," Flora said.

"What she got to worry about? They married. Married folk got problems."

"Y'all heard Aubrey moved out?"

"Oh, who hadn't done that once or twice?" Agnes said.

"Y'all know how many times I packed me a suitcase and left Ernest?" Betty said. "Went running to my mama's house and after a few days, I was right back. That ain't nothin'. That's what married folk do."

"I heard that Sheppard boy got a wandering eye."

"He a man, ain't he?" Hattie said. "What these girls expect?"

Agnes said, "See, that's the problem with colored girls these days. They too hard. Soft things can take a beating. But you push somethin' hard a little bit and it shatters. You gotta be a soft thing in love. Hard love don't last."

"I still don't see what none of this got to do with Nadia Turner." Betty shook her head, staring back out the window. "Don't say hello to nobody, don't speak. And why she always walking back and forth like that? Like she got so many other places to be?"

What we didn't understand then was that when Nadia dropped us off at Upper Room, she paced in front of her daddy's truck so she could watch cars pass on the road. Sometimes she sat on the steps in front of the church for an hour or two, hoping that she might see a green Jeep pull into the parking lot. She never did. No one had seen Aubrey Evans for weeks.

FOR MONTHS, Nadia replayed in her mind the day her lies had collapsed into one another. A normal day, a day so unremarkable that she wouldn't appreciate, until weeks later, those early nondescript hours when her life had been intact. Those hours had passed quickly and then it was evening and she was stepping out of the shower, toweldrying her hair, when she saw a light flash outside the house. She'd gone to the door and when she'd switched on the porch light and stood on her tiptoes to look out the peephole, she'd found Aubrey sitting on the porch.

"Why're you sitting out here in the dark?" she'd asked, stepping outside. "Why didn't you ring the doorbell?"

She hadn't been puzzled by Aubrey's unexpected visit—they were long past the point of calling before they stopped by—but she hadn't understood why Aubrey was sitting unannounced in front of her house. What if Nadia hadn't noticed her headlights from the shower window? Was she just going to sit there forever without letting Nadia know she'd come by? Aubrey hadn't turned around, and for weeks, when Nadia thought about her, she remembered staring at her back, the delicate curve of her neck. Maybe, if Aubrey had never turned around, they would've remained suspended in that moment forever, between knowing and not knowing, that final strained pull of a friendship fraying at the seams.

"How?" Aubrey said.

She knew the what. She could guess the why. But the how of it all had been what eluded her. The how of any betrayal was the hardest part to justify, how the lies could be assembled and stacked and maintained until the truth was completely hidden behind them. Nadia had frozen, her mind numb and slow, like she was trying to form words in a different language. Then Aubrey had pushed herself up from the steps and started down the driveway, Nadia stumbling after her.

"Aubrey," she said. "I'm so fucking sorry—"

"Funny how sorry you both are now."

"I swear to God, I was sorry as soon as it happened—"

"Well, that's nice of you."

"Please. Please. Just talk to me."

She had banged on Aubrey's car door, tugging at the handle. She would wake the neighbors soon, her father peeking out the window and wondering why she was crying and pleading, why she'd hung on to the door even after Aubrey had started her engine.

"Move," Aubrey had said. Her voice was cold, metallic. "I don't want to run over your foot."

For months, Nadia tried everything she could think. She texted, e-mailed, left voice mails, and called, each layer of technology becoming more antiquated until she finally sent a letter in the mail. Three handwritten pages of begging, each request diminishing as if they were in some unspoken negotiation: first, for her forgiveness; then for a moment to explain; until she was only asking that Aubrey read her e-mails or listen to her voice mails, even if she never spoke to her again. The three-page letter returned unopened. She began driving by Monique's house in the afternoon, crawling up the street and peering out the window, but she never saw Aubrey come or go. She knew she should stop—someone might notice her car circling the block and call the cops, thinking she was a deranged stalker or a crazy ex-girlfriend—but she drove by every day for three weeks. In a final act of desperation, she parked one evening and rang the doorbell.

"You can't come by here no more," Kasey said, "you know that."

She leaned against the doorframe, her arms folded across her chest. She didn't look angry, just annoyed, as if she were staring at a cat she kept tossing out the back door who'd managed to claw his way back inside.

"Is Aubrey here?" Nadia asked softly, staring down at the welcome mat.

"Can't you understand that she don't want to talk to you? Jesus, between you and him . . ."

Nadia toed the loose gravel, blinking back tears. The crying started suddenly these days, like a nosebleed. She could imagine how Aubrey must have reported the betrayal, how horrified Monique and Kasey had been, because who wouldn't be? A girl who had lived in their very home, a girl they'd treated like family, a girl they'd whispered about late at night, wondering, did she seem quiet at dinner? Do you think something's wrong with her? Her mother had killed herself—how could something not be wrong with her?—but do you think she seemed sad today?

Kasey sighed, stepping out onto the porch. "Don't think this means we're friends again," she said. "I just can't stand to see you cry."

On the porch step, Kasey rubbed Nadia's back while she wiped her eyes.

"Jesus," Kasey said. "What were you thinkin'?"

"I fucked up."

"Well, no kidding."

"She won't let me apologize—"

"What do you expect? She's still hurting, honey."

"But what can I do? What am I supposed to do?"

"It just takes time. You gotta let it alone."

But she couldn't. She couldn't stop calling or writing or driving past the house. That was what it meant to love someone, right? You couldn't leave them, even if they hated you. You could never let them go. She tried calling the house phone once or twice, until Monique answered one evening.

"You've got some goddamn nerve," she said.

"Please," Nadia said. That was the only word she seemed to say now. "I just want to talk to her. Please."

"I don't think it matters what you want anymore," Monique said.

349

Soon, a month, then two months passed. She brewed her father's coffee in the morning—half regular, half decaf, the way he liked it. She drove the Mothers to Upper Room and she cooked dinner for her father in the evening. She thought about leaving—but then the holiday season arrived, announced only by twinkling lights strewn in palm trees and thick cotton rolled on lawns like snow. She had not spent a single Christmas at home since her mother died. She'd imagined them, eight years with no traditions, eight holidays where she was emptied with loneliness. No one to hang the stockings or press silver cookie-cutters into dough or wrap garland around the mantel. No one to root through the garage for the boxes her mother had carefully labeled **wrapping paper** or **porch decorations**. Just a California Christmas with none of the trimmings, an ordinary sunny day. But this Christmas, she knelt in the garage with a pair of scissors, gently opening the sealed boxes. She hung two stockings, not three, and popped red and green bulbs into the post lights along the walkway. She bought a fake tree from Walmart, nothing like the seven-foot Douglas firs her father used to haul through the door, and assembled it in the living room, pushing the wiry branches into place. She clutched handfuls of the felt tree skirt, lush and green between her fingers, and sniffed it, hoping to catch a wisp of her mother. She only smelled dust and pine.

After Christmas, she thought about leaving again—this time, she'd even bookmarked flights—but each time, she felt something hold her back. Not yet. She couldn't leave her father again, not yet. In the evenings, she lugged a kitchen chair to the coat closet so she could reach the photo albums her father had stored on the top shelf. The album resting on her knees, she turned each page slowly, staring at pictures of herself as a newborn, pale, wrinkly with beady eyes, bundled in a yellow blanket. Her mother holding her in the hospital bed, hair stuck to her sweaty forehead. She looked exhausted but she was smiling. Her body had split open, and she was smiling. Nadia turned the page. Now she was a baby, crawling near anonymous feet; she was a chubby toddler, chasing ducks at the park; she was a preschooler, laughing and missing teeth. She passed the photo of herself curled in her father's lap, the one she'd studied when he was overseas, as distant and foreign as war itself. He was smiling into the camera, a tired smile like the one her mother had worn, but he still looked satisfied—happy, even.

Sometimes, on his way to walk his slow laps in the backyard, her father leaned over the couch to take a look at the albums. She turned pages chronicling her first birthday, past photos of her in a high chair, a party hat cocked to the side of her head. One night, she reached a new page at the end of the album that held pictures of her mother as a girl, in a dress and frilly socks, standing in front of a house with the flatness of Texas stretching behind her. In another photo, her mother was a baby, fists buried in a birthday cake, red and green icing smeared on her face. A taller boy hugged her, grinning into the camera. He'd smeared icing on his face to match hers.

When her father bent over the couch, she almost shut the photo album. But he stuck a finger on the page, next to the picture of the smiling baby who would become her mother and then his wife.

"Who's this?" she asked, pointing at the boy.

"That's your uncle Clarence," he said. "Crazy as can be. I wish you could've known him. But those drugs got to him." He shook his head. "I always thought the war would kill us. Then we get back and Clarence does it to himself. He introduced me to your mother and now it's just me. I'm the only one left."

She and her father were survivors, abandoned by everyone but each other. She watched television with him after dinner and drove him to church every Sunday morning. He could drive himself now but he still climbed in on the passenger's side and she wondered if he worried that she might leave if she no longer felt needed. One Sunday, she followed him into the lobby, glancing around, as she always did, hoping she might see Aubrey. Instead, Mrs. Sheppard pulled her aside.

"You heard from Aubrey?" she asked.

"Not lately," Nadia said.

Mrs. Sheppard cocked her head to the side a little, unsure of whether to believe her. Then she folded her arms across her chest.

"She won't talk to me," Mrs. Sheppard said. "I don't understand it. I went down there the other day and rang the doorbell, but she pretended she wasn't home. And that white woman told me Aubrey's not receiving visitors. Since when have I been just a visitor?"

A familiar jealousy wedged between her ribs. "I'm sorry about that," she said.

"She's pregnant, you know."

Nadia's breath caught. "She is?"

"She's carrying my first grandbaby and she won't even talk to me." Mrs. Sheppard straightened her shoulders. "Luke won't tell me what happened, but I know you had something to do with it. I tried to tell her. I tried to warn her about you— girls don't listen to their mothers, they never do."

That Sunday morning, the pastor dabbed his forehead with his handkerchief as he delivered his invitation, calling all who wanted to welcome Jesus into their hearts to step forward, and she watched as people knelt at the altar, their palms lifted to the skies. Their shiny faces, heads tilted back, hands raised as they swayed and sang. During prayer, Nadia would always peek at the others who bowed their heads and closed their eyes, their hands floating toward the rafters, while she stood motionless, her arms pressed against her sides. She felt it then and she felt it every time during praise sessions, when she glanced around the room of believers—the starkness of her own loneliness.

As the choir sang "I Surrender All," she hunched over the pew, unable to stop her tears. Her father shifted beside her, and then she felt his hand on her back. His other hand reached for hers, his rough palm against her smooth skin.

"Do you want me to pray with you?" he whispered.

He lived in prayers and sermons, in scriptures she didn't understand, and even though it had always made her feel so far from him, she nodded. She closed her eyes and bowed her head.

THE MORNING SHE THOUGHT about returning home, Aubrey lay in bed, fumbling with the lid on her prenatal vitamins. She should be up by now—she'd set her alarm for a half hour ago—but pregnancy made her sleepier than she'd ever imagined. When she first moved back to her sister's house, she'd slept endlessly, so many long, unaccounted hours that Monique thought she was depressed. She'd laughed at the suggestion—couldn't she just be sad? Couldn't she be devastated without there being some physical, chemical explanation?—but when she'd seen Dr. Toby, he asked if she might be pregnant. She did the backward math in her head and flushed, remembering that sloppy night on the living room couch. The doctor had been right, after all. She'd just needed a glass, or four, of wine.

"I thought you should know," she'd told Luke.

The phone line had gone silent, and she'd checked her screen to make sure the call hadn't dropped. When Luke finally spoke, he sounded choked-up, and in spite of everything, her eyes had watered too.

"Can I see you?" he'd said.

"Not now."

"I won't come over. I don't have to come over but what about the doctor. Can I come to the doctor's?"

"I'm not ready," she'd said.

He hadn't asked when she would be. He had abandoned his early, insistent attempts to convince her to return home. Now he circled from a distance; she felt him swooping around her, waiting. She hadn't invited him to any of her appointments but she'd informed him of important updates, like when she learned that the baby was a girl. "A girl, wow," Luke kept saying, and she thought about Russell asking if Luke wanted a boy. But each time he repeated "A girl, wow," she felt his voice lifting into awe. A gender made a baby seem real, no longer a wish. She imagined Luke lifting a little girl above his head, a girl with her mother's tight curls or her father's wispy ones, all gathered in a puff. A girl who would not travel from home to home, who would not fear men

clicking down hallways, who would not fear anything, stretching her arms as Luke lifted her high,
always sure that she would land safely against her
father's chest.

"Knock knock." Monique leaned against the
doorframe, yawning. She was holding a glass of
water.

"I was about to get it myself," Aubrey said.

"I know. I was up."

"You don't have to check on me."

"No one's checking on you. I was up."

The only thing more annoying than her sister
checking on her was how she always pretended
that she wasn't. Monique eased over the scattered sneakers on the carpet, the boxes Aubrey
still hadn't unpacked although she'd moved back
in months ago, and set the water on the nightstand. Then she leaned toward Aubrey's belly and
said, "Good morning, baby girl." She always told
Aubrey that she should talk to the baby more.
At twenty weeks, a baby could hear. At twenty
weeks, a baby could recognize her mother's voice.
But Aubrey talked to her baby the same way she
talked to God, never aloud, only inside herself.
She swallowed her vitamins and hugged her belly.
There. I hate swallowing those and I did it for
you. Anything for you.

"Where's Kasey?" she asked.

"Sleeping," Monique said. Then she smiled. "Hey, why don't we get some exercise? Let's go for a run."

"I don't feel like it."

"Why not?"

"You run too fast."

"I'll jog, then. Come on—let's just get out of the house. It'll be good for you."

Monique stooped, picking up the pair of sneakers off the floor. She couldn't resist it, fixing things.

"I think I'm going by the house today," Aubrey said. "Just to pick up a few things after work."

Monique paused, kneeling in front of the closet. "Are you sure that's a good idea?" she said.

"It's my house. You said that."

"But you still refuse to kick him out."

"Where's he supposed to go?"

"I don't know. He should've fucking thought about that before."

"It's not a big deal, Mo," she said. "He works late today."

"Do you want me to go with you?"

"It's fine," she said. "I'll be in and out."

That night, she unlocked her front door and pushed it open slowly, like entering a stranger's home. She did not hang her keys on the hook she'd made Luke nail to the wall because he always forgot where he put his. She did not slide her jacket on a hanger in the closet or even take off her shoes. She paused at the side table where they set the mail—a stack of letters from Nadia. She did not open them, because she knew what they would say, but she flipped them over to ensure the seal was intact. Luke hadn't opened them either. She thought, as she often did, of the two of them whispering about her in bed. Stop, she told herself. A cord stretched from her to her baby girl, but she wondered if, along with food and nutrients, she was sending other things to her child. If a baby could feed off her sadness. Maybe that cord never broke. Maybe she was still feeding off her mother.

She flipped on the light in the guest room that she and Luke had imagined as a nursery. Before their years of infertility, back when they were newly married and hopeful, pointing at blank spaces and conjuring a crib, a planet mobile, walls painted a color soft and dreamlike. Her sister had brought her paint swatches to study, but she'd stared at lemon yellows and waxy greens, nothing quite right as she and Luke had imagined. She heard the lock click in the doorway and closed her eyes. She'd lied to her sister earlier—she knew Luke came home early on Thursdays but she was too ashamed to admit she missed him. She was not supposed to be the type of woman who forgave so readily—but she didn't feel like a woman at all anymore. She carried a girl inside her, a girl both she and Luke, and she had become three people in one, an odd trinity.

"Wow," Luke said, when she turned around.

He had not seen her since she'd called to tell him she was pregnant. She felt his eyes slide over her body, her swelling stomach, the ugly maternity sweatpants, and he seemed to marvel at the sight. Maybe she wasn't as beautiful as Nadia, as brave, as smart—but she was the mother of his child. She and Nadia lived on a forever tilting floor between love and envy, and she finally felt that floor tilt until she could stand. She was birthing the kept child. She had something Nadia never would, and for the first time, she felt triumphant over Nadia Turner.

"Do you still see her?" she said.

"No," he said. "Never. Aubrey, I just—"

"Or talk to her?"

He shook his head. She didn't ask if he still loved her, because she feared the answer.

"I didn't come back to see you," she said. "I've

been thinking about the nursery and my sister's house is too small—"

"Of course," he said. "Let's do it here. What do you want? I'll get it."

She imagined the two of them assembling the nursery piece by piece, the way she and her sister had redecorated the guest room when she first moved in. They'd created the bedroom from Aubrey's fantasies, a room she had imagined while sleeping on trundles and couches and motel cots, a room she had assembled in her mind when she needed a place to hide. Her mother's boyfriend touched her and she hung a picture frame, spread a thick quilt on the bed, traced the floral wallpaper with her fingernail.

She and Luke could create a beautiful world for their daughter and she wouldn't know any different.

"I have to think about it some more," she said.

"Okay," he said. "Okay. Think all you want." He slid his hands in his pockets, taking a tiny step toward her. "Can I—is she kicking yet?"

"No," she said. "Not yet. I'll tell you when she kicks."

She headed to the front door, past the key hook, the coat closet, the side table. Then she paused and grabbed Nadia's stack of letters. The most recent one had no return address, only the words **Please forgive me** written on the envelope in smudged blue ink.

By FEBRUARY, Nadia's father had started taking slow walks around the block in the evening. He wore a navy blue windbreaker zipped up to his neck and she perched on the front steps, watching him make one slow loop and then another. He no longer needed her help, but she still did small things for him, cooking dinner and washing his clothes. Every two weeks, she cut his hair with her mother's clippers, wondering what her mother would say if she could see them now, if she'd be surprised by how their lives had melded, if she'd foreseen this in the moment she pushed her little girl forward and urged her to kiss her daddy hello. The February bar exam came and went, and Nadia started thinking about July. She could take the California bar, not the Illinois, and move back home for good. Find a job somewhere close, maybe downtown San Diego, only a forty-minute drive away, so she could still take her father to church on Sundays. She could do what every girl in Oceanside did: marry a Marine and dream of nowhere else. What was not to love

about this place where there were no winters and
no snow? She could find a nice man and live in
this eternal summer.

One evening, while she watched her father disappear around the corner, Luke's truck pulled up
in front of the house. Her breath hitched, and she
clambered to her feet as he headed up her driveway.

"Hi," he said. "Can I come in?"

She stepped inside silently, Luke following
her. She suddenly felt exposed—she was wearing
bunchy sweatpants and a baggy Michigan shirt,
her hair pulled into a sloppy bun—and she glanced
around the living room, the floor she hadn't yet
swept, her stacks of books on the coffee table. But
why did it matter? Those days of impressing him
were over, weren't they? Besides, he knew her.
What part of her life was unseen to him? They
both paused in the entrance, as if venturing further into the house breached an unspoken agree-
ment. Then she started into the kitchen—a safe
room—and he followed her slowly, his hands in
his pockets.

"Heard from Aubrey?" he said.

"No," she said.

"She took your letters."

"She did?"

"The ones you sent to the house. I don't know if she read them but she took them."

For the first time in months, her chest felt lighter. Aubrey might never forgive her, but at least now she might know how sorry Nadia was. She filled a glass with water and handed it to Luke.

"I heard about your baby," she said. "Congrats."

He took a long sip before setting the glass on the counter. "My mom?"

"Your mom."

"It don't feel real yet," he said. "I don't know if every guy feels like that or if it's just—I mean, she e-mailed me the sonogram. I guess I always thought I'd be in the room to see it."

Nadia thought of her own sonogram, the faceless splotch against the dark backdrop. She'd never told Luke that she had seen it. It would hurt him, knowing that she'd seen their baby and he hadn't. He leaned against the wall, sliding his hands back into his pockets.

"I got something to ask you," he said.

"What?"

"Can you talk to Aubrey?"

"I told you, she won't talk to me—"

"Maybe it's different now," he said. "She took the letters. You can tell her what happened—how you were sad about your dad and how shit just got

complicated because of everything that happened
before—"

"You want me to take the blame," she said.

"Don't say it like that."

"That's what you're fucking saying—"

"I want to see my daughter," he said. "I want to
know her."

So they were having a girl. In a way, she felt
relieved. She'd been hoping their baby would be
a girl. Baby was, or had been, a boy, and if this
new baby had been a boy too, it would've felt like
Baby had been not just replaced but overwrit-
ten completely. But that was a stupid thought.
She had no way of knowing whether Baby was
a boy or not, and how dare she care if he'd been
replaced, a child she hadn't even wanted in the
first place. Not the way Luke wanted his girl. She
could do this for him, take the fall. She imagined herself delivering this version of the story,
the version that his mother undoubtedly already
believed. That she had seduced Luke, that she
had ensnared a good man who was only trying
to help her care for her sick father. Would Aubrey
believe this? Would any woman truly believe this,
besides one who needed to?

"I hope she forgives you," she said. "I hope
you're there for her. You were never there for me.

You left me in that clinic. I had to handle everything on my own—"

"Nadia—"

"I'm sorry," she said. "But I'm not lying for you.
I'm not lying to her anymore."

Luke left quietly. She followed him into the
entrance, where her father was standing in the
entryway, unzipping his jacket. He frowned as
Luke brushed past him.

"What's going on?" he said.

"Nothing," she said. "Just Luke Sheppard saying hi."

A CHILDHOOD'S WORTH of terrible Christmas
gifts lived in Nadia's drawers. Her father found
them all the afternoon he searched her things.
He wasn't a good gift-giver—his wife had always
bested him—but he'd still spent hours every
December inside department stores, picking out
necklaces with little swirly shapes, charm brace-
lets, anything covered in pink rhinestones. Pretty,
frilly things he thought a girl would want, like
pajamas with an actor's face on them, clunky jewelry, a lavender cell phone case. He found most of
these still in her nightstand drawers as he sifted
through her things. He liked to think that she kept

them because she treasured his gifts, but he knew better. His daughter was not sentimental, not about him. Love was not the same as sentiment. Most likely, she couldn't be bothered to throw his gifts away. In the bottom of one drawer, he found the gift he'd been most proud of, a ceramic box covered with lavender flowers. It had reminded him of a jewelry box his mother used to own; as a boy, he'd run his fingers over the sculpted flowers, amazed by the types of things women owned, prettiness for pretty's sake.

He didn't know what he was looking for. A receipt? A medical document? Some evidence that the clinic he'd overheard her arguing with Luke Sheppard about wasn't the one downtown. By the time his daughter pulled into the driveway, he had emptied her nightstand drawers, covering her bedspread in metallic wallets, fuzzy socks, sparkly earrings still attached to cardboard. She walked in to find him sitting on the edge of her bed, the ceramic box in his lap. In his hands, he held a golden pair of baby feet.

FOURTEEN

In the early morning, Upper Room was cloaked in quiet, which Nadia knew, because years ago, she'd spent a summer of mornings there. In those days, when she was seventeen and wounded and desperate to prove herself worthy of anyone's attention, she had traveled the silent hallways alone, carrying a mug of coffee from the pastor's office to the first lady's. She'd made that journey each morning, and when she'd poured the steaming cup under Mother Betty's watchful eye, she'd glanced at the pastor's closed door and wondered what he was doing inside. His work seemed mysterious, unlike his wife's, which was industrious and practical. Sometimes he'd entered the office after she had, smiling at her as he bustled past, a thick Bible under his arm. Other times he was on the phone when she walked in, his back turned although she could see his hands playing with the curly cord. Once, she'd watched him guide a couple into his office for counseling and she imagined how the pastor might conduct a session. How he would lean back in his creaking leather chair at strategic moments—away when he made a point, toward them when they spoke—how he would seem wise and understanding. That summer, she'd wondered about the types of people who arranged to see the pastor early in the morning. These were the most damaged people, probably, the ones who needed the most help, the ones most worried about what might happen if anyone else in the congregation discovered their problems. She'd never imagined that years later, she and her father would be two of those people, arriving at the pastor's office as the sun lightened the sky.

The pastor jolted when they walked in. He'd been sitting behind his desk, bent over an open Bible and stacks of legal pads, writing a sermon, probably, which made arriving at his office unannounced seem even more wrong. But her father had walked into her room that morning and said, "We're going to see the pastor," with such firmness, she couldn't contradict him. She'd spent a long, sleepless night, picturing her father sitting on her bed, surrounded by her emptied drawers, holding the baby feet. His eyes had shimmered with tears.

"You went through my stuff?" she'd said, weakly.

"You did this thing?" he said. "You did this thing behind my back?"

He'd refused to name her sin, which shamed her even more. So she'd told him the truth. How she'd secretly dated Luke, and discovered that she was pregnant, and how the Sheppards had given her the money for the abortion. Her father had listened silently, head bowed, wringing his hands, and when she finished, he sat there a moment longer before standing up and walking out of her room. He was in shock, and she didn't understand why. Didn't he know by now that you could never truly know another person? Hadn't her mother taught them both that? Now she and her father stood in the pastor's doorway and the pastor gazed up at both of them. Then he cleared his throat, gesturing to the burgundy chairs across from his desk.

"Why don't you two sit down?" he said calmly.

"No," her father said. "You don't give me orders.

She was just a girl, you son of a bitch, and you knew what your boy had done to her—"

"It was handled, Robert—"

"Handled how? Handled by you? You the one who made her do this? Or your boy?"

"Let's just talk about this now," the pastor said, easing out of his chair. "Anger won't solve anything—"

"Damn right I'm angry! You wouldn't be angry, Pastor? If this was your girl?"

Her father wanted someone to blame, and how easy it would be to give this to him. She could be the innocent girl, bullied into that unnatural surgery by a selfish boy and his hypocritical father. Across the desk, the pastor rubbed his eyes, like he was suddenly fatigued by the truth.

"I knew," he said. "I knew that we shouldn't have given you that money. It's arrogant. Interfering with a life the Lord has already created."

"No," she said. "No one made me do anything. I couldn't—I didn't want a baby."

"So you kill it?" her father said.

He was disgusted with her, which was worse than his anger. After all, hadn't he and her mother not been ready to be parents? And hadn't they raised her anyway? What was wrong with her? Why couldn't she have been stronger?

"No one made me do anything," she said again. Her mother was dead now, long gone, but she might have been proud to know that her daughter did not blame anyone for her choices. She was that strong, at least.

ON HER LAST NIGHT in California, Nadia asked the cabdriver to stop at Monique and Kasey's house on the way to the airport. She sat at the curb for five minutes, watching the meter tick up, until the husky Filipino driver rolled down the window to light a cigarette.

"You going in or . . ." he said.

"Give me a minute," she said.

He shrugged and tapped his ashes outside the window. She leaned against the glass, watching the smoke lick and curl. Her father had stood in the doorway of her bedroom, watching her pack her suitcase. "You don't have to go," he'd kept saying, out of a desire for her to stay or just politeness, she couldn't tell. He would be settling into his armchair right now, growing re-accustomed to the silence. He might turn on the television to fill the home with sound. Maybe he missed how simple his life had been without her, all his easy routines. He would have to find a new church now—he hadn't even looked the pastor in the eye when they'd left his office—but what other church would have a need for a lonely man and his truck? She imagined her father traveling from church to church, forever carting someone else's load, keeping nothing for himself.

She finally climbed out of the cab and rang the doorbell. After the second ring, Aubrey cracked open the door. Her stomach curved like a beach ball over her maternity pants. She was pregnant in a way that Nadia had once feared; in the days following her pregnancy test, she'd lifted her shirt in front of the mirror and stared at a flat stomach that ballooned in front of her eyes until it hung immovably over her jeans. When she'd called to make her appointment at the clinic, the man who answered the phone told her that before he could finalize the date, she had to listen to a recording explaining her other options. "I'm sorry," he'd said, "it's just something the clinic is required to do." He did sound genuinely sorry, and when she'd fallen silent on the other end, he told her that he had no way of knowing whether she actually listened to the whole thing. So as soon as the recording started, she'd quietly set her phone on her desk. She didn't need to listen to know that she didn't want to be heavy with another person's life.

But Aubrey didn't look scared. She seemed comfortable in her big sweater, a hand resting on her stomach, as if to remind herself that it was still there. She wanted this baby and that was the difference: magic you wanted was a miracle, magic you didn't want was a haunting.

"Congratulations," Nadia said.

She tried to smile—this was the hardest part, wasn't it? When the ease of friendship began to instead require drudging effort. When you stood on the welcome mat instead of trouncing right through the door. She searched Aubrey's face, for kindness or for anger, but found neither, only a quiet steadiness as Aubrey glanced down, wrapping her sweater tighter around herself.

"You lied to me," she said.

"I know."

"For years. You both did."

"And I'm so sorry. I just didn't know how to—"

"Is that your cab?"

She felt Aubrey gaze past her shoulder to the cabdriver smoking at the curb. "I'm flying back tonight," she said.

"For how long?"

"I don't know."

"So that's your plan. You do this to me and now you're just gonna leave."

"Can I come in a second?"

Aubrey hesitated. For a long moment, Nadia thought she would say no, then she stepped aside and Nadia entered the little white house that had once been her home, past the cardboard boxes scattered on the floor, into the kitchen where a sonogram hung on the refrigerator. She leaned closer. There she was, a baby girl. Twenty weeks old and healthy, ten fingers, ten toes. At twenty weeks, a baby looked human.

"My dad found out," Nadia said. "About my abortion."

"Oh." Aubrey's voice was soft. "Is he mad?"

Nadia shrugged. She didn't want to talk about her father, not now. She turned back to the sonogram on the refrigerator, imagining herself in the room, holding Aubrey's hand as the doctor slid the wand on her stomach. The doctor would laugh when he squeezed into the crowded room—he usually didn't see patients bring in their entire families. No one would correct him that Nadia wasn't family. She'd join the circle forming around Aubrey—Monique holding her other hand, Kasey touching her shoulders—as all four women watched the baby appear, backlit and washed in white light. Could she feel their awe while they watched her on the screen? Could she feel that she was already encased in love? Or could a baby sense when he was not wanted?

"What does it feel like?" Nadia asked. "Being pregnant."

"It's strange," Aubrey said. "Your body isn't yours anymore. Strangers will just touch your stomach and ask how far along you are. What makes them think they can do that? But you're not just you anymore. And sometimes it's scary because I'll never be just me again. And sometimes it's nice because I'll be more than that." She leaned against the wall. "But other times I think, what happens if I don't love this baby?"

"Of course you will. How could you not?"

"I don't know. That's what happened to us, right?"

Sometimes Nadia wished that were true. It'd be much simpler to accept that she had been unloved. It'd be much simpler to hate her mother for leaving her. But then she remembered her mother offering her seashells at the beach and sitting up with her all night when she was sick, pressing a hand against her hot forehead and then kissing her, as if that kiss could detect fever better than a thermometer. Nothing about her mother had ever been simple—her life or her death—and her memory wouldn't be either.

"Maybe they did," Nadia said. "At least the best they could."

"Then that's even scarier," Aubrey said.

She hugged her stomach. Inside of her was a whole new person, which was as miraculous as it was terrifying. Who would you be when you weren't just you anymore?

"Do you have a name for her yet?" Nadia asked.

Aubrey paused, then shook her head. She was lying. She had probably thought up lists of names since the baby was just a prayer. But she didn't want to tell Nadia and Nadia had no right to know. Still, after she hugged Aubrey good-bye, after she climbed back in the cab, after she leaned against the airplane window and watched San Diego shrink beneath her, she imagined herself in the hospital one morning after she received the call. She would pace outside the nursery, looking past the rows of newborns in pink and blue beanies, until she found her. She would know her by sight, the swirling light wrapped in a pink blanket, a child sown from two people she would always love. She would know the baby she will never know.

———

IN THE BEGINNING, there was the word, and the word brought about the end.

The news spread in only two days, thanks to Betty. She would later tell us that she had not meant to cause any harm. Yes, she had leaked personal, private information but that was only because she hadn't realized it was so personal and private. She had just been going about her business one morning, unlocking the doors around the church, when she'd heard loud voices in the pastor's office. Of course she'd gone to check on what was happening. Wasn't that her duty? What if the pastor had needed help? Crazier things had happened. She'd read in **USA Today** about a minister in Tennessee who had been stabbed by a crazy congregant. And she'd seen a segment on **60 Minutes** about a church in Cleveland that had been robbed by a few hoodlums who had suspiciously known exactly where the tithes were kept. When we asked what exactly she aimed to do if the pastor had, in fact, been held at knifepoint in his office, she had dismissed us with a wave and insisted we let her return to her story. So she had gone to investigate the loud voices, and when she'd drawn near, she had peeked around the corner through the crack in the pastor's door and guess who she'd seen inside?

"Robert Turner," she whispered across the bingo table. "Yellin' and carryin' on. He called Pastor an S.O.B.—can you believe it?"

Of course we couldn't, which was why Betty looked so delighted to tell us. We could hardly imagine Robert even getting angry, let alone swearing at the pastor in his own office.

"For what?" Hattie asked.

"I don't know," Betty said, but her slow smile told us she had a good idea. "But his daughter was there and Robert kept saying 'she was just a girl' and the pastor said he was just helping the girl but Robert said she's his child, it's no one's place to be helping her with nothin'." She paused. "Y'all know what I think? I think there were a baby and now there ain't one."

We were disgusted but not shocked. You read about it in the papers every day, girls getting rid of their babies. Weren't nothing new about it. When we were coming up, we all had a girlfriend or a cousin or a sister who had been sent off to live with an aunty when her shamed mother learned that she was in a family way. Some of our own mothers had taken these girls in and we'd peeped them changing through cracks in the door. We'd seen pregnant women before but pregnancy worn on a girl's body was different, the globe of a belly hanging over cotton panties embroidered with tiny pink bows. For years, we'd flinched when boys touched us, afraid that even a hand on our thigh would invite that thing upon us. But if we had become sent-off girls, we would have borne it like they did, returning home mothers. The white girls ended up in trouble as often as us colored girls. But at least we had the decency to keep our troubles.

"Y'all think—"

"Of course."

"Lord have mercy."

"Y'all think Latrice know?"

"Is there anything around here she don't know?"

The Turner girl and her unwanted baby. For days, we could think of nothing else, and although we'd promised to keep the secret amongst ourselves, the truth trickled out anyway. Later, we would blame each other even though we never determined who'd been the first one to run her mouth. Was it Betty, who'd loved the attention so much when she shared the story that she hadn't been able to stop herself from giving a repeat performance to someone else? Or Hattie, maybe, who had shared a ride home with Sister Willis, a woman who couldn't, as we all knew, hold water? Or maybe someone had just overheard us at bingo and the story had spawned from there. We were all guilty in a way, which meant that none of us were guilty and all of us were surprised that next Sunday, when Magdalena Price walked out of service right in the middle of the pastor's sermon. The pastor glanced up, watching her go, and stuttered for a moment, like he'd lost his place. He was preaching on overcoming fear, a sermon that we'd heard him deliver dozens of times. What could he have said to offend her? Then that Wednesday, during midweek Bible study, we heard Third John tell Brother Winston that the pastor had paid Nadia Turner five thousand dollars to not have that baby, how else do you think she was able to go off to that big school? In Upper Room's imaginings, the girl grew younger, the check larger, the pastor's motives darker. He'd paid her to kill her child because he'd been afraid that the pregnancy would hurt his ministry or maybe he just didn't want his kin mixing with Turner stock. Remember how crazy her mama was? Remember, as if any of us could ever forget.

Then the reporter came. A white boy fresh out of college, wearing melon-colored pants and a blond ponytail. We didn't take him seriously at first, melon pants and all, until he told us that he'd heard that our pastor had paid off a pregnant girl, a minor too, and did we care to comment? He stood on our front steps in a wide stance, pen above his notepad, the way policemen always stand, a hand near their holster, as if to remind you they could take your life anytime they wanted. We told him we didn't know nothing. He sighed, flipping that notepad shut.

"I figured wise women such as yourselves would want to know what your pastor's been up to," he said.

We wanted to chase him off those steps with a broom. Get! Get out our house! Who was he to poke around, turning up our rugs? Who was he to tell our stories? But he wrote it up anyway. One of the photographers had an aunty who went to Upper Room and was willing to talk. Some folks will say anything just to see their name in print. At that point, it didn't much matter if his story was true. The earthquake came, the one we'd been expecting over the years. New members dried up. Old members stopped coming. Pastors around the city turned down invitations to visit and stopped inviting Pastor to their churches. Some days, Betty said, she sat in the pastor's office with nothing to do, no schedule to fill, no appointments to make.

Years later, after Upper Room's doors had finally

shuttered, we paid Latrice Sheppard a visit. She invited us inside, offered us tea and cookies, but never an apology.

"I did what any mother would've done," she said. "That girl should be thanking me. I gave her life."

But none of us were sure what type of life Nadia Turner was living. We hadn't seen her in years. Hattie said she'd settled down in one of those big East Coast cities like New York or Boston. She was a big lawyer now, living in a tall building with a doorman who tipped his cap to her when she came bustling in from out of the snow. Betty said she never settled down and she was still flitting around the world, from Paris to Rome to Cape Town, never resting anywhere. Flora said she heard about a woman on CNN who'd tried to kill herself in Millennium Park. She hadn't caught the name but the photo looked just like the Turner girl, the same ambered skin and light eyes. Could that be her? Agnes said she didn't know but she'd felt in her spirit that the girl would think about killing herself later in life, maybe even more than once, and each time, she would instead live. She got her mother in her, holding the knife, and her own spirit flinted over, and each time they struck, she would spark. Her whole life, a spark.

———

WE'VE SEEN HER one last time.

A year ago, maybe, on a Sunday morning that, like all Sunday mornings since Upper Room died, we have spent together. We're too old to find a new church now, so each Sunday, we gather to read the Word and pray. No one leaves us prayer cards anymore, but we intercede anyway, imagining what the congregation might still need. If Tracy Robinson still has a taste for liquor, if Robert Turner has finished mourning his dead wife. We pray for Aubrey Evans and Luke Sheppard, who, in the dying days of Upper Room, we'd seen together in the lobby with their baby—together, but not quite so, the way you can fix a hole in a worn pair of pants but they never look new. On Sunday mornings, we pray for everyone who comes to mind and after, we sit on the balcony outside Flora's room and eat lunch. But that Sunday, we'd glanced out and seen Robert Turner's truck heading down the street. We were delighted to catch a glimpse of him but instead, we saw his daughter driving. She was older then, in her thirties maybe, but she looked the same, hair flowing down to her shoulders, sunglasses covering eyes that glittered in the sun. Her left hand hanging out the window held no ring but we imagined she had a man somewhere, a man she could get rid of when she had the mind to because she would never put herself in the position to be left. Why had she returned to town? Flora thought Robert might be sick again, but Hattie pointed out the flattened boxes filling the truck bed. Maybe she was helping her daddy move. Maybe she was bringing him home with her, wherever her home now was, and maybe that was why she'd seemed so peaceful, because this was the last time she'd ever step inside her dead mother's house. Agnes swore she saw a pink Barbie bag on the passenger's seat—a gift, perhaps, for Aubrey's daughter. We imagined her walking up the steps with the present and kneeling in front of the girl, a girl who wouldn't exist if her own child did.

Then she disappeared around the corner, and as quickly as we'd seen her, she was gone. We will never know why she returned, but we still think about her. We see the span of her life unspooling in colorful threads and we chase it, wrapping it around our hands as more tumbles out. She's her mother's age now. Double her age. Our age. You're our mother. We're climbing inside of you.

ACKNOWLEDGMENTS

Endless thanks to the following people, without whom this book would not be possible:

Julia Kardon, the agent of my dreams, who saves me daily with her guidance and wit. Thank you for always believing. There's no one else I'd rather have in my corner. Everyone at Mary Evans, Inc., especially Mary Gaule, whose feedback and support has meant so much to me. Sarah McGrath, whose incisive edits improved this book at each step, Danya Kukafka, for her invaluable help behind the scenes, and all the good folks at Riverhead, whose contagious enthusiasm has made the process of publishing my first book so much fun.

The faculty and staff at the Helen Zell Writers Program, particularly Peter Ho Davies, Eileen Pollack, Nicholas Delbanco, and Sugi Ganeshananthan, who guided me in shaping a rough draft into a thesis into a book.

My inordinately talented cohort, who challenged me each workshop with their insight and feedback: special thanks to Jia Tolentino, who edited and published my first essay; Rachel Greene; Derrick Austin; and Mairead Small Staid, whose kindness and good humor kept me warm through three Michigan winters. And to Chris McCormick, fellow country mouse, for the impromptu brainstorming sessions and hastily planned trips and endless advice. I applied to graduate school only hoping to improve my writing. What a gift to have met you all.

To the creative writing faculty who mentored me at Stanford, particularly Ammi Keller, who encouraged me during that first scattershot draft, and Stephanie Soileau, who challenged me during my first real revision. You both approached those early drafts with such seriousness and generosity, and I'm forever grateful.

To Ashley Buckner, who knocked on my dorm room one evening to invite me to dinner and, years later, became someone I cannot imagine my life without; Brian Wanyoike, who pushes me to live largely and think intricately; Ashley Moffett, my oldest friend and first reader. To my family, for all your love and support. And to all the writers and artists and scholars who mothered me, who gave me language, who gave me life.